HOUSE FOR SALE
NAVY SEAL INCLUDED

By Cora Seton

ISBN: 9781988896601

Author's Note

House for Sale Navy SEAL Included is the first volume in the Elliotts of Chance Creek series, set in the fictional town of Chance Creek, Montana. To find out more about Carter, Amanda, Lincoln, Hudson, Nate, Gage and the other inhabitants of Elliott Ridge, look for the rest of the books in the series, including:

House for Sale Soldier Included
House for Sale Airman Included
House for Sale Marine Included
House for Sale Ranger Included

Visit Cora's website at www.coraseton.com
Find Cora on Facebook at facebook.com/CoraSeton
Sign up for my newsletter HERE.
www.coraseton.com/sign-up-for-my-newsletter

CHAPTER 1

Last Year

"**Y**OU CAN'T SELL Elliott Ridge," Carter Elliott sputtered into his phone. "Dad—that's our home." He stood in the middle of his quarters at Naval Base Coronado, where his SEAL team was stationed. During the past twelve years, his missions had pushed him to his mental and physical limits, but the pain that lanced through him now was unlike anything he'd known before. His family had owned Elliott Ridge in Montana for generations. Carter still had nightmares about the day he'd left it. He'd sworn he'd get back there somehow. Planned to make things right so his whole family could return.

"Couldn't have been much of a home considering how fast you ran from it," his father countered gruffly. Carter's parents lived in South Carolina now, driven there by his father's ailments. His dad would be pacing their condo's small, modern living room, a caged tiger fretting against his constraints. "I seem to remember you cast the final vote to leave, but all five of you boys

1

couldn't wait to get out of there. Now you're spread around the world playing superheroes. What do you care if I sell the Ridge?"

Guilt surged through Carter, and his fingers gripped his phone hard. "You know I cast that vote to save your life. I couldn't stay there and watch you kill yourself."

"You boys made a mountain out of a molehill."

"No, Dad. It was the other way around. You were trying to make a molehill out of a mountain. Trying to pretend the six of us could run a mill and logging business it took dozens of men to operate. I did what I had to do, just like my brothers. You're still alive, so it was worth it."

"Meanwhile you've spent the past twelve years trying to get *yourself* killed," his father said. "Doesn't matter what happens to the Ridge anyway. None of you are ever coming back."

"Like hell I'm not." Carter surprised himself with his vehemence, given that until this moment he'd had no immediate plans to leave the SEALs. He'd never figured out how to fix what he'd done. Didn't even know where to start when it came to reclaiming the little town where he'd grown up. Now it seemed like he'd run out of time.

He refused to believe that, though. Carter thought fast. This couldn't be the way things ended. The Ridge gone, his family scattered to the four winds. "Look, my current term of service expires next year. I haven't extended it yet. I can be back at the Ridge next April. You can wait that long, can't you?" He didn't give himself time to think over the implications of his words. He'd be turning his back on a career he'd invested his entire adult life in. Walking away—again.

"Why would you do something like that?"

"So I can bring the place back to what it should be." Wasn't that what his father wanted? It was what he wanted, career or no career. Elliotts belonged in Montana. They belonged at the Ridge.

"Can't be done," his father said. "The Ridge emptied out for a reason."

"Because the price of lumber crashed along with everything else. No one was building houses. Things are different now." This defeatist attitude wasn't like his dad at all. Had something happened he didn't know about? "Are you having heart problems again?"

"I'm fit as a fiddle."

Thank god. "Except that hip of yours," he pointed out to cover his relief.

"After the surgery it'll be good as new."

So why was he set on selling the Ridge now?

"Thing is." His father hesitated. "I got a good offer."

"For the property?" Carter's stomach knotted, and he sat down on the edge of his bed. He hadn't expected things had progressed that far. Who could afford to buy an entire town?

"That's right."

"You really want to sell, Dad?" He couldn't fathom it. Carter hadn't been back there since he left, but the Ridge still anchored his world. He knew every inch of the place.

Loved it.

There was a long silence. "No one said anything about *wanting* to sell."

Relief flooded Carter all over again. His father wasn't committed to selling yet, which meant this phone call was more of a fishing expedition than an announcement of his intentions. Well, Carter supposed he'd been hooked. Hell, now that he'd considered going home, he couldn't wait to be reeled in.

"Then let me give it a go."

"You won't get your brothers back to Montana."

"Yes, I will. Lincoln and Hudson miss the Ridge. Nate, too." They talked about it from time to time, swapping reminiscences when their mother roped them into family video chats.

"What about Gage?"

"Haven't talked to him lately." He neglected to say he rarely did. There were things between them that hadn't been right since they left Montana.

"He's a stubborn one."

"And you aren't?" Carter asked.

"Maybe I am. Maybe you are, too," his father said. "But stubborn won't pay our debts."

"How bad are they?" He turned and paced the other way. His father had upgraded the mill equipment right before the crash. If he hadn't, they might have been able to ride out the years where it was almost impossible to sell lumber.

"There's the monthly payment and then there's the

balloon payment to close out the loan we got to buy all that equipment. The balloon payment is due two years from now." His father named the sums, and Carter whistled. He did some calculating in his head. It was June now, and it took time to separate from the Navy, but if he could get home to the Ridge by next April, that would give him just over a year to get the mill up and running and earn enough to make that large final payment. "If you can't pay off that loan, I'll have to sell," his father continued. "I just liquidated the last property we own in town. That'll cover the payments and taxes and so on until you get there next spring, but that's it. The rest is on you."

Carter swallowed. There it was: the bottom line. The real reason for this phone call. Without more town properties to sell, his dad couldn't hold on to the Ridge by himself. He needed Carter and his brothers to get the mill running again in order to keep up with the payments.

That meant Carter would have to scare up buyers for their lumber. He'd need sources for logs once they ran out of the surplus they'd left behind. He'd need to get their own logging operation up and running again. He'd need to find dozens of men to sign on and do the work. His mind ticked through the steps. This wasn't going to be easy.

"If I'm going to take this on, I want more than just your promise not to sell," he said, realizing he was giving up a secure career for a very risky proposition.

"Oh yeah? What else do you want?" his father challenged him.

"The day we pay off those debts, I want you to sign over the Ridge to the five of us. If I'm going to throw heart and soul into the place, I need to know I can stay there—for the rest of my life. There'll always be a place there for you and Mom, of course."

He waited for his father's answer. He'd never bargained with him before, man to man. When he'd left home, he was barely eighteen. The baby of the family.

"Deal," his father said. "The whole point of the Ridge is to pass it down. But no one gets a piece of it unless they help. You tell your brothers that. If they don't show up next spring and stay long enough to pay off that loan, don't bother showing up at all."

Carter heard the steel in his voice and knew his father meant it. He hadn't forgiven them for walking away last time, even if they'd done it to save his life.

He swallowed the words he wished he could say. The apology he could never seem to choke out. "Will do, Dad. What about that offer you got, though? You might not get another one if you pass it up. What if we fail?"

"That offer isn't going anywhere. I'll get your mother to write up something for you to sign. We'll make this official. Better call your brothers," his father said. "You've got your work cut out for you."

When he hung up, Carter lowered his phone and wondered what had just happened. Whose idea was it for him to leave the Navy and resurrect Elliott Ridge— his or his father's?

Somehow he wasn't sure anymore.

Carter decided it didn't matter. It was his vote that had shut down Elliott Ridge twelve years ago. It was his job to bring it back to life. It was the best kind of mission, after all. One that required strategic planning, careful consideration, tactical maneuvers and determination. For once, no one would be shooting at him while he worked, either.

Could he pull it off?

His father was right; it wouldn't be easy. He lifted his phone again. Called his brother Nate, the best listener of the bunch. He'd help figure out the best way to approach the others.

"Carter? What's up?"

Carter took a deep breath. "You ready to go home?"

This Year

"DAD? I'M HOME." Amanda Stakewell entered her ground-floor apartment, kicked off her high heels and breathed a sigh of relief. It was only nine o'clock in the evening, two full hours earlier than she'd told her father to expect her. She'd been prepared to find him parked in front of the television or fixing himself a snack, but although the lights were on throughout her apartment, the television was off and the visible rooms empty. Amanda locked the door behind her, hesitated, then checked to make sure the bolt had engaged.

Maybe he'd decided to do some painting. Usually, he did so only while she was at work. He'd told her the light was better during the day and he could paint for only an hour or two at a time, since his back gave him trouble. Strange to think of her father as old enough to have ailments like that.

He'd definitely changed in the eleven years he'd been away. His hair was streaked with gray now. He was thinner, too. Amanda remembered a man who'd loved a good dinner more than anything, but these days he picked at his meals and swallowed vitamins several times a day.

"Dad?" she called again. She switched off the lights in the kitchen and headed down the hall to where the bedrooms were tucked away. "I'm back early. Want to watch something?"

The night hadn't been a success. She'd joined the other women in her office to celebrate her boss's twentieth year with Biddington Foods, but all anyone wanted to talk about was the rising cost of living in Los Angeles. One of her coworkers, a smug sixty-year-old who owned a bungalow in Los Feliz, grilled her on how much she'd saved since she'd come to work five years ago. Amanda was proud she'd put anything aside, but Gwen had tsked at her. "You'll never even own a condo at that rate."

Didn't she know it.

Every year prices rose while her salary stayed pitifully low, and Amanda had begun to feel a sense of rising panic every time she consulted a real estate website. When she'd first come to LA, she'd amused herself attending open houses in desirable neighborhoods, dreaming of the day when she'd take possession of her first home. In those fantasies she always had a handsome husband—and a pregnancy bump. She wanted a family. A partner. She wanted to be making progress in her life.

Somehow she never seemed to get anywhere.

When Gwen switched to grilling her about her love life, Amanda decided she'd had enough. She'd said her good-nights and come home instead.

At least her father was here now, she told herself as she passed her bedroom, always neat with her bed made and decorative pillows in pretty array. He'd resurfaced in her life several months ago, swearing he wanted to start over and be the dad she'd always deserved. Ever since, she'd been putting him up on the sofa bed in the small "bonus" room she'd been using for her office. She braced herself to face the chaos she knew she'd meet when she got to his door. He had a habit of tossing covers and clothes on the floor, as if waiting for someone else to come and clean up after him. Lately, Amanda had stopped doing so. He was a grown man, after all, and a guest stopped being a guest after they'd been living with you for months. When the mess bothered her too much, she simply closed the door.

Right now his door was open, giving a full view inside, and Amanda stopped short when she noticed his sofa bed was tidied away and the top of his tiny dresser was bare.

"Dad?"

His portable easel was disassembled, and several canvases were propped against the hide-a-bed. Her father's suitcases sat on the floor beside them. One was closed tight. The other lay open, full of clothing and the notebooks he was always filling with sketches and ideas. Amanda moved into the room. He was ready to leave, by the looks of things. There was his shaving kit and toiletries bag. There were all the clothes she'd washed and folded just yesterday.

There was—

What was that?

Amanda bent down to see. An unframed canvas was rolled up and tucked among his clothes in the open suitcase. As she drew it out, she could see it had been previously stretched on a frame but removed for transport, something well within her father's capabilities.

She gingerly picked it up, unrolled it and gasped.

Amanda knew that painting.

She'd seen it at the Warden Gallery only two weeks ago with her father. It was part of a traveling exhibit featuring famous works by Deloitte, but at the time, Amanda wouldn't have cared if it featured finger paintings by local kindergarteners. When she was viewing art with her father, she could pretend he'd never disappeared from her life at all. He was so engaged then, so talkative, his sly humor resurfacing, the way it had when she was a girl.

Afternoon in Sunshine and Shadow was one of many of Leonard Deloitte's paintings featured in the exhibition. A small canvas among larger, showier ones, it was considered one of his best. It had to be worth millions.

Why was it here in her father's luggage?

Amanda closed her eyes. She knew exactly why it was here. They'd been down this road before, and her entire family had paid for it dearly.

She replaced the canvas carefully before picking up the top sketchbook from the pile she'd moved.

Page after page of studies confirmed her suspicions. Her father had been planning this for months. Years, maybe. When had he found out this painting would be part of a traveling exhibit? How many museums had he visited along the way to study it as it moved across the continent from city to city?

More to the point—when had he decided to come back into her life? Before or after he decided to steal a masterpiece?

Pain spiked through her again. Amanda knew the answer to that question, too. Which meant every moment she'd savored with her father had been just another lie.

She thought again of their trip to the exhibit. Her father had excused himself at one point, needing to visit the men's room, and now that she thought about it, he'd been gone awhile, but that wasn't out of the ordinary. She'd figured some other work of art had caught his attention on his way back to meet her. Her father could stand lost in contemplation of a painting for hours if no one was there to herd him onward.

Had he made the switch then?

No. That would be impossible. The place had been full of people.

Maybe he'd taken a page from his old partner, Buck

Bronson, and found a connection who worked at the gallery. Maybe someone had met him at the back door after-hours, taken his forgery and switched it for the original when no one else was around. Her father could have gone back to fetch the real masterpiece any day when she was at work.

It didn't matter how he'd done it.

Afternoon in Sunshine and Shadow sat here in his bag, and her father was ready to run.

He was ready to leave her without saying goodbye.

Again.

Her throat ached with the betrayal she felt. How could she have been such a dupe? What kind of father used his daughter as cover when he was plotting a crime?

Where was he now? Was he meeting with some new criminal friends? Or a go-between who'd turn over the painting to a rich benefactor who wanted to build a private collection? Last time Buck had been the one with all the connections. Could her father really pull off a transaction like this all on his own?

Amanda texted him.

Dad? Where are you?

The answer came almost immediately. *Where are you?*

Home.

There was a long pause. Amanda stared at the tiny screen, willing him to offer her an explanation. Something that would stop the sting of shame that filled her, knowing he'd treat her like this, when she'd been so happy to welcome him back into her life.

Get out of there. Now!

Amanda wasn't sure what she'd expected him to say, but it wasn't this.

Why?

Buck's coming! Amanda, leave right now!

Buck? Amanda stood up fast. Buck Bronson knew where she lived?

Amanda told herself to get a grip. Why wouldn't he? Buck had served for years with the Dallas police, and his friends always seemed to have his back no matter what he did. He used to brag he knew cops all over the country. If he wanted her address, he could get it—even in LA. If he was out of jail already, he could be anywhere.

There was no time to ask for details. She grabbed the canvas, raced to her bedroom, wrapped it in a T-shirt and shoved it in her gym bag. She threw her purse over her shoulder and checked her phone again. More messages from her father.

GET OUT OF THERE! Now, Amanda!

Buck knows everything!

He's been tracking us!

He's on his way!

Did her father mean Buck knew he'd stolen a masterpiece? Was he coming to exact revenge for what happened last time?

He'd want the painting for himself.

Her heart pounding, Amanda turned to leave and heard a sound at her front door. Cold fear gripped her.

Buck was already here. He was breaking into her apartment. She spun around, looking for another way out.

Her bedroom window was low and wide, already open to let in a spring breeze. She popped its screen, threw a leg up and over the sill, hopped outside and thrashed her way through the decorative bushes to reach the sidewalk. The concrete was cool under her bare feet in the gathering dark. The parking lot quiet.

Amanda ran.

Her footsteps sounded loud in the quiet of the night. Gravel sharp against the tender skin of her soles, she picked up speed.

Buck had been tracking them? For how long? How much did he know about her?

Did he know the make of her car? Her license plate number?

Had he hacked her phone?

Nearly stumbling, Amanda bobbled the small gadget she still held in her hand, caught it and threw it into a garbage can as she raced past.

When she finally reached her Toyota, she used the key to manually unlock it, not wanting to call attention to herself by pressing the button on her fob and activating the lights. She got in as quickly as possible, locked the door and started the engine. She kept her headlights off, hoping she could sneak past the building without Buck noticing her progress through a window.

She had a pair of runners in her gym bag. As soon as she was safely away, she'd pull over and put them on, but there wasn't time for that now.

She had to get out of here.

There was no sign of Buck as she drove past the entrance to the building. No sign of anything amiss at all. Amanda pressed the gas pedal and sped away. Was Buck rummaging through their things even now? Did he know she'd taken the painting with her?

She should have left it behind. Should have never let her dad back into her life in the first place.

Should have known he hadn't come back to make amends.

By now he'd be long gone. Ian Stakewell wasn't the kind of man who stuck around when things got hard.

She needed to disappear, too.

Buck Bronson was a killer. He hated her family. She'd been safe while he was in prison, but now she needed to get out of town, fast.

After she returned the painting.

Amanda slowed for a moment, then pressed the accelerator again.

She wasn't like her father. She had a moral compass. There was no way she was allowing this beautiful piece of art to fall into the wrong hands. Besides, if she returned it, her father wouldn't be a criminal anymore. No harm, no foul. He could disappear again, and Buck would lose interest.

She would have her life back.

Such as it was.

Amanda shook the wayward thought from her head, pulled into the parking lot of the Warden Gallery, slowed to a stop and realized she hadn't thought this through. It was well past closing time, and no doubt the gallery was wired with alarms. Cameras were probably recording her right now. She couldn't just march up the steps and leave a masterpiece outside the door to be discovered in the morning.

In fact, she couldn't return it herself at any time. There'd be too many questions she didn't want to answer.

She couldn't afford to wait for daylight, either. If Buck was tracking her, she had to make use of her head start.

All her bravado gone, Amanda started the car again, gripping the steering wheel tightly as she accelerated out of the parking lot. She swung onto Highway 15 and headed toward Las Vegas, as good a town as any from which to disappear.

She'd have to ditch her car. Pay cash for a flight out of town. Find somewhere to hide.

Who did you call for help when you couldn't call the police?

Maybe no one, Amanda thought. She was on her own.

But she had her credit card. She could go anywhere.

As long as it wasn't home.

CHAPTER 2

C ARTER THREADED HIS way through the crowd in the arrivals area of the Chance Creek Regional Airport, trying to get close to the large plateglass windows overlooking the tarmac. It was early May, after four in the afternoon on a Wednesday. He'd already been back in town for a month. Gage, Lincoln and Hudson, who were right behind him, had arrived a couple of weeks after him. They were here today to pick up Nate.

"You're wasting your money," Gage said when they found a spot to stand in. "There's plenty of room in Mom and Dad's house for all of us to stay for now. There's no sense buying and fixing up another one when we might all have to leave next June."

"I'm not leaving Elliott Ridge again, no matter what. The price we agreed on for the house is dirt cheap. Besides, this way I get something tangible for donating money to the family cause."

Carter had gone over this a dozen times already to-day and a hundred times since he'd claimed one of the

Ridge's houses for himself. It was situated in a corner of town his father had planned to subdivide before the crash happened. He'd done all the required steps and had just been about to hand in the final paperwork when the town emptied out instead. Carter had resubmitted the forms as soon as he came home. They were waiting for a decision from the county, so he didn't technically own the house yet, but he'd forked over the money for it into the family account. He'd already moved his things out of house number one, where he'd grown up, and taken them to number twenty-three, the house he'd claimed. He'd drawn up plans for the renovation and gotten to work on it, too. They'd sort out the paperwork when the subdivision came through.

Number twenty-three, on Second Avenue, was a sensible three bedroom, two bath home, the perfect place in which to start a family.

Now all he needed was someone to share it with.

"You've been fixing up Mom and Dad's house," Carter added. "Why isn't that a waste of money?"

"That's different," Gage said. "They might come to visit while we're here, and they deserve to be comfortable. You don't even own number twenty-three yet. You shouldn't be renovating it."

"I've handed over the cash."

"Which is bad enough. Why throw good money after bad? It's far from clear that we can make this all work," Gage said. "We need more contracts, more workers—more everything. If Dad ends up selling to Warrington and we all leave, you won't want to stay."

Gage had a point. It hadn't exactly been smooth sailing so far. Given they were starting from scratch and didn't know if they'd succeed, they'd hired the first batch of workers on a temporary basis and were having trouble holding on to them. This morning three more men quit, complaining about the low wages, the Ridge's crappy internet connection—and the lack of women. It had been more difficult than Carter had expected to find mill workers in the first place. These days the housing market was booming, which meant people with experience in the field were in high demand all over. There were plenty of large operations that could afford to pay better wages—and offer better benefits. That meant the folks Carter had managed to hire were less than optimal. Drifters and troublemakers who preferred not to put down roots.

Once—and only once—he'd tried to interest some of them in settling down at the Ridge. He'd told them there'd soon be houses to buy for low prices.

"You could give them away, and I wouldn't want to stay," Terry Brook had said contemptuously. "I'm gone the minute I get a better offer."

The others seemed to feel the same.

"We're going to make this work," he told Gage.

"Not if you can't attract some better workers. How are you going to do that?"

It annoyed Carter that his oldest brother still had an inch of height on him and that his cold, dark gaze never flinched no matter what.

"The men are right; no one is going to want to stay

here. This isn't a real community. There aren't enough people here. There aren't any women. Which isn't surprising. What woman in her right mind would want to move to a ghost town? Women like stability. There's nothing stable about a mill town these days."

Gage was just mad because Hudson and Lincoln had said they wanted to buy houses, too. They hadn't chosen them yet, mostly because Lincoln was out looking at horses every spare moment and Hudson was out chasing women, but they were enthusiastic about the idea, and that seemed to get under Gage's skin.

"Women are just as adventurous as men," Carter argued. "If they understood the possibilities, they'd be flocking to live at Elliott Ridge." As far as he was concerned, the place was paradise.

"There's the plane," Hudson said. They moved closer to the windows and watched its approach.

"Flocking?" Gage repeated. "You've been recruiting workers since before you even got here. Has a single woman applied for a job?"

Carter sighed. "Women don't need to work in the lumber industry to move here." He was close to losing his patience, but he didn't want to make a scene in public. The rough men they'd employed to work at the mill were giving them a bad enough reputation in Chance Creek as it was. Cab Johnson, the local sheriff, had been out to the Ridge twice to deliver men who'd spent a night in the county lockup for drunk and disorderly conduct. "They can do all kinds of remote work as soon as we get a better internet connection."

"When's that going to happen?"

Carter couldn't answer that. He hadn't anticipated it would be such a hard problem to solve, but there was only one company that serviced the area. All he could do was be patient and hope they saw the value in extending fiber optic cable to Elliott Ridge. It was the kind of chicken-and-egg problem that could drive a man to drink. The internet service provider would be more likely to upgrade their connection if more people lived at the Ridge, but more people wouldn't settle there unless they could be sure of a high-quality internet connection. Gage would say he'd misjudged the difficulty of solving the problem because he was too optimistic.

He was too something.

"I don't see why women wouldn't flock to the Ridge," Hudson put in. "We've got a lake, the forest— me."

Gage snorted. "We've got snow, mosquitoes, a forty-minute commute to town... and I hate to tell you this, Romeo, but you're not that much of an attraction."

"Am, too."

"We've got a lot of houses. Maybe we should give a few away—like they did in those towns in Italy. Remember?" Lincoln said. "They sold them for a dollar to people who agreed to fix them up."

"We can't give them away. We need to sell them to cover our costs," Gage said.

"Here come the passengers." Carter cut off his brothers. He didn't need to hear any more of Gage's grumbling—or Hudson's bragging. He'd had enough of both these past few weeks. They had just under thirteen months to get the mill up and running at full capacity, the logging operation restarted and enough money coming in to cover their balloon payment and their ongoing bills.

That wasn't all. Carter was determined to bring his parents back to Elliott Ridge, and he wasn't going to move them into a ghost town. That meant filling all those empty houses with people who meant to stay. Not just single men, either. Gage was right; he needed women.

Trouble was, he couldn't figure out how to attract them here. Men were easy. They'd come for the mill and logging jobs. Not many women were interested in those.

In fact, young single women were scarce in Chance Creek, too, which was why his temporary workers kept getting in trouble when they went to town. Add twenty extra unattached men to a night at the Dancing Boot, and suddenly you had an alarming imbalance of the sexes.

He focused on the people filing down the metal steps from the small plane. Most of them looked like regular folks coming to visit family or returning from vacation. A few groups seemed ready for outdoor adventures. They had probably come for the fishing. There were one or two businessmen and women, but not too many.

Where was Nate?

Carter's gaze lifted to the top of the stairs when a pretty blonde came into view. She surveyed the little airport and tucked a strand of long straight hair behind her ear. She was dressed in jeans and a blue casual top. She had a large purse strapped across her body and carried a gym bag as well.

She didn't look particularly happy. She looked… alert, Carter decided. As if something might happen at any moment—something just as likely to be bad as good. Her chin was high. Her shoulders back. Her attitude half-defiant and half-anticipatory.

What was she expecting to find here in Chance Creek?

Intrigued, Carter edged closer to the window.

A flight attendant leaned toward the woman from the interior of the plane and gestured as if to say, "Please head down the stairs."

The blonde nodded but didn't move. Was she lingering to savor the moment or to give herself time to prepare for whatever came next? She was beautiful, Carter decided.

The flight attendant gestured again.

Come on, Carter willed the pretty blonde. *You're going to like it here.*

He wouldn't mind making it his business to ensure that.

You don't even know her, he told himself. She probably had a boyfriend or husband waiting to welcome her home. A woman like that wouldn't be single.

His brothers were watching her, too, now. They must have noticed that someone had caught his attention and followed his gaze to see who it was. Despite their differences, they'd always been in tune in some ways.

The flight attendant leaned closer to the blonde. Carter was no lip-reader, but he could guess what she was saying. "You're holding everyone up. You need to keep moving."

The blonde nodded. Lifted her chin and made her way down the stairs. Halfway across the tarmac to the terminal, however, something caught her eye and she slowed, tilting her head back. Carter looked up, too. High above the single airstrip, an eagle circled. A smile curved the blonde's mouth, and she nodded again, but this time it was as if she were communicating with the bird, acknowledging it had its priorities right.

Her smile seemed to say she was also ready to soar. That she was done with her past and ready to take flight.

A visceral thrill shot through Carter's body. That's how he felt coming home to Elliott Ridge. Like his real life was finally about to begin.

And suddenly he knew.

I'm going to marry that woman.

The thought seared through his brain like a sniper's bullet through flesh, even as Carter shook his head at the folly of it. There was no way he could know a thing like that. He hadn't even spoken to her yet.

She could belong to someone else.

Still, he knew his hunch was right, as crazy as it was. He'd taken a bullet once. Had the scars to prove it. He knew what it felt like when a round hit home.

This felt like that. The utter truth of it going so deep

it was viscerally clear.

He was going to marry her.

He was going to bring his family's town back to life—with this woman by his side. He'd never felt so certain of anything, and the revelation shocked him into a higher awareness. Did his brothers feel it, too—this startling clarity?

"Speaking of women," Hudson said. "There's one now. I wouldn't mind if she settled at the Ridge."

"She'd do just fine," Lincoln agreed, leaning forward to get a better look.

Gage shook his head. "No women. No settling. We're going to have to sell the Ridge in the end."

"No, we're not." Carter watched the blonde enter the building. He'd been determined before, but now he was committed on a whole new level. He needed to make a home for this woman who was going to be his wife. He needed to build a whole world for her.

"There's Nate," Hudson said.

WHO KNEW BEING chased by a killer could set you free? Amanda exited the small airplane that had brought her to Chance Creek, Montana, and stood at the top of the metal steps leading to the tarmac. She was taking a leap of faith coming here, banking that Buck hadn't heard of the little town and wouldn't think to come looking for her in such an obscure place.

Two weeks ago, her father's panicked texts had shattered the spell she hadn't known she was living under. For years she'd crafted an existence so small she'd thought it would make her invisible. She'd let shame dictate every move, running more than a thousand miles from home and accepting a position she was overqualified for, so she wouldn't have to face anyone who knew the truth.

When her father returned, she'd thought maybe there was a way to erase the past. She'd hoped he'd paint something so brilliant that his new success would blot out his old crime, and everyone would forget about it.

It hadn't worked.

Her father had barrelled on, heaping a new helping of shame on her family, and Amanda knew that even if Buck hadn't come, she'd have run from Los Angeles anyway now she knew what her father had done. He wasn't the kind of criminal strategist who could pull off a crime like this one. He would've been caught again sooner or later. And his shame would be hers to share. She wouldn't have been able to stand going to work and facing her peers—*Gwen*—once they found out she was the daughter of a forger and thief.

That didn't matter, though.

These past few days, she'd realized even if she could go back, she didn't want to. Buck's re-entry into her life had made her rethink everything.

All of it.

She was angry she'd wasted so many years twisting her life into knots because of what her father had done. Why should she feel shame for crimes she had no part in? Why was she punishing herself when she'd done nothing wrong?

Her father hadn't been in touch since the night she'd fled LA. Did he think warning her about Buck was the extent of his obligation to her as a father?

Where was he now?

She hadn't contacted him, either. Didn't want him in her life anymore, anyway.

"Thank you for flying with us," the flight attendant said.

Amanda nodded, still hesitating at the top of the stairs. As soon as she made her way down them, she'd start a brand-new life. Her father obviously hadn't spared a thought for her since he'd warned her to leave, so she'd put him out of her mind, too. She'd move forward to the future she deserved.

She'd left nothing behind in Los Angeles she would miss. Just an average apartment. Possessions she could replace.

A job she didn't care about one way or another.

A few acquaintances but no close friends.

Gwen.

She'd been sleepwalking through her days. Now she was awake. Should she thank her father?

Should she thank Buck?

"Ma'am, you're holding up the other passengers," the flight attendant said.

Amanda nodded again. She would still have to be careful, so Buck couldn't trace her here. She had to get rid of the masterpiece hidden in her bag. But once she was free of that cargo, she'd craft a brand-new existence. One that was vibrant, authentic. That included real friends—

A man.

Children.

Purpose.

"Ma'am?" the flight attendant prompted.

Everything changes right now, she told herself. She lifted her chin and started down the stairs. When she was on solid ground, she strode across the tarmac, almost giddy with the possibilities. Maybe she was fooling herself.

Maybe Buck would find her—again.

But maybe, just maybe—

A movement overhead caught her attention, and Amanda stopped.

It was an eagle. The best of omens. An eagle meant strength.

Freedom.

She could do this.

Feeling a triumphant smile tug at the corners of her mouth, she squared her shoulders and started for the terminal again. Somewhere in front of her was the life she'd always wanted.

She'd be damned if she missed one more second of it out of shame or fear.

She pushed open the door and stepped into the building, but the crowd in the waiting area brought her up short. There was a single baggage carousel on the far side of the room. In between her and it were enough people to fill several Greyhound buses. This had to be the smallest airport she'd ever seen.

Find my suitcase. Rent a car.

She didn't let herself think about what she'd do after that. She needed to find accommodations, of course, but she didn't want to stay in another motel, which would require showing her credit card again. Bad enough she'd have to use it to get the car. That couldn't be helped, she supposed, but if it was at all possible, she wanted to find a private rental cabin she could pay for with cash.

As she inched forward among the knots of passengers being greeted by their loved ones, she couldn't help feeling like the odd person out. An extended family exuberantly greeted a grandmotherly woman who'd been seated several rows in front of her on the plane. A serious man with a military bearing who'd been a few rows behind her edged past and joined a group of other men. His brothers, maybe? There were five of them all told, of different heights, a couple of them wearing the cowboy hats that seemed so popular in these ranching states. They all had the same broad shoulders and upright bearing. Handsome and strong—and happy to see each other.

One of them caught her looking. Amanda quickly turned away. The baggage carousel wasn't running yet, but she wasn't sure what to do with herself while she waited.

She glanced at the five brothers again. They'd coalesced into a tight group, taking turns shaking the hand of the one who'd just arrived, all talking at once. There was some sort of argument going on between them, but the newcomer made a comment and all of them laughed.

Amanda's heart squeezed. She and her sister, Melissa, hadn't laughed like that in years. They were never in the same place at the same time anymore, and when they talked on the phone, they often disagreed. The few times they'd met up since leaving home, Melissa had seemed like a stranger, someone she had to take care not to upset. She missed their younger years when they'd been inseparable.

A sound chimed, and the carousel turned on. As the crowd surged toward it, the brothers moved, too, but not before the one who'd caught her gaze before turned to look her way again. He nodded at her, as if to encourage her to come fetch her luggage, too.

Amanda was surprised and a bit unnerved by his sharp brown gaze. Men like him didn't usually pay attention to women like her. Not that there was anything wrong with her, Amanda told herself. It was just there wasn't anything extraordinarily right. She'd made sure of that, after all. She liked to blend in. Just pretty enough and no more.

He was certainly extraordinary, though. The kind of man who would catch everyone's attention no matter where he went. He had ash-brown hair, warm brown eyes and shoulders that strained the seams of his shirt. He wore no uniform, but she would bet her life he'd served in the military. One of her roommates in college had dated a man in the ROTC, and all his friends had a certain bearing. This man had it.

His gaze held hers as if he was searching for answers and thought he could read them there. Maybe he could, Amanda thought. She wouldn't put anything past a man like him. Then one of his brothers said something, and he turned away.

The moment passed, leaving Amanda breathless—and slightly amused at herself.

She was supposed to be looking for a place to live, not a man to dream about.

Although she wouldn't mind one of those, too.

This stranger would do for her dreams, she decided as she drifted in the direction of the baggage carousel. He was the perfect fodder for nighttime fantasies, which was as close as she'd been to a man in quite some time.

She couldn't see the stranger anymore in the throng of passengers trying to find their luggage. Her suitcase wasn't in sight, so she pulled out the pay-as-you-go phone she'd bought during her travels to replace the one she'd thrown out the night she'd left LA.

Most of the local vacation rentals seemed affiliated with national companies and required a credit card to make a reservation. Amanda paged through them, her concern growing, and nearly dropped her phone when someone tapped her shoulder. The same man who'd nodded at her a few minutes before.

"Waiting for your family?" His voice was deep and matter-of-fact, as if he had every right to inquire into her circumstances.

"Uh... no." Amanda was too shocked to lie. Strangers didn't talk to you in Los Angeles, but this man was standing close to her, using his body to create a pocket in the crowd, a space for just the two of them.

"Did you come to Chance Creek for vacation?"

"I'm… planning to stay awhile, actually." She was close to panic, but he seemed fully at ease. Amanda wondered what it felt like to be so comfortable in your body. To plant yourself with feet spread and know that the world would part around you instead of running you down.

"You don't have a reservation anywhere, do you?"

How could he know that? Her surprise must have shown, because he lifted his hands in a placating gesture.

"Easy guess," he told her. "You look like I feel when I land in a town without a plan. I like things nailed down."

She could understand that, at least. "I do, too," she confessed. Her whole life up to this time had been planned out and carefully constructed to keep her safe.

Talking to this man felt anything but.

He smiled, and Amanda's heart stuttered to a stop before catching up double-time. It was a wonderful smile, the kind that warmed everyone in the vicinity.

"There's always the Evergreen Motel. It's plain but comfortable enough. At least it was twelve years ago—I haven't been there since I've been back."

A motel? That wasn't going to work. "I… was looking for something more like a rental. Something long term. Out of town, preferably?"

She'd barely spoken a word to anyone in the past

two weeks, and now she felt out of practice. She pressed her lips together to stop herself from revealing any more than she already had.

The man straightened. Stuck his hand out and waited for her to take it. When she did, his fingers closed around hers, and Amanda's breath caught all over again. It was as if the floor had dropped out beneath her feet. Like a tide had taken her and was dragging her out to sea.

"My name's Carter Elliott," the man told her. His grip was strong and sure, a lifeline to cling to. "I've got the perfect place for you to stay."

"You do?" Hope surged within her, followed by a swoop of fear. Amanda refused to give into it. Nothing about Carter Elliott suggested he was anything like Buck. Besides, he had a rental. She wondered what kind.

"I do." He tilted his head, studying her for another moment. "The house is a little rough. I've just started renovating it, but if you don't mind a little dust while I finish the work, I can give you a good discount."

"How much of a discount?" She was worried about money. She'd withdrawn a stack of cash at one of her layovers, and it was burning a hole in the purse she wore strapped across her body. It represented a large portion of her life savings, which she was spending far too quickly these days. She wasn't going to have a paycheck anytime soon. She'd emailed her boss and told her a family emergency had taken her out of town and that she wouldn't be back.

Carter sent a glance toward his brothers, who were

still waiting by the baggage carousel.

"When you say long term, how long term are you talking about?" he asked in a lower tone, leaning closer.

"Maybe forever." The words popped out of her mouth before she could consider them. She hadn't meant them to sound flirtatious, but somehow they did. It was true, though. She couldn't go back to LA. Buck's prior crimes included theft, battery, arson and *murder*. Who knew what he'd do to her if he ever caught up with her again? She suppressed a shiver.

Carter's brows raised. "Forever?"

"Maybe." It felt reckless to say it but exciting, too.

Carter smiled again, a slow grin that sent a thrill through her body straight down to her toes. "That's perfect."

"It is?" She felt breathless. Something had propelled her to Chance Creek. Was she supposed to be here?

Supposed to meet this man?

"Here's the thing," he said. "My brothers and I just took charge of a town. It's a really small town, but we've got over a hundred houses to fill. We need people."

Amanda wasn't sure what to make of that. Her confusion must have showed, because Carter added, "It's a great place to live. Inexpensive, too."

"How inexpensive?"

His gaze sharpened. "How inexpensive do you need it to be?"

Amanda pulled back. What kind of game was he playing? Did he have a place for rent or not? She'd hoped rural Montana would be a lot cheaper than Los

Angeles, but maybe she'd been naive. "Pretty inexpensive," she said dryly. Her pocketbook wouldn't stand for anything else.

He hesitated. Looked toward his brothers again. When he turned back, there was a glint in his eye she couldn't decipher. "Have you heard of those towns in Italy—the ones offering houses for a dollar to people who pledge to fix them up and live there?"

"The towns that are dying out?" She'd read an article about them a few years ago.

"We're doing something similar at Elliott Ridge. Giving away a house for a dollar to one lucky person. You pay a buck, sign a contract, and it's yours."

"For how long?" Amanda was intrigued. A house for a dollar? In an abandoned town?

That was a hell of a lot more interesting than her apartment in LA.

"Forever. You need to help me fix it up, of course, but we can arrange that so it won't get in the way of your work. What is your work?"

A personal question she didn't really want to answer. She liked Carter—so far. That didn't mean she trusted him all the way yet.

"Just how rough is this house?" she asked, buying time.

"It's got four walls and a roof. Two stories. Three bedrooms, two baths, a kitchen that was last redone in the '80s." He made a face. "We'll fix that, though. It will be thoroughly modern by the time we're done."

There was something endearing about a man who

wanted to renovate a house with you, Amanda thought.

"Will I need to buy the building supplies and appliances and all that?" Would she have any savings left if she did?

He shook his head. "I've already ordered them. You'll want to furnish it when we're through, but it comes with a bed and a few other things."

"What's the catch?" This was all far too good to be true. She tried to look like the kind of woman who couldn't be fooled, but the truth was it sounded perfect. She wasn't afraid to get her hands dirty and wouldn't mind getting to know Carter better. Besides, she needed somewhere to go.

"The catch is that right now Elliott Ridge really is a ghost town. We're starting from scratch except for the buildings and the mill. It would be great if you were willing to pitch in and help us get the place up and running, but it's not necessary." He paused, and his smile turned sheepish. "Look, I know this is sketchy as hell, approaching you in an airport when you don't know me. It's a long story, but the upshot is I thought our town was done for, and now I've got the chance to resurrect it. It's not going to be easy, but I've got to try. I need a few hundred people to agree to settle there, and I've got only a year to make it happen, so I'm kind of desperate." He lowered his voice again, speaking confidentially. "So far all I've got are men."

"No women?" Amanda stepped back. That didn't sound safe at all.

"It's just me, my four brothers, a caretaker and

twenty temporary mill workers who don't really count. They're quartered in the old bunkhouses and won't be around long term. That's why I need someone like you to buy my house."

His smile tugged at something deep within her. She tried to sneak a glance at his hand without being too obvious. No ring.

He could still be spoken for, she cautioned herself, but she didn't think so. If Carter was in a relationship, there'd be at least one woman living at Elliott Ridge.

"*Your* house?" she repeated.

"The house I'm currently renovating," he amended. "I need a woman to move to the Ridge as a proof of concept—to show that women are actually willing to live there."

"Why wouldn't they be?"

Carter sighed. "Because it's been abandoned for a number of years. It's forty-five minutes out of town, and there aren't any amenities out there—yet."

"You're right; that does sound sketchy." As Carter's face fell, Amanda rushed to soften her words. "But it also sounds like exactly what I'm looking for."

"Really?"

"Maybe," she hedged. "I'll have to see it before I know for sure."

"You'll love it," he assured her. "It was great to grow up there, and I know it can be like that again."

Amanda read sincerity in his words. He spoke of the Ridge in a proprietary way she hadn't felt about any- where since she was living at home—before her father took up a life of crime. Renting an apartment always felt so tenuous. She'd been craving stability for years but had never got any closer to securing it.

"Maybe you'd prefer to be right in the thick of things in Chance Creek, though," Carter added, misinterpreting her silence.

"No." Amanda caught herself. "I mean, I'd like to live in the country." Somewhere Buck would never think to look.

"You ought to check out Elliott Ridge, then. After all, you can't beat a house for a dollar." This time when he met her gaze, she felt like they were co-conspirators, and another thrill coursed through her. Maybe resurrecting a ghost town was exactly what she should do next. "I don't suppose you've ever worked at a lumber mill?" Carter added.

Amanda laughed at the absurdity of the question. "No." She hadn't done that. "I work at a corporate office for a grocery conglomerate. I'm in purchasing."

Carter blinked. "Can you do that remotely?"

"No," she said. "I mean, maybe I could, but that's not why I'm here. I quit." Carter's brows rose, and she struggled to make sense. "I needed a change."

He waited, as if suspecting there was more. That was all she could tell him, though.

"I'm sure you'll be able to find work around here," he said when she didn't go on. But he didn't sound confident.

Disappointment spiked through her. She needed to find a job sooner or later. "Are you sure you still want me?" she asked. "Sounds like you were looking for people with practical skills." She held her breath, worried he might change his mind. Should she have lied about her credentials? Amanda decided against it. You couldn't fake experience working with heavy machinery.

Carter's gaze ran over her like he was considering her question in a way she hadn't meant. When his gaze met hers again, the frank appreciation she saw in his eyes sent warmth radiating through her body.

"I want you," he confirmed. "We'll find something for you to do."

She nodded, distracted. Was Carter Elliott attracted to her?

She was definitely attracted to him.

"Have you spotted your bags yet?" He gestured to the carousel. It looked like his brother had grabbed his. A large duffel sat on the floor beside him.

"I just have one. I'm traveling light." Still off-kilter from their heady conversation, she went to fetch it, and he followed. "I'm on a journey of discovery," she added, not wanting him to ask any more questions she couldn't answer. "I've been all over the country." She'd taken plane after plane to try to throw Buck off her track. "But like you said, you can't beat a house for a dollar." She grabbed the handle of her suitcase and hauled it off the belt.

"A house for a dollar," a new voice repeated. "Where would you find something like that?"

Amanda dropped her suitcase on the floor with a thump, then caught it before it fell over. When she straightened, she realized the men she'd seen with Carter before had come to join him.

"At Elliott Ridge," Carter said firmly. "This is Nate," he said to Amanda. "And that's Lincoln, Hudson and Gage. My brothers." Nate was the shortest and stockiest, his hair a shade lighter than the others. Lincoln and Hudson had to be identical twins. They were about the same height as Carter, their hair a shade darker. Gage shared their hair color but struck her as the oldest of the bunch. He had sharp features and deep-set eyes. All of them were tall and handsome. Impressive, Amanda thought.

Carter hesitated. "I didn't catch your name."

"Amanda Stakewell," she supplied, then cringed, wishing she'd thought to give him an alias.

"Amanda Stakewell," Carter repeated to his brothers. "She's new in town and looking to settle here. I told her about our newcomer deal."

"Newcomer—" Nate's words died on his lips. Amanda looked to Carter. Had she just missed some kind of communication between him and his brothers? He hadn't said a word or moved, as far as she could tell, but all of them had gone on alert in a way that set her warning bells ringing. Now they surveyed her with renewed interest.

"The newcomer deal," Carter repeated. "The one we're offering to the first woman who settles on Elliott Ridge. Amanda is buying the home I've been fixing for a dollar. She'll help me with the renovation and has agreed to try to be useful to our community. Nate hasn't been around for all our conversations, Amanda," he went on. "He's just home from the Marines."

"It's nice to meet you." Amanda shook his hand, still uncertain about what had just happened or why Carter's voice suddenly had an edge to it. Nate had a firm grip.

"Nice to meet you, too, Amanda," he said. "Glad you're joining us." Despite the curious tension among the brothers, she had the feeling Nate meant it, and she relaxed a little again. Whatever undercurrent she'd felt must be a family issue, she decided. Maybe Carter was staking a claim to her. Telling his brothers in some unspoken way to back off.

That gave her ego a little boost, even as she told herself not to get her hopes up.

"Lincoln and Hudson are twins, as I'm sure you've noticed," Carter said. "Lincoln's been with the Army for the past twelve years. Hudson was a pilot with the Air Force."

The two did look a lot alike, but Lincoln was more reserved as he shook her hand, while Hudson held hers a little longer than necessary, letting go in a way that was almost a caress.

"Knock it off," Carter told him. "Stay away from Hudson," he told Amanda. "He's a love 'em and leave 'em kind of guy."

"But I always leave 'em happy," Hudson said, eliciting several groans from his brothers. "What? It's true."

"Gage, here, was with the Rangers." Carter spoke right over him.

Gage shook her hand but didn't say anything, leaving Amanda to wonder if he welcomed her or not. After all, Carter had invited her to their town without consulting anyone.

"I didn't mean to intrude on your reunion," she felt compelled to say. "I'm sure I can find a place to stay in Chance Creek." What if Gage thought she was an opportunist?

"Don't mind Gage. He's a dour old bastard, but he's harmless," Hudson said. "We're happy to have you."

"Yeah," Lincoln said. "We only just came up with the newcomer deal, that's all."

"Gage is surprised Carter found a taker so fast," Nate said. "We'd love to have you, right, Gage?"

Gage heaved a long-suffering sigh. "Whatever. Time to go." He stalked off toward the main entrance.

Nate leaned closer to her. "Can't have five brothers without one of them being defective. Are you ready? Do you have a car?"

She shook her head. "I was going to rent one for now."

"Why don't you ride with me?" Carter asked. "We've got plenty of vehicles between us. If you decide to stay and want your own car, I'll run you back to town so you can pick one up."

Amanda hesitated. Shouldn't she rent one right now so she could escape if this turned out to be a bad idea?

"Here." Carter tossed her the keys. "My truck is yours as long as you want it. Like I said, we've got plenty of vehicles to share. That way you can leave anytime you like. Just tell me where you've parked it so I can pick it up if you skip town."

Carter's humor was reflected in the faces of his brothers, who were watching this exchange curiously. Amanda was still wary. "This is the only set of keys?"

Carter nodded. "I'm at your mercy."

"We're good people, Amanda," Nate said. "Ask anyone in Chance Creek. They all know us."

"A girl can't be too careful," she said.

"That's true," Lincoln said.

Gage walked back to them. "What's the holdup?"

"Amanda's not sure if we're trustworthy," Carter said.

"We're trustworthy," Hudson protested.

Gage surveyed her, his frank gaze leaving her feeling exposed. "You're safe with us. Come on." He stalked off again.

"You heard the man," Carter said. "Coming?"

"I guess so," she heard herself say. Why not take a chance? She couldn't be in more danger on Elliott Ridge than she already was, if Buck was trying to find her. Maybe she'd be safer, considering Carter and his brothers were all military men. They'd know how to deal with a killer if Buck showed up, wouldn't they?

She hoped it never came to that.

"See you there," Hudson told Amanda. "Happy to finally have a woman around the place."

"Get out of here." Carter shoved him away good-naturedly.

Lincoln and Nate followed their brothers.

"Ready?" Carter asked and led the way out of the terminal.

CHAPTER 3

"J UST HOW FAR is this place?" Amanda asked thirty minutes into their drive from the airport.

"We're almost there." Carter noticed her knuckles were white on his truck's steering wheel, and the anticipation he'd felt since meeting her turned into concern. "You said you were looking for a place out of town," he reminded her, hoping she wouldn't chicken out before they reached Elliott Ridge. He was already bracing himself for a showdown the next time he was alone with his brothers. He'd silently invoked an old rule from their childhood days, when they'd devised a secret code sign language, and he was more grateful than he could say that it still worked.

He'd pursed the fingers of his right hand together, then spread them wide. The signal meant, "Shut up and go along with what I'm saying—no questions asked." According to their old code of conduct, his brothers had no choice but to back up his story.

That didn't mean they'd be happy about it, though.

Carter had only invoked the rule twice before—both

times to avoid punishment when he'd snuck out at night as a teenager to meet girls and hadn't made it back before sunrise. He wasn't so proud of that now, but the rule sure had come in handy today at the airport. Frankly, he was amazed they'd gone along with it considering Gage had shot down the house-for-a-dollar idea the first time Lincoln raised it. They must think he was out of his mind.

Maybe he was. Paying for the house and its renovation had eaten up a large share of his savings—and he was going to give it away to a woman he'd just met?

He knew what Gage would say the next time they were alone. If he was willing to sell "his" house, he should have done so for a profit. They were desperate for cash to make their monthly loan payments.

He hadn't known what else to do to make Amanda give Elliott Ridge a chance, though. He couldn't simply let her walk away—out of his life. Not when his gut told him she was *the one*. He wasn't the kind of simple-headed romantic who fell for every woman who gave him the time of day, either. In fact, he'd never had any kind of premonition before. What he'd felt at the airport when Amanda crossed the tarmac was something new and different. He had to know if it was real.

"The drive is worth it, believe me. You're going to love Elliott Ridge," he told Amanda firmly. She had to, or he didn't know what he'd do. So far, very little was going right in this enterprise, and he needed his luck to change. No way was he going to let Blake Warrington buy his family's property out from under him.

According to his father, Warrington had been disappointed when his initial bid to buy the place had been thwarted, but he'd resolved to be patient. "When those boys of yours discover it's harder than it looks to settle a community, they'll come running to me for the cash," he'd told Carter's father, which made Carter more determined to succeed.

The road began climbing, and soon the ranches they'd been passing were replaced by scrub forest and small hamlets of houses.

"You don't belong to some kind of cult, do you?" Amanda kept her eyes on the highway, but she was driving more slowly, as if regretting coming at all.

"Definitely not."

"How can one family own a whole town?"

"The Ridge has been in our family for generations," Carter explained. "We used to be kind of rich, I guess." A long time ago now. "One of my ancestors found silver here in the late 1800s. He opened the mine. Brought in workers. Built housing for them and collected the rent. Elliott Ridge was a company town. Near as we can make out, the workers didn't profit much. Between paying rent for their houses and buying their food from the company store, a lot of their earnings went right back into my ancestors' pockets. The place eventually hit hard times, though, and the mine petered out."

She glanced his way. "But your family held on to the place?"

"My great-great-grandfather looked around, saw

trees everywhere and started a forestry and lumber operation. As the years passed, the workers still rented their houses and could buy food from the store if they wanted to, but Chance Creek was growing by then. People could drive into town to do their shopping. There was more fun to be had in off-hours. Earnings went up, but rents climbed more slowly. Elliott Ridge boomed. Unfortunately, when the price of lumber tanked in the early 2000s, the bottom fell out of the business. My dad had to lay people off, and those people left the area. Pretty soon the town had cleared out."

"What makes you think you can bring it back to life?" Amanda asked.

He'd been over this so many times with his brothers he could recite his explanation in his sleep. He bit back a smile as Amanda pressed down on the accelerator again, caught up in his story. "People don't need to live where they work anymore. Not all of them, anyway. Remote workers are looking for places that offer amenities but are cheaper than expensive cities. No one can afford housing in San Francisco, but out here…" He waved a hand at the forest around them. "Homes are cheap. Even housing prices in Chance Creek have gone up these past few years," he added, "but Elliott Ridge is a bargain."

She nodded slowly. "Hard to beat a house for a buck. But… If you previously rented these homes, are they zoned for individual sale?"

He had an answer for that, too. "Not all of them,"

he admitted, pleased she was showing so much interest. "But Elliott Ridge is made up of multiple lots, all owned jointly by my family. A number of years back, Dad started the process of subdividing one section of the town. I got the process moving again when I got home. Approval should come through any day now."

"So I really will *own* a house," she said.

"Once we get that approval—and once you've signed the paperwork, you will. Turn there." He pointed to a road that branched off the country highway, and she took the turn onto the winding road that led to the Ridge. "This is Elliott Way," he told her, relieved they'd made it this far. "My ancestors liked to put their name on everything they could."

She nodded again. They were silent until they rounded a final bend in the road and the community spread out before them. It resembled a Western ghost town more closely than Carter wished, but this was home. He was confident he could persuade Amanda to stay now that he'd gotten her here.

"It must be gloomy in the wintertime." She peered up at the ridge above them. "Does the sun stay behind that most of the day?"

"It's not as bad as you think," Carter lied, captivated by the way her hair swung forward in a shimmering wave as she bent over the steering wheel. The truth was, the Ridge cast deep shadows in the winter months. "Besides, wait until you see the lake. Prettiest thing around." It was the sunniest location, too. "This is the Circle," he said as they drew up to where the road looped around a central field. "Stop here for a minute. That's my parents' place. Number one. It was the first house built at Elliott Ridge." The white clapboard house was old-fashioned, with a deck that wrapped all the way around it. The back of the house faced the lake. A black flag with green and silver stripes hung from a pole by the front door.

Amanda pointed to it. "I've never seen a flag like that."

"It's the Elliott Ridge flag. The black is for the Ridge, the green is for the forest and the silver is for the... well... silver." He chuckled. "At the top of the Circle is the town hall. Those other large buildings used to be a general store and a hotel with a bar on the first floor. There's the town chapel." Peeking out from behind the other buildings, it was a small structure with a steeple. It had been sparsely used in his childhood, but it could be spiffed up again if it was wanted. "We used to have a minister living on site, but he passed away in the 80s. After that, we had visiting ones now and then." He pointed to the left. "Go three-quarters of the way around the Circle and turn onto Center Street." Amanda followed his directions. "Turn left onto Second Street. That's the one." He pointed to the house he'd begun to renovate—number twenty-three.

As she parked the car in front of it, a simmer of unease settled in his stomach. What if she hated it? What if she drove straight back to town? Gage would take that as a clear sign they were doomed to fail.

It was do or die time, Carter decided as Amanda

surveyed the house. If he wanted her to stay—and he definitely did—he needed to use all his powers of persuasion to try to show her what the Ridge—and the house—could become. He'd have to find another house to live in for now, but his mind was already swarming with images of the two of them sharing this one. Watching the game on the couch in front of a wide-screen TV, prepping dinner for friends in the kitchen, heading up to bed together—

Don't get ahead of yourself. He was spinning a story about a future Amanda might never want. He needed to wait and watch the new arrival before he allowed himself to act on his attraction, no matter what thoughts he'd had at the airport. As long as he could get her to stay, there'd be plenty of time to get to know her and see if she was really the woman he wanted for his wife.

"Who's that?"

Amanda pointed to a man walking down the street toward them. Dennis Crutchfield was seventy-two, with a heavy paunch, a halo of thinning white hair and a perpetual frown. He'd seemed old when Carter was a child, and he never seemed to change. Still wearing the same work-worn pants and torn flannel shirt over an undershirt that once must have been white but now was an indeterminate yellowish-tan, he was as much a part of the place as the evergreens that marched up the slope to the rocky summit of the Ridge.

"That's Dennis. Don't mind his appearance. He's a sweetheart," Carter told her. He got out of the car. Amanda followed suit more slowly. He wondered what she thought of the place. Wished she could see it through his eyes.

It was cooler up here than it had been in town. Quiet, too. They were far from the road and miles away from any other habitations.

"Who the heck have you got there?" Dennis boomed at them as he came striding up in his hitching, painful-looking way.

Carter stiffened. Hell, this wasn't the impression he wanted to give Amanda. He strode forward to head the man off.

"Dennis, let me introduce you to Elliott Ridge's newest inhabitant." He spoke loudly to divert Amanda's attention from Dennis's stormy attitude. "This is Amanda Stakewell. Amanda, Dennis Crutchfield, caretaker of the town and all-around handyman."

Dennis scowled and looked Amanda up and down. "Newest inhabitant? Since when?"

"Since about an hour ago."

"Thought you boys were selling the Ridge."

Amanda's eyebrows shot up. Carter knew he had to do damage control—fast.

"You know darn well we're not. We're selling the houses, one at a time, starting with the downslope subdivision. Remember how Dad put the process in motion? It will get approved any day now, so we're starting to bring in buyers." When Dennis's frown deepened, Carter added, "Come on, we're bringing the Ridge back to life. Aren't you happy about that?"

"What's a girl like you want with living out here?

You in trouble?" Dennis asked Amanda, ignoring Carter.

Her eyes widened. "N-no."

"Not very convincing. You'll have to work on that."

"Dennis!" Carter couldn't believe this. "You can't talk to Amanda that way. She's new here, and she deserves respect."

Dennis wasn't cowed at all. He shook his head. "Knew this was coming. Felt it in my bones. It's another Calamity Year."

This was a disaster. Carter turned to Amanda. "Don't listen to him. Living alone all this time has turned his mind. Pull it together," he told Dennis.

"I'm not losing my mind. Might not be as fast on my feet as I once was, but I'm not senile." Dennis turned to Amanda. "There was another time like this one, in the 1920s. My father told me all about it. Heard about it from his father. The mine petered out. The town emptied. Old Cade Elliott came up with a new scheme. Started bringing people back. And then the *women* came."

"Dennis," Carter warned.

"What women?" Amanda asked.

"Troubled women. Women running from something. Drifting in from all sides of the country, one after another. There was hell to pay." He looked to Carter. "Take one of them, you'll get them all. Mark my words."

Amanda crossed her arms, holding her shoulders high and tight. Dennis was ruining everything, and

Carter wasn't going to stand for it. Too much was at stake.

"You're talking nonsense. Amanda was bored with her job, so she's taking time to see what she really wants to do with her life. She's interested in what we're planning here, and she's pledged to help us grow this town. Isn't that right, Amanda?"

Dennis cocked his head and held Amanda in his steady gaze. Amanda looked back at him. Carter bit back a curse. How had the caretaker taken control of the situation?

Amanda nodded finally. "That's right." She held her hand out to Dennis. "Nice to meet you. I look forward to getting to know Elliott Ridge and helping any way I can."

Dennis turned to Carter. "You've still got a chance," he said. "You can stop this right now."

A surge of anger rushed through Carter. He was working his ass off to bring this town back to life. He wanted Amanda to be part of that.

He wanted Amanda, period.

You don't know her, his conscience reminded him. Maybe Dennis was right; maybe this was a big mistake. Why was he rushing to install her here—daydreaming about making her his wife?

Because he was attracted to her?

Because he was sick of being single?

Because he was desperate to rebuild the community he'd never wanted to leave in the first place?

Or all of the above?

It didn't matter, Carter decided. He trusted his gut, and his gut told him to do anything it took to keep Amanda here. It told him she was special. Necessary, even.

He stepped closer to her. "I've offered Amanda a home, and I mean to stick to my word. I don't care about your stories. The past is the past."

"The past is never the past, but it's your funeral. Have it your way." Dennis reached out his hand and grasped Amanda's. Shook it long and hard. "Welcome to Elliott Ridge, Amanda. What's done is done. Don't blame me for the consequences."

And he walked away.

"CHEERFUL GUY." AMANDA hoped her voice wasn't betraying the state of her mind. How on earth did that old codger—there was no other word for him—know she was running from trouble? And what did he mean there'd be hell to pay?

"I hope he didn't scare you off." For the first time Carter seemed to have lost his confidence. He stared after Dennis, tracking his progress down the road. "He's got a house up the Ridge. He was born there. I really didn't think he'd lost any of his mental faculties while we were gone, but I've never heard him talk like that before. Usually you can't get two words out of him."

"Maybe he was surprised to see me." Amanda supposed any other woman might be hightailing it out of here by now, but Dennis didn't scare her. She didn't think he was losing his faculties, either. He struck her as a man who'd been alone too long—and gotten used to it. In school, when she was a cashier working swing shifts, she'd dealt with plenty of people young and old who were so starved for attention they made up drama however they could.

People did strange things when they got that lonely.

Like inviting their father back into their life, ignoring the potential consequences until it was too late, she thought ruefully.

Carter was watching her again, searching her face as if worried she might run. She met his gaze frankly, wanting to reassure him she wouldn't. Carter intrigued her, and so did this empty little town. She got the feeling the rows of houses were leaning toward her, willing her to stay and help bring other people to fill them. Now that she'd made the drive out from Chance Creek, she understood what Carter had told her earlier. Elliott Ridge was remote. Men might come for mill jobs, but they wouldn't see it as a place to settle down unless enough women settled here, too. Getting women here could be a problem.

Could she help Carter solve it?

"Let me show you the house," Carter said. "You can leave your luggage in the car until you see if it will suit you."

"Sure." She could put up with a character like Dennis if it meant she could hide away from the world for a while. With housing taken care of, her savings would easily feed and clothe her for months—if not longer. By then, she'd know if she wanted to stay or not.

Even if her attraction to Carter faded away, or wasn't reciprocated, she might find someone else here to share her life with. She could learn about the lumber industry. Explore a brand-new state. Maybe she'd start a whole new career—or go back to school. There had to be a university in Billings, which wasn't too far away. Besides, there were online classes these days.

She could do damn well anything she wanted—at least until her money ran out.

She caught Carter watching her. "What?" she asked him.

"You look—happy."

"I am happy." She realized it was true. Buck would never think to look for her here. She had no dull job to go to tomorrow. She could wake up and be whoever she wanted to be. "I like it here. So far. This place is special, isn't it?" she asked him. "More so than just your average little country town." Was it her imagination, or had the rows of houses practically swelled with pride?

A silly thought, but one she found hard to shake off. She wanted Elliott Ridge to like her as much as she liked it.

"The Ridge is more than the sum of its parts," Carter agreed. "When people live here, it's—I don't know. A community in the best sense of the word."

"We'll make it that way again," she assured him. "All the place needs is a little hard work, right?"

"That's right."

She slung her purse over her shoulder and followed Carter up the little path to the porch. Five steps brought her level to the door, where she waited for Carter to open it and usher her inside. As he did so, his hand lightly touched the small of her back.

Amanda liked that courteous touch. Her heart lifted as she stepped into an entryway connecting to a hall that divided the house in two. A central staircase led to the second floor. To her right was a living room that spanned most of the house. To her left sat a dining room separated from the kitchen with a doorway.

"I plan to knock out the wall between the dining room and kitchen. Open it all up," Carter said. "There's a powder room in back." He pointed down the hall. "Upstairs are the bedrooms." He led the way.

Amanda followed him, expecting small dark rooms, and was pleased to find that wasn't the case. Two of the bedrooms had a Jack-and-Jill bathroom between them. The master bedroom was quite airy and held the only furniture she'd seen in the house—a bed and dresser. Its ceiling followed the roofline, and several windows looked out over the community.

"I started renovating in the master bathroom," Carter told her, "so it's the only thing that's done so far." He let her pass him to look inside, where she saw gleaming tiles, a standalone tub and separate shower, and a modern double-vanity topped by an enormous mirror with brand-new light fixtures overhead.

Her respect for Carter increased. He'd done a professional-looking job.

"It's like something out of a magazine."

Carter beamed at her. "Exactly what I was going for.

You like it?"

"I love it!" It would be like having a home spa if she lived here.

"By the time we're done, your whole house will be up to this standard." He moved back into the bedroom.

Despite herself, Amanda warmed to that "we" as she followed him. Carter meant for them to be a team. When her father showed up again in her life, she'd hoped he'd feel that way about her, but of course that hadn't happened.

Thinking of her dad—and of Buck—brought her back to her senses, and her good mood evaporated. She might have found a safe haven, but that didn't mean she could let down her defenses.

She'd be alone in this house tonight, with no one around but six strange men, counting Dennis.

And twenty others in the bunkhouses, wherever those might be.

Amanda shivered.

"Cold?" Carter frowned. Amanda knew why. It was a perfectly nice May afternoon.

She shook her head. "Guess someone walked over my grave. It'll take a lot of work to finish this house," she added to deflect him. She was only saying what she thought he would expect to hear, though. The truth was, she couldn't wait to get started. The house suited her way more than her apartment had.

"But once you sign the contract and hand over that dollar, you don't just get the house, you get me, too." His mischievous smile lit a spark inside her that quickly fanned into a flame.

Amanda bit back a smile of her own, entranced by his easy masculinity, even as she told herself not to get carried away. Carter simply meant he would take charge of the renovations. Didn't he?

"I guess that will help, as far as renovations are concerned."

His gaze searched hers. "But you're still worried about something."

"We're standing in a ghost town in the middle of nowhere. I don't know anyone here."

He leaned against the massive old dresser that stood against one wall. "I wish I could set your mind at ease." He thought a minute. "Maybe I could call around. See if I can find a woman to come stay with you for your first few days here. I bet some of my old high school friends are still in town."

A feeling spiked through her she couldn't name. "That's all right," she hurried to say, picturing one of Carter's old flames cozying up to him, all in the name of making her feel comfortable.

She didn't like that image at all.

"Are you sure?"

She didn't know how to answer that without giving her thoughts away. His concern seemed real, and the purely sexual interest she'd felt a moment ago shifted into something else. Something far more potent.

More proprietary.

"What?" he asked a little defensively when she continued to study him.

"Just trying to figure you out," she admitted. "What are your intentions, Carter Elliott?"

She was unprepared for his reaction. "Hell," he said and straightened. "I…." He cut off and looked away a long moment. Turned his brown-eyed gaze back to hers. "I guess my intention is to get you to stay. I've taken a shine to you, Amanda Stakewell."

His confession stole the breath from her lungs until Amanda reminded herself this was a man trying to resurrect a ghost town. He needed her to stay. He didn't mean anything else. He certainly didn't mean he wanted—her.

Or did he?

"Okay." She wasn't sure what she was agreeing to. Giving Elliott Ridge a try?

Giving *him* a try?

"I mean… I can't turn down a house for a dollar, right?" she scrambled to add when the moment got too much for her. She couldn't tell what she was reading into the situation and what was real.

Carter nodded slowly. "Staying is the only sensible thing to do," he agreed.

Another wave of desire swept through her. What would it be like if this man decided he wanted more than just to use her as a beacon to draw other women to his town?

How would it feel to be in his arms?

In his bed?

When he started toward her, Amanda drew in a breath and held it, but he moved past her toward the closet. "I've been sleeping here while I worked on the place. Let me grab my things, then I'll fetch your suitcase and leave you to get settled in. I can bring you a set of sheets and towels from my parents' place to tide you over for now."

"Thanks, I appreciate it." She watched him fetch a bag from the closet and sweep his things into it. He moved around the room efficiently, and in less than a minute or two, all traces of him were gone.

"Be right back." He clattered down the stairs. A few moments later he reappeared with her things. "Why don't you come to the town hall when you've settled in? We've been eating together there to save time. Someone should have supper on by now. It's the big building at the top of the Circle," he reminded her. "I'll bring the sheets and towels so you can have them after dinner."

"I'll be there soon," Amanda promised him.

He hesitated, leaning against the doorframe, his biceps straining his shirtsleeves. "You sure Dennis didn't scare you off?"

"Of course not." She was still nervous, but she was determined to give this place a try.

"Good. Anyone who does is going to have to answer to me."

He wasn't joking, Amanda realized. For a moment she saw the man Carter could be when he was ready to be protective.

When he'd retreated downstairs and shut the front door behind him, Amanda set her suitcase near the dresser, her gym bag on the bed and looked around, glad to be alone for a few minutes to get her bearings. Carter had done a number on her, turning her head until she felt like a schoolgirl. She paced the room until her heartrate slowed, then focused on the task at hand. Luckily, she didn't have much to unpack. Just one very important item she needed to hide.

The master bedroom was still in mid-repair, which meant Carter would be in and out of it until it was done, a thought that left her a little too giddy for her peace of mind. She trailed into the bathroom, the last place she'd usually consider hiding an important piece of art. The painting remained rolled up, protected by a towel and sealed in several plastic bags. Airport security hadn't batted an eye when she'd put her gym bag on the conveyor belt through their scanners. Amanda considered the large double vanity. It was as good a place as any, she supposed. She opened one of the cabinet doors and placed the bag at the back before shutting it.

Tonight, when she was truly alone, she'd go online and figure out where to take the painting. Surely after it was out of her hands, Buck would lose interest in her.

Coming out of the bathroom, she surveyed her new home. Maybe she could stay long-term here at Elliott Ridge. Make a new life here.

See if the sizzle between her and Carter could start a fire.

That was getting ahead of herself, though. One thing at a time.

Amanda took a moment to splash cold water on her face and freshen up. She gave herself a once-over in the mirror, then went downstairs and out the door. She retraced her way to the Circle and followed it to the cluster of larger buildings Carter had pointed out before.

When she stepped through the front door of the town hall, she found herself in a large foyer. To her left and right were double doors. In front of her ran a counter. Behind it was a rectangle of metal post-office boxes, enough for every house in the community, and a large bulletin board that must once have held notices of interest for the people who lived here.

She could hear muffled voices. Was Carter arguing with his brothers somewhere in the building? She stepped over to the double doors to her right and peered in to see a cafeteria. Tables were scattered around it. At the far end a large pass-through opening gave her a glimpse into an industrial kitchen. The men seemed to be gathered in there.

Amanda wondered what the problem was. Had Dennis been repeating his suspicions about her? There was no way he could know she was running from trouble. It had been a good guess, that was all. She was a woman alone, with little luggage, who'd agreed to buy a house without ever having looked at it. It didn't take a genius to realize something wasn't right.

She needed to get her story straight, or Carter or his brothers might start doing some digging online. There'd been nothing about the art theft in the news yet as far as she'd seen, but someone at the Warden Gallery might spot the forgery at any moment. Her father was good at what he did, but no one was good enough to fool the experts forever.

Amanda squared her shoulders and pushed open the doors. She crossed the cafeteria to the kitchen. Inside, the men were arrayed around the room, preparing the meal. Gage was heating soup on the stove. Lincoln and Carter were chopping vegetables for a salad. Hudson was pulling plates out of a cabinet. Nate was reaching for something in the refrigerator.

Lincoln nudged Carter as soon as he caught sight of her, and Carter came to greet her. "Find everything you need in the house?" He gestured to a bag on a nearby counter. "There's your bedding."

"Thanks. Everything is perfect." At least, the master bathroom was. She hoped the rest would improve with time. "Is there a problem I should know about? I heard you arguing."

Carter exchanged a look with his brothers. "Not at all. It's just... like I said, we haven't been home that long, and Nate has only just gotten here. I guess none of us expected we'd make a sale so soon. We aren't completely prepared for it."

Lincoln and Hudson looked guilty. Nate's expression was neutral. Gage was somewhere between irritated and angry.

Ah. He must be the problem, Amanda thought. He'd been grumpy at the airport, too.

"Do you want me to leave?" she asked the men bluntly. Gage stopped stirring the soup. The others quickly shook their heads. Just as she thought. Too well bred to be rude straight to her face.

"There's one issue," Lincoln spoke up. "Carter might have given you the wrong impression about where we're at with the subdividing process. We expect approval any day now, but we haven't gotten it yet, so there's always the chance it will be turned down. When and if it goes through, we'll need a contract drawn up before we can sell you a house officially. We need to consult our real estate agent and a lawyer. It could take a while."

"We need to consult Mom and Dad," Gage put in.

"Mom and Dad will be fine with it," Carter said. "They want us to do whatever it takes to settle the Ridge again."

Amanda spoke up to prevent the argument from starting all over again. "Carter told me the subdivision process wasn't nailed down yet." But he'd made it sound like practically a done deal. She needed to be certain about where she stood. "Are you saying you might not sell me a house for a dollar, after all?" Might as well sort it out right now. She was already so invested in the idea of living here, it was going to hurt if they withdrew the offer, but that was better than not finding out until she'd lived here for several weeks.

"We're definitely selling you a house for a dollar," Carter said. "Right?" he asked his brothers.

Once again she had the feeling a conversation was happening right in front of her, even though none of the men said a word. Carter's fingers spasmed as if a sudden pain had lanced through them. Gage brought his hands together in front of his body, one fist driving into the other palm.

All the men straightened.

Amanda went on alert. "What was that?" she demanded.

Five pairs of eyes turned toward her. She copied Gage's gesture, driving her own fist into her open palm. "What's going on here that I'm not catching?" She could swear she caught looks of alarm pass between them, but no one moved. Carter was the one who recovered first.

"What's going on is I want you to stay, and I want to sell you that house for a dollar. I believe in this place, and I believe in what we can build here as a family and community. I never wanted to leave Elliott Ridge in the first place. Now that I'm back, I'm going to stay no matter what." He wasn't looking at her anymore. He was looking at Gage. "I want a chance to try to recapture what I lost. I know it won't be easy. I know we've got a steep climb ahead of us to make this work, but I deserve the chance to try."

She looked from him to his brother. "You don't want Carter to try?" she asked Gage. All the joy she'd felt at the prospect of fixing up number twenty-three—and spending time with Carter—was slipping away.

"I don't want anyone to get their hopes up. It's easy to get attached to an idea, then disappointed when it doesn't pan out." Gage spoke quietly. To Amanda's surprise, she heard pain in his voice. What had made a man like him so cautious? Was it being forced to leave here once before?

"You don't think Carter can succeed?" she asked him. "Because it seems to me if anyone can bring a town back to life, he's the man to do it."

"What makes you say that?"

She thought she'd surprised Gage. What's more, he seemed genuinely curious to hear her answer.

"Have you seen the master bathroom in number twenty-three? It's beautiful. If Carter can take a plain old house and make it shine, he can take this empty community and transform it, too. Don't you think?"

Gage surveyed her. "You're willing to risk more than a year of your life to find out if you're right? We've got a loan coming due next June. If we can't pay it off, we'll all have to leave. You understand that, right?"

She hadn't known that.

"I was going to explain everything," Carter said to Gage defensively. "There was no use going into all the details until Amanda decided if she even liked the place or not."

"Whatever time and money you put into the Ridge could all be gone next year," Gage continued as if he hadn't heard him. "You could lose everything. We already did once."

His warning only stiffened her resolve. She'd lost everything before—twice. And yet she'd survived. "All I'm risking is my time. I'm willing to wager that. Besides, I… could use something to believe in."

Gage let out an impatient breath. "Don't believe in Elliott Ridge. It'll break your heart."

She expected the others to balk at his dramatic

speech, but none of them said a word. Instead, they watched the two of them, as if their confrontation would determine the outcome of their attempt to bring the town to life.

Once again, she felt the yearning of the place to be given a chance.

She was supposed to be here. Somehow she knew that. It was as if Elliott Ridge needed her as much as she needed it.

Carter and his brothers needed her, too.

She remembered how she'd felt when her father left the first time. Her once-happy life had been reduced to memories in an instant. Often she'd wished she could go back. Carter and his brothers had a chance to do so. To reclaim their former happiness—their family legacy.

Amanda faced Gage. "My heart's already broken," she told him honestly. "But look. I'm still standing. My hands work. My brain works. I'm not ready to give up hope that something in my life can turn out right."

"Nothing turns out right."

"Really?" She held Gage's gaze. "You're what—thirty-two? Thirty-three? And you're ready to give up on everything? What are you going to do with the rest of your life? Sit around and whine?"

He blinked. One or two of his brothers chuckled.

"Look," she went on. "Maybe you're right. Maybe we'll fail. Maybe I'll be out a dollar and a year of my life. Who cares? I'll have met some new people. Learned some new skills, most likely. I'm willing to give it a try. Aren't you?"

"Yeah, Gage. What do you say?" Nate asked.

"She's got a point, doesn't she?" Lincoln asked.

When Gage didn't answer, Amanda felt her bravado slipping away. She was the wrong person to fight for this cause. After all, an hour and a half ago she'd never heard of Elliott Ridge.

Now she'd seen it, though. She'd met Carter. She'd been offered a beautiful house and its wonderful master bathroom.

She wanted to see what would happen next.

"Sounds like you've made up your mind," Gage said finally.

"That's right."

"And you want to help?"

"Of course I do." Amanda braced herself, though. His tone had shifted. Now it was faintly mocking, which told her he was going to test her determination. He'd probably assign her some stupid task she'd hate, just to prove she couldn't go the distance.

Well, she'd show him she wasn't easy to shake.

"We need someone to shop, cook and clean up from meals. Not just for us but for our workers, too. They're sick of having to fend for themselves."

"But—" Carter stepped forward. He'd been watching their exchange warily, eager to find a way to end it, Amanda thought.

"But nothing. Everyone needs to do their share. Amanda's share is three meals a day, including the shopping and cleaning up." Gage folded his arms over his chest, daring her to refuse.

"I can do that," Amanda snapped before anyone else could intercede on her behalf. Typical man, assigning her the girly work. "Anything else?"

Gage stared at her.

"You could grab the mail when you're in town. We've got a post-office box down there. Mom used to pick it up when she went shopping," Lincoln said.

"I can do that, too. What else?" She turned to Hudson, since he hadn't said anything yet.

Hudson smiled wolfishly. "Well, now that you mention it, I wouldn't mind—"

"Watch it!" Carter warned him.

"I wouldn't mind if you would run some other errands in town now and then. If we need anything," Hudson finished. He sent an innocent look Carter's way. "What did you think I was going to say?"

Carter shook his head. "You're impossible. And the rest of you are taking advantage of Amanda."

"How's this?" Amanda spoke up. She needed to assert herself so they didn't think they could ride roughshod over her, but she also needed to thwart Gage's attempt to scare her off. "I'll take care of the shopping, the mail, some errands, and I'll cook lunch and dinner. The rest of you take care of breakfast, and we'll all take turns cleaning up. Deal?"

"Deal," Lincoln said.

"Deal," Hudson said.

"Deal," Nate said. She had the feeling he was enjoying all this, even though he'd kept his peace until now.

"I still don't think you should have to do any of

those chores," Carter said.

Amanda waited for Gage's response. In the end he heaved a sigh. "Fine. Have it your way. We've already agreed to waste a year of our lives here. You can waste a year, too. But when the time is up and this all turns out to be a disaster, you realize we're going to sell the rest of the property to someone else, right? Blake Warrington is building a golf resort on the other side of the Ridge. He wants this side, too. If you buy that dollar house, you'll end up tucked away in a corner of his empire, watching rich people live like kings."

"In that case, Blake Warrington will probably want my property as well. I'll sell it to him for two dollars and double my investment."

Gage threw up his hands. "Whatever. It's your funeral."

Amanda bit back a laugh at his frustration. "I don't think a little hard work is going to kill me."

"You won't last a month," Gage said as he returned his attention to the stove. "Food's ready," he announced. He turned off a burner and used mitts to lift the big pot of soup and carry it out of the room to the table.

"You'll last a month, won't you?" Carter asked when he was gone. "You don't have to do all that stuff, you know."

"I'll last a month," she assured him. "And I'm happy to help."

CHAPTER 4

"THANKS FOR HAVING my back in there," Carter said after the meal was done. He ushered Amanda out of the town hall and set off toward number twenty-three. The sun was getting low in the west, but the temperature was still comfortable. Nights like this when he was young, he and his brothers would play baseball with the other kids in town, protesting heartily when their mother tried to call them in at bedtime.

He wished he could enjoy this evening, but his gut was knotted up from this latest confrontation with Gage—and he was still off-balance from Dennis's earlier accusations. At the time he'd told Amanda he'd never seen the old man act that way.

That was a lie.

Dennis had predicted the crash when Carter's father had taken out the large loan to upgrade the mill equipment.

He'd confronted Carter's father one afternoon in front of everyone. "You're a fool," he'd shouted. Carter had stood staring with the rest of the employees as the reclusive man faced off with his father. "You've got to hunker down when trouble's brewing! You don't give away your ammunition right before the war starts!"

His father had laughed. "There's no war starting. We're in great shape. We've got trees for miles, Dennis. Enough contracts to keep us busy for a lifetime."

"That's when trouble comes—when you think you're on the top of the world."

They'd all thought he was crazy. Three years later, the Ridge had emptied out.

"No problem. Four brothers must be a handful," Amanda said, breaking into his thoughts. Carter pulled himself together. Dennis had made a lucky guess back then, that was all. He couldn't know the future.

"You've got that right," he said.

"Must have been fun, too. When you were growing up here?" She tilted her head to look at him.

"Most of the time. Other times I wished I was an only child." He'd been wishing that again when Amanda had stumbled on him and his brothers arguing in the cafeteria. He'd had to invoke the rule again—the one that said his brothers needed to go along with what he was telling Amanda. Gage had tried to overrule it. Smashing his fist into his palm to tell the rest of them he was done with all that. He'd been about to ruin everything.

Amanda had saved the day. She'd stood up to Gage the way few people did, and in the end Gage had to back down.

"I have just one sister," Amanda said. They made

their way around the Circle and turned onto Center Street.

"Older or younger?"

"Younger—by a year," Amanda said.

"Are you close?"

"Not anymore." Her voice was wistful. "We were thick as thieves as kids, but when we were teenagers, we stopped seeing things eye to eye."

"Boys? Politics? Musical tastes?"

"Family matters." Amanda kept her gaze on the ground ahead of them. "My parents split up when I was fifteen. She took Dad's side."

"That's rough." Kids shouldn't have to take sides in a situation like that, to his way of thinking.

"Melissa ran away a few times," Amanda said softly. "She left for good when she was sixteen."

"Did something happen to her?" Carter stopped walking and faced her.

"No." Amanda shook her head. "I mean, yes, it did. She moved in with her boyfriend's family. Refused to come home. Mom finally agreed to let her stay. Kicked in money for groceries and rent in return for Melissa's agreement to remain in school. It worked. She graduated. Even got a scholarship to an arts program where she studied dancing. But she never forgave Mom for driving Dad away, as she put it."

"That must have been hard on your mother. On you, too."

"People leave," Amanda said. "That's just life."

Her calm words covered a world of pain. Carter

wished he could wrap his arms around her. Protect her from the cold, hard world. It was too soon for that, though.

Someday, he promised himself.

"I won't leave," he told her, starting to walk again. She followed suit. "You get sick of me, too bad. I'm staying right here."

A ghost of a smile flickered over her face.

"I know," he told her. "That doesn't get your sister back."

"I can understand why she lashed out as a teenager. What I don't understand is why she hasn't moved on. She never apologized to Mom. Barely talks to me."

"I'm sorry to hear that." They reached number twenty-three. "Here we are." He walked up the steps and opened the door. "Do you have everything you need?" He willed her to invite him in. He wished he'd thought to install a porch swing or furnish the living room with a comfortable couch. There was nowhere for him to hang out with her except the bedroom.

It was too soon for that.

Unfortunately.

"I'll be fine," she said firmly as if she could read his mind.

"You sure? We could sit here and watch the sunset."

"I'm sure. I'm tired. It's been a long day."

She couldn't be more direct than that. "Breakfast at seven at the town hall, then." He retreated down a step.

"I'll be there. Good night."

"Night." Carter watched her close the door, swallowed his disappointment and turned away.

Gage was waiting for him when he reached the end of the driveway.

"I'm not in the mood for whatever it is you want to say to me," Carter told him.

"That's a hell of a bet you're taking on a woman you barely know."

"All those years you spent with the Rangers, you never had a gut feeling you had to follow?" More than once one of those feelings had saved his life when he was with the SEALs.

"That's different."

"No, it's not," Carter said. "Maybe you're right and I'll regret what I've done, but not nearly as much as I'd have regretted not following my instincts. She's the one, Gage. I'm going to marry that woman."

"That's what you think."

"That's what I know."

AMANDA WISHED SHE'D asked Carter to stay.

She'd been fine while the sun was up. She'd taken her time looking over the house again, trying to envision what it would be like when all the renovations were done. She'd discovered a back deck and a small yard, and spent some time mentally designing a kitchen garden and a place to put a barbecue.

Upstairs, she'd arranged what little possessions she had and tried out the shower. Now it was nearly ten. It had been dark for more than an hour. She'd checked the locks downstairs three times, but she'd left the windows in her bedroom open a crack to cool the place down. Luckily there were screens, or she was sure the bugs bumping up against them would flock inside. The occasional metallic tap and buzz of wings kept startling her. So did the rustles and noises she heard outside.

She told herself over and over they were natural sounds. Small creatures skittering among the accumulation of dead leaves. The wind in the trees. Things like that. In LA she'd grown used to a constant hum of traffic. The absence of it here left her uneasy. She kept imagining Buck prowling around in the shadows outside her house.

She assured herself that wasn't the case. He had no idea where she was.

Still, maybe she should have said yes when Carter offered to call an old friend to come stay with her. He'd done everything he could to make her comfortable here, but she'd let jealousy get in the way. Now she was paying for it.

The worst of it was she didn't get cell phone service in this house, and there was no TV to fill the silence with noise. She couldn't even distract herself by searching online to figure out what to do with the painting hidden in her bathroom.

What if something happened and she needed to call for help?

What if Buck tracked her down?

She wondered where Carter was sleeping. At his folks' old house? It seemed a million miles away now that it was dark outside. There were no streetlamps as far as she could tell. Even the starlight didn't penetrate the canopy of trees overhead.

Amanda kept her light on until nearly midnight, but she had a feeling Carter and his brothers would notice if it was on much longer, and she didn't want to give Gage the satisfaction of knowing what a scaredy-cat she was. He'd already chalked her up as useless.

When she turned it off, the night pressed in from all sides. What had she gotten herself into? She didn't know when she'd last been this afraid—except for the night she'd run from LA.

Buck can't find me here, she told herself.

And she prayed for dawn.

"WHERE'S AMANDA?" HUDSON asked the following morning when he entered the town hall kitchen.

"I'll go check on her when breakfast is ready." Carter tossed the last eggshell into the compost bin and washed his hands. He did a couple of neck and shoulder stretches, trying to get the kinks out of his body.

"Where'd you sleep?" Hudson asked. "With our newest townswoman?"

"Across the street in number twenty-four. On the floor," Carter said. "Wanted to stay close in case Amanda had any trouble." A beep alerted him the latest batch of waffles was done.

"Sucker. I would have told her if she wanted to take my bed, she needed to take me with it."

"Which is why the ladies are falling all over you." Carter indicated the room, empty except the two of them. He opened the waffle-iron Lincoln had bought when he'd come home, peeled off the waffles and set them on a pan in the oven with the rest to keep warm.

"If I'm single, it's because I want to be," Hudson said.

"Keep telling yourself that." Carter poured another round of batter into the waffle iron and closed the lid. Hudson had always been cocky, but these days he was worse. He wasn't finding much action in town, as far as Carter could tell. Maybe he was frustrated and that's why he was laying it on so thick. "Can you take over making the waffles? I'll see if Amanda is up."

"You could text her. Oh, wait, our connection sucks." Hudson pretended he'd just remembered.

"Yeah, yeah. I'm working on it. Get those scrambled eggs going, too."

"If I'd known I was going to get stuck with kitchen duty, I'd have stayed in bed," Hudson called after him.

"Whatever."

As his brother got to work, Carter made his way through the cafeteria to the town hall's front door and exited into a soft, warm morning that made his heart lift. His plan had worked better than he could have expected. He'd lured a beautiful woman to Elliott Ridge, and now he'd get to spend time with her fixing up a house. What more could he want?

When he reached number twenty-three, he raised his hand to knock on the door, then thought better of it. Amanda might still be sleeping. He'd poke his nose in, see if she was up, and if he didn't hear anything, he'd simply close the door again. He could come back later. When he turned the handle, however, the door was locked from the inside.

Carter pulled his keys out of his pocket, realizing belatedly he probably should have given them to Amanda. He'd do that today.

The lock stuck, as usual, leaving him swearing under his breath before he got it open.

He swung the door open slowly, peered around it—

And ducked as a tile shattered against the wall next to his head.

"What the hell? Amanda? It's just me—Carter." He recognized that tile. It was from a box he'd left stacked near the stairs a couple of days ago, meant for the kitchen backsplash. He waited a moment to see if the coast was clear, peeked around the edge of the door and opened it wide.

Amanda crouched a yard or two away, breathing hard, scanning the room as if looking for something else to throw at him. When she saw him, she straightened. "Carter? Why are you breaking into my house?"

"It was my house up until yesterday." He held up the key. "Guess I wasn't thinking straight. I didn't want to wake you if you were still sleeping. I thought I could open the door and suss out the situation."

She ran her hands through her hair. "I was just coming down the stairs when I heard the key in the lock, then the door started opening. It was like something out of a horror movie."

He didn't point out it was broad daylight, and technically he still owned the place—or at least his family did. He took the house key off his ring. "Here. It's the only copy. I swear. You're safe here, Amanda," he added, seeing the humor in the situation now that he wasn't in danger of losing an eye. "This is the country. No one goes around breaking into houses."

She flashed him a skeptical look. "You sure about that? There's crime everywhere, isn't there?"

"Not here." He couldn't remember anything being stolen when he was a kid. People were in and out of each other's houses all day back then. Everybody knew everybody.

Of course, Elliott Ridge wasn't a ghost town at the time.

"Anyway, breakfast is on. We've got waffles and eggs. You hungry?"

"I—guess."

That didn't sound promising. He'd scared her. She was probably re-evaluating whether she wanted to stay. "Come on, I make fantastic waffles. We'll eat and go over your house plans before I head to the mill." He tried to sound enthusiastic.

"Fine. Breakfast. I can do that." But she didn't look happy as she walked past him out the door.

SHE WAS SAFE here.

Amanda hoped that was true, but her heart was still pounding when they arrived at the town hall cafeteria. She was embarrassed she'd nearly brained Carter with a tile, but it was his fault for scaring her. She hoped he'd bought extras.

It didn't help she'd barely slept last night. She'd tossed and turned for hours. When her phone alarm had chimed a half hour ago, she'd bolted straight up out of a nightmare, convinced a smoke alarm was going off.

Fortunately, that was her mind playing games. Some bird had been peeping outside her window, and her brain had turned the sound into an angry shrill. She'd inspected the house top to bottom before getting dressed. Nothing was amiss.

She thought she'd pulled herself together by the time she walked downstairs to go to the town hall, but when she heard the key in the lock, instincts had taken over. Thank goodness Carter had good reflexes.

He ushered her to the same long table they'd eaten at the previous evening. She caught sight of Hudson in the kitchen. Carter joined him there and came out again with a platter of waffles, scrambled eggs, some sliced fruit, plates and silverware. The rest of his brothers assembled one by one as she helped set the table, and soon they were sharing the food around. With each passing moment, her fears quieted, leaving her shaking her head at her own antics. She was a grown woman, for heaven's sake. She shouldn't be afraid of the dark.

She had every right to be afraid of Buck, though. It made sense to be worried about the masterpiece in her bathroom cabinet, too. Later, when she managed to get alone, she'd have to try her phone in different places at the Ridge. Maybe there was somewhere she could get a signal, so she could go online and figure out what to do with it.

"What's on the agenda today?" Lincoln asked.

Amanda returned her attention to the men around the table, especially the man on her left. Carter looked just as good this morning as he had yesterday. Better, maybe. He smelled shower fresh. His muscles strained against the fabric of his shirt. Every once in a while, his shoulder brushed hers, sending a little thrill of anticipation through her.

"I want to put in a couple of hours on Amanda's bedroom before work." Carter interrupted the fantasy that began to spin in her mind. "We'll get started on the drywall. Most of it is okay, but there are a few places that need to be patched. When we're done, we can paint."

"Always smart to start in the bedroom," Hudson joked, then flinched when Lincoln punched him in the arm. "What?"

"There's a lady present."

"If there wasn't, the joke wouldn't be funny."

"It's not funny," Carter told him.

"Amanda thinks it's hilarious."

Was she smiling? If so, it wasn't because of Hudson. It was the way the brothers interacted with each other. She could almost imagine how they'd been when they were children.

Gage thumped a fist on the table, making the plates, glasses and silverware jump. "Smarten up," he growled at Hudson. He turned to Amanda. "I'm not related to any of these idiots." He helped himself to a stack of waffles and passed the plate.

Amanda laughed despite herself. The other four men looked affronted.

"Gage is not the funny one," Carter said.

"Definitely not," Hudson said darkly.

"He's a little funny," Amanda pointed out and was rewarded with the ghost of a smile from the man. Carter, catching it, leaned forward.

"Anyway, we'll start in the bedroom…"

Lincoln, Hudson and Nate all guffawed, and Amanda couldn't help laughing, too. "You're just making it worse," she told him.

He sat back and crossed his arms. "Fine. We're going to work on Amanda's house. Then I'll get over to the mill. Lincoln, can you hold down the fort until I'm there? Maybe it's time you took the lead anyway. You know a hell of a lot more about lumber than I do."

"Hold on. Wait a minute," Lincoln said, setting down his fork. "Not sure I'm ready for that. Things didn't go so well last time I tried to step into that role."

"That was different," Carter said.

"Was it?" Lincoln held his gaze for a long moment before heaving a sigh. "Maybe it was. I just don't want to screw it up, you know?"

"You won't screw it up. Hudson will help you, right, Hudson?"

"I'll be there," Hudson said.

"I can help out, too," Nate said.

"I know you'd rather be in Grandpa's shop," Lincoln said.

"Lumber is a business, woodworking is a hobby. That's what Dad always said, right?" Nate said mildly.

"That's what he said. Doesn't mean you have to agree with it."

Nate didn't answer that.

"What are you going to do today?" Carter asked Gage.

Gage just shrugged.

"We could use an extra pair of hands," Lincoln told him.

Gage grunted but kept eating.

Amanda focused on her plate, finding she was hungry now that she wasn't alone or frightened anymore. Buck would have a hard time getting past all these men to cause her harm.

"Is there a Wi-Fi password I should have?" she asked when the silence stretched out. "I couldn't even get online last night."

"There is, although I'm not sure it will help you much." Carter told her what it was. "Our service isn't great. I'm working on that."

"It's satellite," Lincoln told her. "Slow as hell when you can connect at all."

"That's okay," she said doubtfully. "I didn't come here to hang out on the internet." She did need to find a way to get rid of the painting, though. She reached for the syrup. Maybe she could run into town to a coffee shop.

"If you get bored, you come find me," Hudson drawled. "I'll keep you company."

"No thanks." Her answer was automatic.

The rest of the men laughed.

Lincoln mimed a plane crash, complete with sound effects.

"Guess she told you, buddy," Carter said. "Better luck next time."

"She doesn't know what she's missing." Hudson stabbed another bite of waffle with his fork.

"Sounds to me like she's got a pretty good idea," Nate said.

"I'll give you a pretty good idea—"

"Settle down and eat," Gage roared.

Everyone stilled before Lincoln shook his head. "Sure thing, old man."

"Don't call me old man," Gage said, but the bickering ended, and the men got down to the business of consuming their food. Amanda followed suit. She was starting to like the Elliott brothers. Even Hudson, the dedicated flirt—and Gage. She got the sense that despite their arguing, they all believed in family. She had no doubt they would rally together against a common enemy.

Conversation turned to general topics as Amanda ate her waffle and eggs. The meal done, she went back to her house, Carter promising he'd join her there soon. Last night, when she'd gone to bed, she'd been very aware that Carter had slept in it only the night before. Had he moved in purely for the sake of efficiency, like he'd said, or had he meant the house to be his before she arrived? Once or twice she'd wondered if the

Elliotts had really planned to sell a house for a dollar, or if that was a story Carter made up on the fly. After all, she'd heard him fighting with his brothers about something in the town hall kitchen last night.

Now she surveyed her limited wardrobe with frustration. She'd bought a couple of things during her two weeks on the road, but only what she could find in airports. The clothes she was wearing would have to do for renovation work, which left her only a couple of other casual outfits and one dress she'd bought in desperation her first day on the run. One of these days she would go to town and stock up, but she wasn't in any hurry to leave the safety of the Ridge.

She closed the closet door when she heard knocking and went downstairs. Carter was standing outside.

"You really don't have to keep your door locked if you don't want to."

"Habit," she said.

"Ready to put up some drywall?"

"Sure." She led the way upstairs, glad she'd tidied what little she had away. The room felt smaller with Carter standing in it, and even though all she'd done here so far was sleep, it still made her feel vulnerable to have him in her bedroom.

"Have you ever done this before?"

"No," she admitted, "but I'm sure I can learn."

"Let me show you what to do."

For the next hour, Amanda helped hold sheets of drywall while Carter screwed them into place, a job that forced them practically into each other's arms.

Carter smelled good, some mixture of shampoo and soap she couldn't identify but appreciated. She was getting a fine view of his muscles as he moved and appreciated that, too. More than once his arms made a cage around her as he accomplished his work. It was all she could do not to picture him putting down his tools, backing her against their newly repaired wall and kissing her thoroughly.

She'd enjoy that, she had to admit.

As they worked he described what the community had been like when he was young, and she did her best to concentrate on what he was saying. "My brothers are staying in Mom and Dad's old house," he said as he measured the last gap they needed to cover in the wall. A remnant of old drywall remained in the corner. When he'd put away his measuring tape, he bent to wrest it off.

"Where do your parents live now?"

"South Carolina. When the mill shut down and everyone left, Dad was having health issues. Mom put her foot down and made Dad move closer to my grandmother and other members of her extended family. She didn't think it was a good idea for them to live up here all alone. Turned out for the best. Dad was in the hospital several times with heart problems during the next few years, and Grandma passed away. In late June Dad's getting a hip replacement."

"But they didn't sell the Ridge? Isn't there property tax or something that would make it hard to hold on to a huge place like this if no one was living here?"

"My family amassed a lot of different properties over the years, including a number of houses in Chance Creek," he explained. "Dad's been selling them off one at a time in order to hang on to the Ridge. Can you help me move this?" he added, gesturing to an old dresser that had been left in the house by its previous owners. Carter told her he thought it could be stripped down and stained, and it would be good as new. In the meantime it was still functional.

Amanda came to help him move it away from the wall, staggering a little under its weight. When it was sitting several feet away, she caught sight of something on the floor.

"What's that?"

Carter picked it up. It was a small porcelain figurine of a cuddly black bear.

"That's cute." Amanda reached for it. Carter passed it over.

"It is?"

"I like it. Jasper," she pronounced. "That's his name." She set him on the dresser. "He can be my good-luck charm."

"Jasper, huh?" Carter repeated.

"That's right. He'll be my first decoration." Amanda chuckled. "Probably not the vibe you were going for when you planned your renovations."

"I was thinking modern rustic," he admitted, scratching his jaw. "But sure, go all country schoolmarm on me. Collect a hundred figurines, if you want. I won't mind."

"Country schoolmarm it is." She warmed under his regard. Something about the way he looked at her told her Carter was ready to like just about anything she did. He was disposed to like *her*. Was he simply bored living way out here in the country with his brothers, or was there something about her that had caught his eye?

She wished she could ask him, but she couldn't imagine doing so. What if it turned out she was reading him all wrong?

When they'd replaced the last piece of drywall, he showed her how to tape the gaps and apply the "mud." She was good at that, better than Carter at achieving a smooth finish, and soon he designated her "chief mudder." She wasn't sure if that was a compliment or not.

Carter was easy to get along with. He was cheerful, patient and quick to crack a joke when he could find one. She learned a little more about his family and the history of the Ridge. Carter stuck to positive stories, though it was clear times had been hard in his teenage years.

"You said you were in the Navy," she prompted when they'd been working for an hour. "What was that like?"

Carter was quiet a moment. "I was with the Navy SEALs."

Amanda was surprised. She'd always supposed a SEAL would be a flint-edged, scarred warrior. Dour and silent. Brooding. Carter was anything but. When she asked him about it, he laughed.

"It takes all kinds to accomplish a mission. If we all spent our time brooding, we'd never get anything done. Some of us have to be optimists."

"Fair enough," she said, but his stories were generating more questions than answers. She found she looked at him a little differently now. Carter had to be showing her his soft side, but if he was a SEAL, there must be a harder side, too. He must have spent a lot of the past twelve years training for all kinds of missions. That explained the muscles.

Did it explain his determination to reach the goal he'd set for himself?

"I'd better get to the mill," Carter finally said when they'd cleaned up. "I'd rather stay here with you, but there are bills to pay. Will you be all right on your own?"

"Of course." Although she'd miss his company.

A knock sounded on the front door. Amanda followed Carter downstairs just as Gage stuck his head in. "Megan's here. I let Lincoln, Hudson and Nate know, and they're on their way."

"We're coming," Carter told him.

"Who's Megan?" And why did a zing of jealousy zip through her? She barely knew Carter. She couldn't be possessive of him yet.

But she was.

"Real estate agent," Carter answered succinctly. Together they went outside to where a curly-haired redhead was standing next to a light-blue truck. She was far younger than Amanda had expected. Probably in her early twenties.

"Megan Lawrence, this is Amanda Stakewell," Carter said when they'd joined the others. "Amanda, this is Megan."

"Nice to meet you. You must be new in town. I don't recognize you," Megan said.

"That's right."

"Welcome to Chance Creek."

CHAPTER 5

"WELL," MEGAN SAID when they'd made some small talk and all the brothers gathered around. "What's it going to be? Am I selling a hundred and twenty-one houses? Or are you really going to make me sell a whole town at once?"

That was the second time someone had mentioned the idea in front of Amanda. Carter knew that if they didn't stop, she'd be scared off for sure.

"Sell the whole town?" Amanda repeated, looking to Carter for clarification.

"She's talking about Blake Warrington, the guy who's building a resort on the other side of the Ridge. He wants to buy our entire property, but he knows it's not for sale."

"Not yet, anyway," Gage said.

Megan's smile disappeared. "I thought you wanted to stay," she said to him.

"What I want and what's going to happen are two different things. We've got a loan to pay off in just over a year, and we're struggling to keep workers at the mill.

We haven't even started the logging operation yet, which means we're going to run out of logs to turn into lumber at some point. I'm being practical. This probably isn't going to work."

"Ah," Megan said. "You must have been running ragged trying to fix all those problems. Is that why I haven't heard from you in over two weeks?"

Hudson guffawed. "Gage? Running ragged? Hardly. He hasn't set foot in the mill—or near the logging equipment. Seems to me like he's on vacation."

Carter swallowed a smile. Gage looked disconcerted, something that rarely happened. Megan's expression darkened.

"So you haven't been too busy to call me about those listings you promised. What's your excuse?"

What she didn't say was clear to all of them. She'd expected Gage to ask her out after the way he'd flirted with her at Cindy Glendale's wedding last month, and she was wondering why he hadn't. They'd all attended, except Nate, who wasn't home yet. They knew Cindy from school. Carter had enjoyed catching up with other acquaintances at the reception. After the way Gage had singled out Megan for his attention that night, it was clear she was angry he hadn't followed up.

Before she could give Gage a piece of her mind, Carter headed her off.

"We're still waiting to hear about the subdivision, but our answer should come any day now. As soon as it does, we'll be ready to give you those listings. Amanda, here, will be our first buyer," he added.

"You will?" Megan turned to her. "Which house are you buying?"

"Number twenty-three, on Second Avenue," Carter said.

"For a dollar," Gage said.

"A dollar." Shock slackened Megan's features before she pulled herself together. "You're selling her a house for a dollar?" Her voice rose. "We haven't even signed a seller's contract. You sold a house without me—for one lousy buck? Did you list it with someone else?"

"No." Carter wasn't sure why he felt guilty when he knew it was Gage Megan was angry with.

"I don't understand what's happening here." Megan's face was growing red. She turned to Gage again. "You said you wanted me to be your real estate agent. You promised those listings to me in front of my boss! But you never followed up. If you lied, just say so."

"I didn't lie."

When he didn't go on, Megan shook her head in disbelief. "Were you drunk at Cindy's wedding, Gage Elliott? I suppose that would explain a lot."

"I wasn't drunk. I just got… carried away."

"Carried away?" Her disgust was clear. "All you had to do was give me a call and say you'd changed your mind. You didn't have to make me feel like a fool."

She spun on her heel, stalked to her truck, got in it and slammed the door. Her tires kicked up a spray of gravel as she punched the gas and spun her way out of the parking area. They all watched her taillights disappear around a bend in the road.

"That went well," Lincoln said.

"Did you think Megan was going to work for free?" Hudson asked Carter.

"It's just one house. Besides, Gage is the one who talked to her, not me."

Gage kept looking after Megan's truck long after it was out of view.

"Hell" was all he said.

"WANT TO TELL me what that was all about?" Amanda asked Carter when the others trudged away toward the mill.

"Gage being Gage." His older brother could be as stubborn as anything when he wanted to be. "He flirted with Megan all night at Cindy Glendale's wedding last month. She was desperately looking for listings, and he told her she could sell the Ridge one way or the other—either the subdivision houses or the whole shebang next year if we can't manage to keep it. He didn't look drunk to me that night, but maybe Megan's right. Maybe that explains why he never asked her out afterward. I should have told her we're selling only one of the subdivision houses for a dollar." Carter rubbed a hand over the back of his neck. "She left so quickly I didn't have a chance."

"She could have been my first female friend in this place, but now she probably sees me as an enemy."

Carter let his hand drop. "No, she doesn't. She's not mad at you."

"Are you sure about that?" Amanda let out an impatient breath. "Maybe I'm risking only a dollar and my time, but it would make me feel a whole lot better if I thought the five of you shared a common vision for this place. I like Elliott Ridge the way it is now. I don't want to live next to a golf course."

Carter chuckled. "You won't have to, I promise. Don't worry about Gage. He'll come around. He's just scared."

"Of what?"

"Of failing, I guess. I told you the bottom fell out of the lumber industry and the Ridge cleared out. It was a hard time for all of us. Gage doesn't want to relive it."

"So why doesn't he leave?" she pressed.

Carter shrugged. "He loves it here as much as the rest of us, even if he won't admit it. Never mind him. Let's go inside and look at your kitchen. I'll walk you through the changes we'll be making to it. You'll forget Gage even exists."

"Okay," Amanda said slowly, reminding herself that one way or another she'd have free housing—and food, too, it seemed like—for the rest of the year. That left her plenty of time to plan for her future. Maybe she'd get tired of Elliott Ridge and decide to move on, anyway. Just because she was enjoying Carter's company now didn't mean that would last forever.

The thought of leaving didn't sit well with her, though. She was becoming attached to the town. To the Elliotts.

To Carter.

Inside, Amanda realized all over again how much care he had put into his plans for the house.

"These two walls will all be cabinets, with a sink under the window, the stove there and the refrigerator there." He pointed them out. "The island will be eight feet long."

"Eight feet long?" Amanda fell a little in love with him right then. She'd always wanted a kitchen island big enough to roll out pastry or make pizzas with her friends—or seat her children around someday so they could do their homework while she cooked dinner.

She'd just about given up on those dreams, though.

"That's right." Carter looked at her curiously. "You okay with that?"

"It sounds wonderful," she admitted.

"Let me show you something else." He led the way into a gutted medium-size room at the back of the house.

"This used to be a pantry and storage room. On the other side of that wall is the powder room. It's really small. Since you'll have so much storage in the new kitchen, I want to turn this into a laundry room and expand the powder room so it's not such a tight squeeze. I'll install the machines under a counter you can use to fold your clothes on and put some cabinets above it. There'll be a wall here." He indicated it with his hands. "In the new powder room, there'll be room for a toilet, sink and shower. I'll have to get back into your bathroom upstairs to fiddle with the pipes to connect everything, but it shouldn't disrupt things too much."

He'd need access to the master bathroom? Amanda

didn't like the sound of that. She'd better move the painting. Find somewhere else to stash it.

"Sounds perfect," she made herself say. "The whole place is perfect. You're really good at this."

"You think so?"

"I do. What was your specialty in the military?"

His expression shuttered. Amanda wondered if she'd stepped across a line. "Sorry. Too personal?"

He shrugged. "Not something I talk about to just anyone. When you're a SEAL, you learn to keep things to yourself."

So he knew how to keep secrets, too. She supposed that made sense. This man was a highly trained warrior who carried out the kind of missions the public didn't always hear about. Which begged the question: Should she tell him what had happened in LA? Maybe he'd know a lot more about solving her problems than she did.

Just thinking about her father's return to crime— and Buck's re-entry into her life—made her stomach twist. She'd gotten so involved in Megan and Gage's dispute she'd forgotten about the danger she was in. She had a masterpiece hidden in her bathroom, for heaven's sake, and here she was worrying about whether Megan would want to be her friend.

No, Amanda decided. As much as she liked Carter, she didn't know him well enough to dump a crime in his lap. She needed to handle the painting herself. After she'd gotten rid of it, and hopefully rid of Buck Bronson, too, she could fill Carter in on what had happened.

Until then, she needed to keep her mouth shut.

"I was trained in counterterrorism," Carter said quietly.

Amanda took that in. "I suppose you know how to defend yourself in a sticky situation."

"I do." It was a bald statement of fact when she'd half expected a joke or a deflection.

"Should I worry about the baggage you brought home with you?" She tried to keep the question light, but she wanted to know the answer. She'd learned from experience the most charming of men could carry demons with him. Buck had wrapped all of them around his little finger before he'd turned her father down a dark path.

Carter took the time to consider her question. "No," he answered finally. "I'll tell you if I ever change my assessment of that, but I've been lucky. I served with men I respected. Men with whom I shared a common feeling of where the lines were drawn, if that makes sense. There are stories I won't share with you no matter where our relationship takes us, because you don't need that darkness in your life, but I have friends who've been there, too. I don't have to keep it bottled up inside."

She nodded, glad to hear it. She could only imagine the things he'd seen.

"You're wondering if you can trust me," he stated.

"It's not that," she told him truthfully. "You've been brave. You must have faced your fears a thousand times."

"You haven't?"

She was already shaking her head. "I've spent my life choosing the safe route—instead of following my heart."

"You think coming to live in a ghost town is the safe route?" His smile was teasing.

"You told me it was," she pointed out, smiling back at him.

"Guess I did. You arrived here without much of a plan, and you've rolled with the punches ever since. Seems to me like you're shaking things up in your life."

"I guess I am." They were standing close together in the doorway. Amanda wondered if he could hear the way her heart was pounding in her chest. If he reached for her, she would go to him willingly.

She wanted this man.

"Maybe you're following your heart this time, too," he suggested. His voice had gotten husky, and her pulse picked up in response.

"Maybe." She couldn't meet his gaze. She couldn't allow herself to hope that was true.

"Do you like canoeing?"

It took a moment to catch up to his sudden change of subject. "Uh… sure." Was he trying to de-escalate the situation? Maybe it was obvious she was hungry for him, and he wasn't interested.

"I'll come home from the mill early enough so we can go have some fun before dinner."

The way he said it calmed her fears. It was an invitation, not a brush-off.

Good.

"I guess I'd better figure out what I'm serving everyone for lunch." She was supposed to be the new cook, after all. Would she need to go to town already? The idea left her nervous.

"Not today," Carter said firmly. "Today you should settle in. Explore a little. Check out the kitchen and see what we've got in the cupboards. Make a plan for the rest of the week. My brothers and I will handle lunch and dinner, and the workmen can survive on their own for another twenty-four hours. Tomorrow we'll start the new regime—if you're sure you're up for it."

"I'm up for it."

Carter suddenly clapped a hand on his pants pocket. Pulled out his phone and glanced at it. "Hell."

"What's wrong?" Amanda asked when he scowled at something on the screen.

"Flag's gone! That changes everything." He shoved the phone back in his pocket, took her hand and lunged for the door. "Come on!"

"What flag?" she cried as he hauled her outside, slammed the door behind them and pulled her down the steps.

"The Elliott flag. The one hanging on my parents' house." Carter broke into a run as soon as he hit solid ground, and Amanda raced to keep up with him. As they turned onto Center Street, Lincoln dashed past them from the direction of the mill.

"Flag's gone!" he shouted.

"I know!" Carter put on a burst of speed, dragging

Amanda along with him. She sprinted to keep up, but Carter was faster and nearly pulled her off her feet as he jerked her along. When they made it to the Circle, he slowed and pointed a finger. "See?"

The black, green and silver flag that had hung in front of number one was missing.

"Who took it?" she gasped, trying to catch her breath.

"That's the question." Carter scanned the area. "Wasn't me. It isn't Lincoln—he's not a good enough actor."

Amanda gaped at him. "Why would Lincoln take it?"

"That's how the game works. Come on!"

"Game?" This was a game?

Carter was running again, following Lincoln toward the big white house. Amanda had no choice but to keep up.

Lincoln had a wide head start on them and reached the house when they were only halfway across the Circle. He skidded to a stop near the front steps, backpedaled, his head swiveling, then turned on his heel. "It's got to be Nate!" he hollered as he shot past them again.

Carter shook his head. "It's never Nate. It's got to be Hudson. He'll have it up on the Mast." He veered toward the Ridge and higher ground, still dragging Amanda along.

She opened her mouth to protest that she wasn't up to this, but Carter was sprinting again, and she sprinted, too. As the ground began to rise under her feet, she panted harder as she tried to keep pace.

"Hudson is a climber," Carter shouted over his shoulder. "He loves to be up high. Once he's got the flag up there, it's hell to get it down again."

"Isn't that Hudson right there?" Amanda said.

Carter slowed as his brother dashed around a nearby house and raced back the way they'd just come. "What the hell is he doing?" He waited until Hudson disappeared around the side of his parents' house. "He's trying to pretend Gage has it. Gage's favorite spot is Hidden Beach. You've got to swim for it—or take a boat." He looked down at her. "Rule number one in the Game: someone's lying. Come on." He tugged her on toward the slope, speeding up again. "Let's get to the Mast. Are you good at climbing trees?"

"I... haven't... tried... in... years," Amanda said. She hadn't run like this in years, either.

"This might not be the one to start with." He kept going up the slope, and Amanda did her best to follow him. She knew she was slowing him down and redoubled her efforts, but it didn't make much difference. Just when she thought she might sink to the ground in defeat, he finally stopped. "It's that one." Carter pointed to a monster of a tree so tall Amanda had to tilt her head back to see the top of it.

"You're going to climb that?" she asked faintly.

He lifted a hand to shade his eyes. Swore. "It's not there."

"How do you know?"

"Rule number two: you have to display the flag." Carter swore again. Thought a moment. "Hell, what if Gage does have it? We've got to head off Hudson."

"Gage?" Amanda couldn't imagine him stealing a flag.

"You'd better believe it. Let's go!" Carter tightened his grip on her hand and sprinted back down the hill. "If Hudson gets the flag back to my folks' house, he wins. We've got to stop him." Amanda's hand slipped from his, and she stumbled. Carter whipped around, caught her without missing a beat and saved her from a spill to the ground. They stood like that, Amanda clinging to him, desperate to stay upright, until she spotted someone over his shoulder.

"Lincoln!" she cried. "He's heading to the house!"

Carter turned to see. "He's empty-handed, which means Nate didn't take it. It has to be Gage. Hell." He hesitated. Steadied her and took her hand again. "That's okay."

"No, it isn't!" She was invested in the game now. "Get going! Catch him!" She shoved him in the direction Lincoln was running.

"You sure?" Carter called back, already racing away.

"I'm sure!" She raced after him, determined to help if she could but at a minimum wanting to see what happened next. Lincoln caught sight of Carter and sped up. Carter lowered his head and ran after him. Amanda followed them as fast as she could, but the men were far ahead of her, already disappearing around the side of number one by the time she reached the Circle again.

She ran straight across it, darted around the side of the big white house, down stone steps flanked by a fern garden and onto the beach. Carter, Hudson and Lincoln were grappling together at the edge of the water. She dashed toward them as they tumbled over in a tangled heap.

"Carter!" she screamed.

He struggled out from under Hudson and tossed her something. Amanda flinched, then realized it was the flag. She snatched it out of the air with one hand.

"Get to the front porch!" Carter yelled. "Run!"

Amanda ran, the flag streaming out from her fist. She heard footsteps behind her as she raced across the beach again. Were they all coming after her? She picked up speed.

"Don't let it touch the ground!" a chorus of male voices all called at once, some from behind her, one from in front. Gage was on the back porch of his parents' place.

Startled, Amanda whipped her arm up and forward, and the flag fanned out in front of her. Temporarily blinded, she snatched at it again, caught the fabric in her hands and tripped—

Amanda screamed as she launched into the air. Some instinct of self-preservation sent her tucking into a ball. She landed, rolled over, flopped onto her back—

The flag still in her hand.

Before she could take a breath, someone snatched her right off the ground, heaved her over his shoulder and kept going.

Amanda screamed again. The next few seconds were a jumble of sand, bracken, steps and a triumphant roar as Carter hauled her up to his parents' front door and banged on it with the flat of his hand.

He flipped her down into his arms and spun her in a circle. "We won!" he cried as Nate came running up the road.

"Hell, I missed the whole thing, didn't I?" Nate cried.

"We won?" Amanda asked.

Carter pulled the flag from her hands. "We won. Suckers!" he shouted at Lincoln and Hudson as they gathered at the bottom of the porch steps. Gage ambled around the corner of the deck.

"Good job," he said calmly.

"I'm the one who swam it back here," Hudson said. "Kept it dry the whole way." He was soaked, water dripping from his clothes, which were crusted with sand as well.

"Doesn't matter what you did. It only matters that I brought it home," Carter told him. "With Amanda's help."

"That's not fair," Hudson grumbled. "It's supposed to be every man for himself."

"Amanda's a woman, and she's with me. Get your own girl if you want."

Amanda found it hard to catch her breath but not because she'd been running. Carter's arm still rested around her waist as if to make his claim to her more tangible. They were all breathing hard, but despite the complaints all the Elliott men looked happy. Even Gage.

"That's one for Carter—and Amanda," Gage said.

"Next time I'll win," Lincoln said.

"Yeah, yeah." Nate elbowed him. "You always say that."

"At least I know when we're playing."

Amanda let their banter wash over her as Carter turned to look her over.

"You okay?" he asked her. "Sorry if I got a little rough back there. We Elliotts play to win."

"I'm okay." He'd been so strong when he lifted her off the beach and tossed her over his shoulder. How could he run so fast while carrying her? She found herself looking at him with a whole new appreciation. Her body had touched his in a variety of places during his headlong scramble for his parents' front door. Now she tingled all over, aching for more.

She had so many questions about the game. Who had come up with it? Had they been playing it all their lives?

Were there more rules?

"Work!" Lincoln pronounced before she could ask. "The men will be wondering where we got to for so long."

Amanda decided she'd ask another time. Or wait until the next time they played. She was sure there'd be a next time. Despite Gage's grumbling and the way the brothers sometimes bickered among themselves, these were men with a long history at the Ridge. They'd do anything to keep their home.

Even Gage.

"I'd better go. See you later?" Carter asked. He bent closer. "You did really good back there on the beach."

His breath tickled her ear, sending delightful shivers down her spine. Amanda glowed at the praise. "I did?"

"You fit right in here." He touched her hand, then turned to follow his brothers.

She was happy to hear that because she was more determined than ever to stay.

CHAPTER 6

C ARTER SPENT HIS time at the mill getting Lincoln up to speed on where they were with fulfilling their current contracts and to whom he'd reached out about getting more work. Taking the lead at the mill had fallen to him only by default because he was the one to get back to the Ridge first. He'd been so afraid to waste a moment of time, he'd started calling their old contacts months before he even came home. He'd lucked out and secured a large contract with an old family friend that was substantial enough to get them started and allow him to hire twenty workers. His years of military training had given him the confidence to do that much, but it was Gage and Lincoln who'd lived and breathed the work before they'd all left. Since Gage was refusing to take any responsibility, Lincoln was the obvious choice to head their operations.

After they'd finished going over paperwork, they both spent most of the rest of the day helping out on the floor. Carter cut his afternoon short to take Amanda canoeing on the lake before dinner. While he thought she'd had fun this morning, he was afraid his family's hyper-competitiveness might have scared her a little, especially when he'd scooped her off the beach and run with her to his parents' front porch. He wanted to establish that he could be gentle, too. A slow glide over calm water ought to prove that.

Besides, he needed to spend time with her. Throughout his workday he'd had a hard time concentrating. Now that he'd felt her in his arms, he craved more of her. A lot more.

When they reached the boathouse, he was gratified that Dennis had kept the boats in as good repair as everything else at Elliott Ridge. Carter helped Amanda on with her lifejacket, spending more time on the simple operation than it warranted, finding it hard to stop touching her once he'd started. They carried the canoe to the shore, and he steadied it while she took her seat in the bow before climbing carefully into the stern and pushing off.

They paddled along the periphery of the lake at a gentle pace, giving Amanda time to remember her skills. She told him she'd canoed once or twice as a child, but that was the extent of her experience.

"We used to paddle across the lake and camp out on the far side," he told her as they glided along. "Sometimes we were gone for days."

"Your parents didn't worry about you?"

"Nah. There were five of us, and we were pretty handy. They figured we'd make so much noise we'd scare off any bears."

"Bears?" Amanda stopped paddling. "There are bears here?"

"Of course. I thought you liked bears."

"When they're made from porcelain. I'm not sure how I feel about real ones."

He took another stroke, brought his paddle to the other side and stroked again. "Anyway, my parents knew if we ran out of food, we'd either catch a few fish or paddle home."

"They didn't worry about you fighting among your-selves?"

He considered this. "We scrapped all the time, but that's just boy stuff. We always had each other's back when the circumstance called for it."

"Sounds like a great childhood."

"It was." Until times got tough. "We'll have to pack a picnic next time. I'll take you to our diving rock."

"Sounds fun." Amanda took a couple of strokes, then rested her paddle on her knees. "This is the life."

"It is," he agreed. Suddenly he could see a future like this. A time when the Ridge was settled and he had a wife and family. Work to do every day. His brothers around him. A bustling little town like it once was.

They poked around the lake for another half hour, until Carter spotted some wildflowers close to shore. The bank was steep here, jutting right out of the water, so he guided them in close and picked one before pushing away into deeper water again.

"A present for you." He held it up to show her. "Meet me in the middle?"

"Of the canoe? Won't we tip over?"

"Not if we're careful." He wanted to touch her again, despite all his good intentions. With a few strong strokes he got them far from shore, where they could drift without running into anything.

"You go first."

"Okay." Amanda swiveled on her seat, tucked her paddle away, bent to hold on to the gunwales and took a step.

"Keep your center of gravity low," he cautioned her.

She did so, awkwardly stepping over a cross thwart and easing down to her knees when she reached the middle of the canoe.

Carter maneuvered his way to her more quickly but just as carefully. He knelt, too, and presented her the flower.

"Thank you." She hesitated, holding it. "Now what?"

"Now this." Carter took his time leaning down to close the distance between them. He hoped like hell he wasn't making a fatal error kissing her. They'd met only yesterday, but he didn't think he could wait a minute longer.

Amanda didn't pull back. She closed her eyes as his mouth met hers, a small sound escaping her.

She was soft and sweet under his touch, and it took everything Carter had within him to pull back after a few moments instead of taking more.

But when Amanda looked up at him through her lashes, her lips parted and her cheeks flushed, he lost even that small measure of control. He growled low in his throat, cupped her chin and kissed her again. This time he deepened the kiss, determined to show her how he really felt.

When she leaned into him, bracing her hands on his chest, satisfaction filled him. His risk had paid off.

She wanted him, too.

He needed to slow down. Take this one step at a time.

Carter didn't want to. He was hungry for her. Wanted to feel her in his arms. Wanted to—

Amanda pulled away. Sat back on her heels.

Disappointment left Carter reeling. Kissing her felt so good. Didn't she feel it, too? Was she angry with him?

Would she—

A breath escaped him when he noticed what Amanda was doing.

Her fingers were working at the top button of her checked cotton shirt, the one that made her look as sweet as an old-fashioned dairy maid. She wasn't being sweet now, though.

She worked her way through the buttons and drew her shirt off. Carter was glad they were out of sight of his parents' house here. He didn't want any of his brothers to see just how beautiful she was.

Did she mean what he thought she meant? He'd taken Amanda for a woman who'd want to go slowly. Someone who'd require him to prove himself before getting any closer.

But she'd left her life behind recently. Maybe she wanted to kick caution to the wind.

Or maybe she simply wanted to be with him.

He watched her set her shirt carefully behind her on the floor of the canoe. Turning back to him, clad only in a lacy bra, she folded her hands primly in her lap.

"Now what?" she asked again.

"Amanda." Her sweet smile set him in motion, tugging his own shirt up and over his head. He tossed it behind him and reached for her, splaying his hands over her sun-warmed back, kissing her thoroughly and giving her plenty of time to pull away. When she leaned in, kissing him back, he fumbled with the clasp of her bra and untangled it from her arms.

Her breasts swung free, and he had to bite back another groan. He traced a finger around one before spreading his hands and cupping both. When he dipped his head to taste one nipple, she clutched his shoulders and let out a moan.

Were they really doing this? Carter couldn't believe his luck. What were the chances he'd run into the woman of his dreams at the airport, and what were the chances she'd give herself so freely to him just one day later?

He'd learned to be suspicious of good fortune, knowing how quickly it could turn. But he knew, too, that when life went your way, you had to grab hold of it and drink it in.

He drunk his fill of Amanda, exploring her body with his mouth until both of them were breathing hard.

"I want to be with you," he said, knowing she'd probably put an end to things now. She didn't know him. Couldn't possibly trust him enough—

"I want to be with you, too."

"Are you sure?" Normally he didn't feel so off-balance with a woman, but Amanda was special—and they were in a canoe.

"I'm sure." She ran her hands over his chest, as if testing the feel of him. Judging by the wonder in her eyes, she liked what she was discovering. God, he hoped so.

"Should we go to shore?"

"No."

Her simple answer floored him. "No? It's not going to be easy…" He gestured to the canoe.

"I don't want it to be easy." Her smile lit her eyes. "You're a Navy SEAL. You'll figure it out, won't you?"

Hell, yeah, he would. "Better get rid of the rest of our clothes first."

"I thought you'd never ask."

The wooden yoke that braced the centerline of the canoe was still between them. Carter fumbled with the waistband of her linen shorts, but Amanda stopped him. "Let me," she told him. She sat down in the bottom of the canoe and wriggled out of them, tugging her panties along with them. As she drew them down slowly over her legs and set them aside, she offered him glimpses of her most intimate places in a way designed to drive him wild.

He followed suit, carefully removing the swim

trunks he wore. Amanda watched him avidly. He couldn't hide his interest from her now, either. She drank in all of him, her eyes alight as she met his gaze again. She rose to her knees and met him at the center yoke.

"Now what?" Amanda asked a third time. They couldn't lie down in the canoe without the crosspieces getting in the way.

"I'm going to sit right here," Carter said, showing her. "And you're going to climb over the yoke as carefully as you can and join me." He kept his weight close to the center of the small boat to help steady them. "Move slowly, or we'll end up in the drink."

Amanda did what he told her, her breasts swinging as she bent forward and climbed over the yoke as gracefully as she could.

"Easy," he cautioned as she straddled his lap.

Her nipples were hard as her breasts brushed against his chest, tantalizing him. The warmth of her core pressed against his hardness as she sat down. Carter kept still, steadying the canoe, but it was agony.

"Do you really think we can do this?" she asked, her hands braced on his shoulders.

"If we go slow." They hadn't talked about protection. "Should I be wearing a condom?"

"I'm on the Pill. I'm safe. It's been... ages."

"Same for me. Safe."

Hands on her hips, he lifted her hips up, then guided her down slowly, letting out a breath as she slid down around him. She was warm and wet, slick and ready. Sitting like this, her breasts were crushed against him, her mouth in easy kissing range.

"Amanda," he said again.

And then he couldn't say anything more.

THIS HAD TO be heaven.

Carter pushed inside her, filling her until she let out a little moan. This position brought him deep. When he flexed his hips, willing her into motion above him, she shut her eyes and allowed the sensation to overtake her.

She'd never been one for quick flings, but everything about Carter made her throw caution to the wind. She'd been thinking about him nonstop since they met at the airport. Fantasizing about how this would feel.

Now she knew.

Was it the chaos of the past few weeks that made her so reckless when she'd played life safe for so long? Amanda wasn't sure. All she knew was she couldn't deny her feelings for Carter.

Didn't want to.

She wanted him right where he was—inside her. His arms holding her tight. Amanda rocked against him, loving the sweet friction that built within her. Carter captured her mouth, kissing her deeply. He cupped her bottom with his powerful hands, lifting her, coaxing her, shifting inside her, revving her up until she lost track of where they were.

The canoe rocked with their motion, but Carter braced it with his thighs, keeping it from spilling them over the side.

He was everything she wanted in a man, Amanda decided. She would never get enough of this—of him. Everywhere they touched her skin was on fire.

She couldn't get her fill of kissing him, either. Couldn't get him deep enough inside her. Couldn't get close enough—

As Carter's thrusts sped up, Amanda cried out as her release overwhelmed her. She clung to his shoulders as wave after wave of sensation passed through her, then held on and savored the feel of him as he kept going. Amanda thought she was done, but Carter's strong movements, his fingers digging into her skin, the pulse of him inside her unexpectedly wound her up to another peak. She strained to hold together, wanting Carter to have his moment, too, but his next thrust brought her over the edge, and she shattered into a million pieces. Amanda cried out, glorying in the feeling. Carter's strong hands cradled her. Kept her safe.

She cried out again, as warmth and brightness pulsed through her. Carter buried his hands in her hair, pressed his face against her breasts and called out, too.

Wave after wave of heat and sensation rocked through her until Amanda went slack, helpless in his arms. When he'd sated himself, he crushed her to him and whispered her name.

"God, you're amazing," he said.

"You're amazing, too." She couldn't stop kissing him.

"I could stay here forever. Just like this." His hands kept caressing her, skimming her body as if he couldn't get enough of it.

"Me, too."

"Except my ass is killing me."

Amanda laughed. "So are my knees."

He looked around, letting out a shuddering breath as if waking up from a dream. "Hell, we're drifting. Better get us to shore." He looked down at her. "I mean it, though. If I could, I'd stay. I never thought I'd meet someone like you."

"Someone who can make love in a canoe?" She let the curtain of her hair cover her eyes, a little shy now that their lovemaking was over but feeling bold at the same time. She liked the way he was looking at her. Like he'd found some unexpected prize.

"Someone I could be serious about."

Amanda's breath caught, and she stilled in his arms. He could be serious about her?

Suddenly she remembered they'd just met a day ago. That she had a masterpiece hidden in the bathroom of the house he'd yet to sell her.

That Buck could be anywhere.

"Did I just scare you? I didn't mean to," Carter rumbled as he kissed her again.

"You didn't scare me." She was lying, though. He had scared her a little. Or at least her circumstances had.

But Carter had also made her heart sing.

HAD HE BLOWN it?

Carter worried that he had as Amanda carefully lifted herself off him. "Take it slow," he cautioned her.

She did so, climbing back over the yoke carefully and giving him a hell of a view.

"Amanda?" he asked.

"Yes?"

"Tell me I didn't just ruin this."

"You didn't." She met his gaze this time as she gathered her clothing. "You surprised me," she added.

"You surprised me, too."

"I guess I did." She looked around. "Should we go for a swim?"

"Might as well. We need to get back soon, though. It's nearly dinnertime." He couldn't shake the fear that as much ground as he'd just gained with her, he'd lost ground, too. "Tell me what's wrong?"

She hesitated, and he could see her thinking over how to answer. "Your brothers. What are they going to think about this?"

His brothers?

Somehow he knew that wasn't her real concern, but he answered as if he thought it was. "They'll never know what we got up to out here."

"They'll know." She made a face.

She was right; they probably would, he thought. There was something about a woman who'd been with a man—and vice versa, he supposed. But what was really bothering her?

He supposed he'd have to be patient. She'd tell him in her own time.

"Let me get us back to shore." He moved to the stern of the canoe carefully, took up his paddle and brought them in where the water was shallow. He braced the canoe while she slipped out, then he got out, too.

"It's freezing," she complained.

"We don't need to stay in long." He fastened the canoe's rope to a nearby tree and came to wade beside her.

The sun was out, but the light breeze was lifting goose bumps on his skin where it was exposed. Amanda waded in deeper and scrubbed herself with her hands. Carter's body responded to the view, despite the chill. He waded in deeper, before she noticed, and did his best to clean up, then helped her onto the bank.

"I think I've got a towel in here." He fetched it from the canoe. They shared it, then dressed themselves again. "Time to get back."

"I'm ready."

She was quiet.

"Amanda." He needed to get something sorted out before they went back and joined the others for dinner.

"Yes?" She finally looked up at him. With her clothing damp from her skin, she looked vulnerable. Younger than her years. Carter figured she was in her late twenties, but now she could pass for a college student.

"I didn't do that to get you out of my system. Like I said, I'm not going anywhere." He hoped she understood what he meant.

"Okay," she said after a moment.

"I really hope you aren't going anywhere, either."

She bit her lip, and color rose to her cheeks. When

she shook her head, relief coursed through him.

"Good. Let's go home."

PADDLING BACK WAS harder than coming out had been. Amanda was chilly in her damp clothes and tingling with an emotion she couldn't quite pin down. Just thinking about being with Carter sent desire racing through her body, and if they weren't due back for dinner—if she wasn't afraid Buck could be watching them even now—she could easily be convinced to find a private spot and explore his body all over again.

She craved his hands on her bare skin again, but she craved something else, too. The way he looked at her. All of her. He'd watched her in her most intimate moments. Had coaxed feelings out of her body she hadn't known were possible. She'd been desired before, but she'd never been wanted in the way that Carter seemed to want her.

He'd made it clear he was interested in more than just a quick encounter.

She wanted something more than that, too.

First she had to deal with the painting.

"Looks like we're having a cookout tonight," Carter said.

Amanda took in the scene on the beach ahead of them. It looked like all of Carter's brothers had gathered to make the meal. A fire was burning in the large firepit. As they drew closer to shore, the smell of hamburgers and hot dogs reached her. Amanda's stomach growled, but she quailed to think of walking past all those men after sharing such an incredibly intimate encounter with Carter.

When they reached the beach, she scrambled from the canoe and darted out of the way when Hudson came to help Carter pull it past the water line.

"Almost ready," Lincoln called to them from the firepit.

"Be there in a minute. We need dry clothes," Carter said.

"What have you two been up to?" Hudson asked.

Carter ignored him, took Amanda's hand and walked with her across the beach. She was grateful he'd taken charge that way—and that he hadn't joked around with Hudson about their disheveled state.

"You all right?" he asked as they made their way to number twenty-three.

"Yes."

"Don't let my brothers get to you."

"I won't."

He stopped at the bottom of the steps to the house. Squeezed her hand. "We've got nothing to be ashamed of."

"I know."

"But you're not comfortable with this." He drew her closer, lifted a hand to cup the back of her head and kissed her softly.

"I'm not comfortable with people making judgments about me," she said when they pulled apart.

"No one's going to judge. They might be jealous, but that's all. I'm not the only one in my family who's thinking about getting a move on and settling down."

Settling down?

Amanda didn't know how to respond to that. Carter gently lifted her chin so she had to face him. "I'm not going to rush you into anything," he assured her. "But you need to know I'm ready for something real."

Meeting his gaze, Amanda thought she could be ready for something real, too—after she got rid of the painting hidden upstairs.

He brushed another kiss over her lips and let go. "Be back in a minute."

As soon as he was gone, Amanda made a beeline upstairs to the shower, where she let hot water chase the chill away. Newly scrubbed and shampooed, she changed into another outfit and felt more in control of her emotions. She tossed her wet things over the porch railing when she came downstairs and spotted Carter waiting for her at the end of her driveway.

That man wants something real with you, she thought, savoring the novelty of it. She'd kept herself too isolated in the past to have many relationships. Those she'd stumbled into seemed to fade away after a few months, just like her friendships with other women had. She had a way of procrastinating before replying to invitations. Canceling at the last minute when she did make plans. Worrying if the relationship would ask too much of her.

So why was she throwing herself at Carter now?

Amanda couldn't answer that question satisfactorily, except for the obvious. She was into him in a way she hadn't experienced with another man. Was it that simple?

Was Carter the one?

Amanda stopped halfway down the steps. At the end of the driveway, Carter turned, caught sight of her and smiled.

"Ready?" he called, beginning to move toward her.

Was she ready?

Amanda wasn't sure. Still, somehow her feet propelled her down the last few steps and toward him. When they reached each other, he touched her arm.

"What's making you smile like that?"

"Am I smiling?" If so, it was because she was happy. She *was* ready—for both friendships and a special relationship with this man. She was ready to finally live.

"You're definitely smiling."

"So are you."

"Because you're here."

The warm May day was softening to a beautiful evening. It seemed natural to take the hand he extended as they walked the short distance to the beach. She had to fight the urge to lean into him. It was as if Carter were a gravity-dense planet and she were a moon who was helpless to do anything else than circle him. Amanda realized how apt the word *attraction* was. It explained what she felt for Carter perfectly.

That's what had happened in the canoe, she decided. She'd lost the battle against physics.

And she didn't mind one bit.

"Hope you're hungry," Lincoln said when they reached the beach. He passed her a plate and gestured to a bag of buns. "Throw one on the grill if you want it toasted. Otherwise, doctor it up however you like. Hudson will get you a burger or hot dog."

She followed his instructions. When Hudson had deposited a burger on the roll she'd toasted for a minute, then slathered with mayo, ketchup and mustard, she joined Carter at a nearby picnic table. The others dropped onto its bench seats one by one when they'd filled their plates.

"I've started working on a hutch," Nate said suddenly to Carter. "Might work in the dining room of number twenty-three when you're done fixing it up."

Carter set his burger on his plate. "Didn't know you'd found time for woodworking."

"Can't work at the mill all the time. Been messing around in Grandpa's shop." He shrugged. "Thought I'd throw one together. A man needs a hobby, right?"

"Nate builds amazing things," Carter told Amanda. "If he's offering a hutch, you'll want to take it."

"I'd love to see it." Amanda wondered how much it would set her back. She didn't have an income anymore, something she needed to rectify. She'd been so distracted by Carter these past twenty-four hours, she wasn't thinking straight.

Buck could be close to finding her. The painting was still in her bathroom cabinet. If she was smart, she'd concentrate on that.

"If you have time for woodworking, you should have time to increase production at the mill. The contracts Carter got aren't going to keep us afloat for long," Gage said.

Nate frowned. "You can ride me about production when you start helping at the mill. I can't work all the time."

"Hobbies are for old people. You need to get out more. Have some fun," Hudson said. "No wonder you never want to go to the Dancing Boot."

"I don't want to go because if I did, I'd have to see our workers making asses out of themselves. The sheriff would expect me to intervene."

"It's been quiet for a few days," Hudson said.

"Let's hope it stays that way."

"It won't," Gage grumbled. "Never does, does it?"

"Always the pessimist, aren't you?" Nate said good-naturedly. "Anyway, it'll take me a few weeks to finish the hutch, Amanda. I'll let you know when it's done."

"Thanks," Amanda said.

After that she was content to listen to the brothers talk. Despite their different temperaments and interests, no one could doubt they were a family.

It had been so long since she'd felt a part of anything like that.

"You're so lucky," she said aloud.

The conversation subsided as they all looked her way. "To have each other," she tried to explain. "To have all this." She tried to encompass the community, the lake, the forest, the sunshine and beach, the common bond that united them.

She was surprised when Gage answered. "We are lucky," he said quietly. "Or at least we were."

"We still are," Carter said firmly.

"I agree," Nate said.

"Me, too," Lincoln said.

Hudson nodded absently, gazing at the lake. He'd been restless tonight, up and down to tend to the grill several times.

They finished the meal. When the other men got up, reaching automatically for dishes and food to carry to the town hall kitchen, Amanda wondered if their parents had raised them to clean up after themselves or if their time in the military had drummed it into their heads. Either way, she approved.

As she stood, too, Carter's hand brushed hers. He leaned in to murmur near her ear.

"I feel lucky to have you here."

CHAPTER 7

H E NEEDED TO slow his roll.

He was starting to sound as lovesick as a teen-ager. It was hard to keep from telling her how he felt, though.

The moment they kissed in the canoe, Carter's desire for Amanda had accelerated from a warm flame into a scorching need. When she looked him in the eye and began to peel off her clothes, he'd been a goner.

But he could blow this.

First he needed to convince her to stay, sign the contract, buy the house and settle in for good. Then, and only then, could he find out if they really had something together. Just because he was itching to find a wife didn't mean Amanda was looking to be one. It was going to take time to find out if their chemistry would last a lifetime.

Carter walked Amanda home slowly, glad to leave his brothers behind at his parents' old house. When they were safely away from prying eyes, standing on number twenty-three's front porch, he let himself enjoy kissing

Amanda until his whole body was buzzing with anticipation.

He didn't ask to come in, however. He had a feeling if he did, she'd let him, but he also knew it could easily become too much, too fast. He didn't want to overwhelm Amanda.

He wanted her to want him as badly as he craved her.

"I'll be right across the street," he told her finally. "I'd love to be here with you," he added when she opened her mouth to say something, "but I also want to give you time to decide what you really want."

She hesitated so long, he thought she'd tell him to stop being dumb and just come inside. Instead, she nodded. "I think it's a good idea to take things slow." Her quick smile was lopsided. "If that's even possible after what we got up to this afternoon. It's not that I don't want to be with you tonight," she added. "It just feels like if I ask you to stay, I'm committing to something. Does that make sense?"

It did, as much as he didn't want it to. "Like I said earlier. I'm looking for something real."

"I want that, too." She met his gaze head-on. "We have to know each other before we can have that, though. Don't you think?"

Carter knew she was right.

"The next time I'm with you, I want it to be because I'm ready for everything it implies."

"How long do you think that will take?" It wasn't a fair question, but he was too distracted to pretend he didn't want to get there right now.

"I don't know, but I want to find out. Are you angry?"

"Angry? Of course not. I can wait as long as it takes, Amanda." He wasn't some kid. He was a man who was thinking about the future he wanted to create.

She was thinking about their future, too. Letting him know it was important to her to get it right.

He kissed her cheek. "Good night."

"Night."

He walked away.

Two hours after settling down for a second night on the floor of number twenty-four, he was still tossing and turning, aching with frustration that the width of an entire street lay between them. It was a warm enough night that he'd left several windows open. A mosquito found its way in somehow and was droning on and on. If he was smart, he'd turn on the light, find and kill it before it feasted on him.

Carter sat up—

A scream pierced the air.

On his feet in an instant, he was outside before he realized he was wearing only boxer briefs. Undeterred, he raced across to number twenty-three and banged on the door.

"Amanda? What's going on?"

He waited, his heart thumping in his chest, but there wasn't an answer.

Carter banged on the door again. "Amanda? You in there?"

He heard footsteps a moment later. The lock turned and the door opened a fraction of an inch. Inside, Amanda wore a tank top, panties and nothing else.

Carter swallowed against the urge to sweep her right into his arms. "You okay?"

"Yes." Her voice was small. "Sorry. Nightmare, I think. I woke up thinking I'd heard something, but it was only in my dreams."

"You sure about that?"

She shook her head. "There's nothing in the house. The door was locked."

"Why don't you let me come in and look around?" Carter heard footsteps behind him and turned to find his brothers pounding up the street.

"Heard a scream," Nate called. "Everything all right here?"

Sounds traveled too well at the Ridge on a quiet night like this one.

"I think so. Amanda had a bad dream, but I'm going to search the house just to be sure."

"We'll check out here."

Carter turned back to Amanda, who let him inside. She crossed her arms over her chest, but that didn't hide the fact she wasn't wearing a bra. All his pent-up desire roared back to life as Carter passed her, and he struggled not to let his body betray the extent of his interest. He made short work of searching the house. Like she'd said, nothing was amiss. He trusted his brothers to make sure all was clear outside, too, but Amanda still looked spooked.

"You want me to sleep here tonight? Down here, I mean. If it will make you feel better."

"I would like that," Amanda admitted more readily than he'd have guessed. She was having trouble looking him in the eye. His lack of clothing seemed to be throwing her off. "I'm jumpy tonight. I don't know why."

"You're in a new place. You're a city girl, right? It's probably too quiet for you here."

"I guess."

"Go on back to bed. I'll bring my things over and settle in. Just call if you need anything."

"Thanks." She waited a moment, biting her lip. Went up on tiptoe and planted a kiss on the side of his mouth. "Good night."

No hiding what he wanted now, Carter thought as his body hardened with desire. "Good night. Get some sleep."

Her gaze dipped for only a second. Amanda bit her lip but didn't say anything, even though he knew she had to have seen his erection. He hoped against hope she'd take pity on him and invite him upstairs. He thought she wanted to, but their earlier conversation had put that out of the question. Both of them needed to keep to the agreement they'd made.

"Night," she said again and turned away.

Stifling a sigh, Carter watched her as she went upstairs, allowing himself to appreciate the view, then took a moment to get his body under control before he walked across the street to fetch the covers he'd left in number twenty-four. On his way he met Lincoln, who said things were all clear outside. His brothers walked back to his folks' house, and Carter continued on to fetch his things. At least Amanda trusted him enough to let him stay in her house, but even when he settled down again for the night, he lay awake for a long time before he finally dozed off.

AMANDA WOKE TO sunshine peeking through a break in the forest canopy outside her window. It was hard to remember why she was so frightened last night now that it was so bright and cheerful in her room. She'd left her windows open when she went to bed. Maybe she'd heard a branch falling or some small animal roaming in the dark, and her unconscious mind had run riot with it, feeding her dreams of someone inside her house.

Now someone was. Unless he'd already left, Carter must be sleeping downstairs. Last night she'd appreciated the way he'd agreed to the boundaries she set, but she couldn't help envisioning what it would be like if he was beside her now. Would they make love again?

She'd be sorely tempted to.

She hated to think of him lying on the hard plank floor of the living room but assumed a Navy SEAL must be used to conditions like that. He'd led a much rougher life than she had—until recently, at least.

Visions of his muscular body filled her mind. He'd been a sight to see in those close-fitting briefs last night. When she'd leaned in for that last kiss, she felt him respond, and the evidence of his desire was obvious given how little clothing he wore. It would have been easy to entice him upstairs. She didn't want this relationship to be a flash in a pan, though, scorching hot and then over before it had began. She was willing to be patient if that meant they had a better chance of creating something that would last.

Amanda slipped out of bed and quickly dressed. She needed to ask where she could do a load of wash today—and she needed to run into town to buy some new clothes. She was halfway down the stairs when Carter came into the hall from the living room. He'd pulled on a pair of jeans but was shirtless, stretching one arm and then the other like a runner might do before a run. He stopped when he saw her.

"Sleep at all?"

"Yes, thank you." It was hard not to look at the play of muscles over his arms and chest as he moved. Several scars marred the smooth planes of his skin, and her gaze lingered on them. She wondered about the stories behind them. He was at ease in his body in a way she'd never been in hers, causing a thread of jealousy to worm through her. What was it like to be that powerful and know you could always defend yourself? These past few weeks she'd been on edge, knowing the advantage Buck would have over her if he ever found her. She felt perfectly safe around Carter, though.

"Hungry?" he asked.

She nodded.

"Let me duck across the street and change. Pick you up in a minute."

Amanda sat on the front steps to wait for him. He was as good as his word, back to meet her fully clothed in no time at all.

"I was worried maybe having me downstairs would make things worse, not better," he admitted as they walked to the town hall.

"Why would you think that?"

"All things considered, you still don't know me very well," he pointed out. "Takes a lot of trust to let someone get that close when you're sleeping."

He was right, of course. There was no reason she trusted him so much when she barely knew him, but she had invited him into her home without a second thought last night.

Of course, she'd invited him into her body before then. How much closer could you get?

"I guess I trust you, then," she said lightly.

His gaze softened a moment, before he schooled his features into neutrality. "Good." He took her hand. Just like yesterday, it felt natural to allow it. She didn't hesitate to curl her fingers around his, then wondered why it felt so comfortable. After everything that had happened with Buck and her own father, she should have a grave distrust of men, but Carter seemed cut from a different cloth from Ian Stakewell or Buck Bronson. Her father spent his days thinking about the angles, figuring out how to cut corners, sure rules didn't apply to him. Buck just took whatever the hell he wanted and meted out punishments if he was crossed.

Carter had his own brand of cockiness, but he had a

code of conduct, too. He had values that seemed to align with hers. She'd learned how important that was.

They walked like that all the way to the town hall, but he let go of her hand when he ushered her inside. Amanda missed the comforting pressure of his fingers but didn't allow her feelings to show. Surrounded by Carter and his brothers, she released any vestiges of the fear she'd felt last night. Even if Buck did show up, he could never take on all these men at once.

They found Nate making omelets and home fries. When her stomach growled, Amanda smiled. She was looking forward to trying both.

"I need to do some wash," she said as they all sat down and served themselves. She was determined to keep her thoughts on practical matters. Time enough later to worry about Buck and the painting. "Are there machines around here somewhere?"

"There's a set in number one," Gage said.

"Throw a load in any time," Carter said.

"And I should head to town," Amanda said. "I need to get some groceries. I checked out your supplies while you were working yesterday and came up with a menu for the week." With no access to the internet, it had helped to pass the time.

"I could come with you," Carter said.

"Not this time," she said. "I appreciate the offer, but I'm going to do some shopping for myself, too. Besides, they need you at the mill, right?" She wanted a chance to use the Wi-Fi at a coffee shop to come up with ideas for how to return the painting without getting caught. She couldn't do that if Carter was with her.

"That's right," Lincoln said, leaning forward. "It's all hands on deck these days."

"Don't worry; I'm sure I can find my way around," Amanda said.

"You'll come back, though, won't you?" Carter asked.

His brothers laughed. "You afraid she's not going to give you that dollar?" Nate teased him.

"That's not it." Carter kept his gaze on her.

"I'll come back with some new clothes, your mail, a bunch of groceries and whatever else that takes my fancy," she assured him.

"How is she going to pay for that?" Nate asked. "The groceries and stuff?"

"We'll have to add you onto my credit card," Carter said. "But I can give you cash for now."

"That will work," she said. For some reason she'd gone all tingly again. Surely not because Carter wanted to put her on his card. For one thing, she had credit cards of her own, even if she couldn't use them at the moment. For another, no matter how domestic the arrangement sounded, it wasn't like he'd proposed. He was setting up a business arrangement. After all, as cook she'd be like the Elliotts' employee—and she wasn't even getting paid for the work.

"I'll come with you next time you head to town, and we'll visit the bank together." Carter got back to eating, but the frown on his face told her he was disappointed she wouldn't let him come along.

"Sounds like a good idea."

When the meal was done, Amanda made the drive to Chance Creek easily, since one country highway took her most of the way there. Navigating the town was simple, too, given how small it was. She found a clothing store run by a friendly woman named Storm Hall. Storm helped Amanda pick out a number of staples for her new wardrobe and a couple of fun extras. Usually she shopped for practicality as well as price. Now that Carter was in her life, however, Amanda found herself lingering over pretty clothes. Storm encouraged her, finding soft colors and styles that suited her, going back to find different sizes and bringing skirts and accessories Amanda wouldn't have chosen for herself.

All the while Storm chatted about the town and its inhabitants. She told Amanda about her favorite local restaurants and bars, and assured her that although Chance Creek was small, it was full of interesting people doing interesting things.

"Give it some time," she advised as she was ringing up Amanda's purchases. "Make sure you attend all the holiday celebrations and activities the town holds. Once you meet a few people, it becomes easier to meet more."

"Thanks, I will," Amanda told her, wanting to believe a life like that was possible for her someday. Laden down with more purchases than she'd intended to make, she walked to her rental car to stow them away before she went to the grocery store.

She felt more conspicuous there. The aisles were

tight, and she found herself looking over her shoulder more than once. There was no sign of Buck, though. Just fellow shoppers intent on loading up their carts. Amanda breathed a sigh of relief when she had checked out and was back in Carter's truck, the groceries stowed away. Soon she'd need to find an alternate form of transportation. Could she afford to buy a beater car? Would registering it somehow flag her whereabouts to Buck? Had buying her plane ticket to Chance Creek already done so?

There was no way to know. Her phone worked here in town, however. She considered finding a coffee shop, then decided she felt more comfortable here in the truck. No one knew about this new number. She hadn't informed anyone when she ditched her old one, being too busy traveling around from place to place to get away from Buck. When she opened her email account, she found her sister had written.

Why aren't you answering my texts? What's going on?

Short and sweet. Melissa didn't waste words.

It was interesting she'd written at all. Usually Amanda was the one who reached out to start a conversation.

Should she answer her sister?

Later, she decided. Right now she needed to figure out what to do with the painting. Then she needed to get back to Elliott Ridge.

She looked up the Warden Gallery and copied down its address. The easiest thing to do would be to simply mail it back. She quailed to think about putting a masterpiece at risk like that, but she told herself mail was delivered intact all the time. If she wrapped it well and bought a cardboard tube to send it in, surely it would arrive all right.

She found the location of Chance Creek's post office and drove to it, happy that parking was so easy in this little town. Inside, she found the kind of mailing tube she was looking for. It was made of rigid cardboard she didn't think she could bend if she tried, but it still made her feel sick to her stomach to trust such a valuable item to the postal system.

"Would you like to purchase that?"

Amanda looked up to find a middle-aged man at the counter, watching her. Even worse, on the wall above him several security cameras were mounted. She looked down quickly, pretending to go through the selection of mailers.

"No, thank you. I just need to pick up my mail." She fished out a key Carter had fetched for her and found the Elliotts' post office box, all the while feeling the gaze of the man behind the counter on her. If she tried to mail the painting, there'd be footage of her doing so. Would the Warden Gallery investigate the return of *Afternoon in Sunshine and Shadow* if she sent it back? Could they track the package to the Chance Creek post office and discover who sent it?

Amanda pulled out a small stack of mail, locked the box again and left the building.

In Carter's truck she slumped in the front seat, defeated.

Mailing the painting back was a dead end.

She had to find another way.

"THAT LASAGNA WAS great. Family recipe?" Carter asked as they finished the dishes that night. He was washing, Amanda drying and putting away.

The simple soup and sandwiches she had served for lunch, the first meal the mill workers had joined them for, had gone over well, and everyone's mood had improved by the time they returned to work that afternoon. There'd been a lot of talk and laughter about how great it was to see a female face around the place. Carter decided they'd better get some more women around soon, before someone decided to hit on his girl.

His girl.

He'd come to like thinking about Amanda that way.

Dinner had been even more of a hit than lunch. Amanda's lasagna was layered high with meat, sauce and cheese, a real stick-to-your-ribs type of meal the men preferred. For the first time in weeks, Carter thought it was possible he might convince some of the workers to stick around long-term. The current crop had agreed to a three-month stint here at the Ridge, and none of them seemed inclined to extend it, but maybe things would be different now.

Amanda had returned from Chance Creek laden down with bags from a clothing store. Carter couldn't help wondering why she'd traveled so light when she arrived here. Most women he knew lugged suitcases brimming with outfits everywhere they went. He noticed she rarely talked about herself. She never mentioned the job she left behind, her home or her family unless he questioned her directly about them.

Determined to find out more about Amanda, Carter took his time with each dish, scrubbing it well before he handed it to her.

"I taught myself to cook mostly," she said.

"Your mom or dad didn't show you how?"

She shook her head. "Like I said, they split up when I was a teenager. After that, Mom worked full-time. I took over the shopping and cooking."

"That's a lot of responsibility."

"It was, but it taught me a lot. I went out in the world knowing how to run a household."

"I guess that's good. Did you see your dad much after the split?"

She slowed as she wiped dry the plate in her hand. "No. Not for years."

He heard the pain in her voice and felt for her. The Elliotts were family people; the first years after they'd left the Ridge had been difficult. He hadn't spoken to his brothers very often, but at least his parents' marriage had been solid throughout all the trouble they'd known. "He must regret that." Amanda gave a little laugh he wasn't sure how to interpret. "What's so funny?"

"These days I'm not sure if my dad ever wanted a family. He sure doesn't act like it."

"I'm sorry to hear that."

"I'm not in contact with him anymore," she said shortly. "As far as I'm concerned, I never need to hear from him again."

Carter touched her arm softly. "Sorry I brought it up."

"It's okay."

It wasn't, though. Carter could see that. He took the plate and dishcloth from her hands and put them on the counter, then folded her into his arms. He held her lightly, willing her to feel safe and comforted. He wanted her to know he would never let her down.

At first she was rigid in his arms, but then she relaxed and rested against him, her head tucked under his chin.

When he released her a few minutes later, she stepped away, picked up the dishcloth and plate and got back to work.

"I like it when you do that," she said softly.

Warmth flooded his chest. "You do?"

She nodded. "You're a good hugger. You feel... safe."

Emotions warred within him. He was glad she thought so, but right now *safe* wasn't the word he'd use to describe the way he felt around her. He wanted all of her again. Not just once or twice, either.

He wanted to make her cling to him the way she had in the canoe. He wanted to see her lose control.

Carter shifted. He'd been half-hard and uncomfortable most of the day so far just thinking about Amanda. He needed to be patient, but that wasn't proving easy.

When they were done, on their way out of the building, Amanda said, "Hold on a minute." She ducked around the counter in the entryway and then into the back room, where there was access to the back of the mailboxes. She came out a minute or two later with a pen and a piece of paper. He waited while she made a list of names. "I'm in number twenty-three." She wrote a twenty-three by her name. "Gage, Lincoln, Hudson and Nate are in house number one, right?"

Carter nodded.

"Should I put you in number twenty-four?"

Was that her way of asking where he planned to sleep tonight? If she was offering him the chance to sleep on her living room floor again, the answer was a big "Hell, yeah." He didn't want to misread the situation, though. Carter thought it over.

"My mail can go to number twenty-four, but I'll sleep in your living room as long as you want me there," he offered. There. Ball was in her court now. If she didn't want him there, she could send him back across the street.

Or invite him upstairs.

She bent over the paper. "Thanks. I'd appreciate it if you stayed with me tonight. Guess I'm still jumpy. Can you give me a list of the mill workers' names? I caught a few, but I don't remember most of them."

He did so, naming them off one by one, then counting them to make sure he hadn't forgotten anyone. All the while, he fought to keep a smile from spreading across his face. She wanted him at her place tonight. That was a promising start.

She assigned each of them a mailbox, even though they were all staying in the bunkhouses, then tacked the piece of paper on the bulletin board near the mailboxes and surveyed her handiwork. "Where are the keys to the boxes?"

"I'll hand them out to everyone at lunch tomorrow. Pretty sure they're at my folks' house. Ready to go?"

"Yes."

He took her hand as he walked her to number twenty-three. Inside, she said, "It's got to be uncomfortable sleeping on the floor like that. Don't you have an air mattress or something?"

"Is this your way of telling me a day isn't long enough to know whether you want to commit to a relationship with me?"

"Two is the minimum, don't you think?" she quipped.

Since he'd known his feelings on the matter the minute he saw her step out of the plane, he couldn't agree. Still, he said, "I suppose that's reasonable. To answer your question, I haven't found our old camping gear. I don't know if it's worth dragging a mattress over from my folks' place—it'll just be in the way when we renovate."

"I should have bought you an air mattress when I was in town. I'll grab one the next time I go."

"Sounds good." He scrubbed a hand over his jaw, very aware she'd just set a firm boundary with him.

"I'm sorry," she said.

"For what?" He was genuinely curious. She didn't owe him anything.

She made a face. "For not asking you upstairs. You

want me to, don't you?"

Busted. "Yeah," he admitted, "I do. Any time you want, I'm your man. I'm not going to push you, though."

"That's gentlemanly of you."

"I can be gentlemanly."

"It's a good look on you." She studied the floor. "I just want to be sure, you know?"

"I know. Like I said, I'm not going anywhere." He waited until she opened the door. "I'll get my things and come back. When I do, I'll stay down here."

"GET YOUR WALKING shoes on, Amanda. I'm going to take you on a tour today," Carter announced the next morning after they'd eaten breakfast burritos with his brothers. Lincoln had manned the kitchen this morning, making burritos spicy enough to make them all comment on it.

"Don't you have work to do?" Amanda asked. They had wandered over to number twenty-three together after the meal. Carter was stowing away his things. She was watching him. She'd had a hard time sleeping last night knowing he was down here. It took all her strength not to creep down the stairs and slide into his sleeping bag next to him. This attraction between them had a life of its own.

"It's Saturday. Besides, you need to know your way around the Ridge if you're going to stay."

She was going to stay, Amanda thought. No matter what it took to get rid of the painting. She had to come up with a new plan, since mailing it wasn't going to work, but she couldn't do that now.

"Looking forward to it," she told Carter before she went to freshen up. By the time she got back, he was on the stoop, waiting for her. They set off toward the lake first, following the road that branched off from the Circle and ran along the edge of it for a short distance.

"We own the land clear around Elliott Lake," Carter told her. "People keep telling us to develop it. We could put several tiers of summer cottages around it and make a good profit, but I don't want seasonal people. I want people who will make Elliott Ridge their home."

"That sounds smart," Amanda said.

"I'll take you to the old mine, next."

The road curved upward in a series of switchbacks for quite some time. It ended in a wide-open area in front of the old entrance to the mine.

"We're about three-quarters of the way up the Ridge here," Carter said. "The main shaft is blocked now. There was some remediation when it shut down, and an inspector comes once a year to check things out."

"Is it dangerous?"

"Not really. There's no reason to come up here, though. I just thought you should know where it was."

"Sure." She wondered what the mine was like in its heyday. It didn't look very big.

"It petered out fairly quickly," Carter confirmed. "But it employed the men of the town for a few decades. Put Elliott Ridge on the map, so to speak."

It seemed lonely here to Amanda. More ghostly than

the abandoned town, somehow. To one side a trio of outbuildings were being reclaimed by nature.

"Steer clear of those," Carter said when he noticed where she was looking. "Those aren't stable anymore. We'll have to knock them down someday so no one gets hurt."

Amanda figured she'd found where to stash the painting. Surely there was some nook or cranny just inside one of these outbuildings where no one would ever look. Carter was busy with her house and the mill. She doubted he'd get to knocking down these places anytime soon. It wasn't like she needed to hide it there for very long. Only until she found a way to return it to its rightful place.

Next he took her to his favorite lookout, a scramble up steep ground to where the trees and brush began to thin and they were climbing over exposed rock. There was a good view of the valley from here, and she could even spot Chance Creek in the distance.

"This is amazing!"

"It's always been my favorite place. It's my thinking spot. Sometimes Dad would join me when he wanted to talk something over."

"It's wonderful."

"I think so. Come on, let me show you something else." He led her along an overgrown trail to the back side of the ridge. Down the slope, she could see a newly cleared area and some kind of construction. "That's Warrington's land. The guy who wants to buy our town. Damn fool is building a golf resort over there. Can you believe it?"

"He's going to have to take down a lot of trees."

"You're right. I wonder who he's selling the timber to." They wandered back to their side of the ridge.

"I like this better," she said.

"Me, too." He hesitated. "It means a lot to me that you like it here."

"Elliott Ridge is a special place. It deserves to be brought to life. It deserves a second chance, you know?" She still got the feeling the town wanted that as much as the Elliott men did.

Instead of answering, Carter leaned down to kiss her. Amanda tilted her head to meet him without even thinking about it. It felt so right to let him take her into his arms, slide a hand under her hair and close the space between them. His mouth was soft on hers at first, but as time went on, he deepened the kiss, waking up a longing deep inside her that flared into hunger this simple connection couldn't quench.

Every time she got near to Carter she wanted to take her clothes off, Amanda thought with amusement.

"What are you thinking?" he asked her, his mouth brushing the sensitive skin under her ear.

"I'm thinking about how it would feel to have you inside me again."

Carter groaned against her throat. "You're killing me. I thought we were taking it slow."

Amanda laughed. "I'm trying."

"Does it count if we're outdoors?" He pulled back and looked down at her.

Amanda thought about that. "No," she said. "I don't believe it does."

"Thank god." Carter turned her in his arms, pressed his front against her back and found the hemline of her shirt. He peeled it over her head, tossed it aside and skimmed his hands across her skin. Amanda sighed with desire. Every touch felt so good.

Reaching behind her, she found the button of his jeans and undid it. When she slid a hand down into his pants and found him hard, straining against his boxer briefs, she smiled with the knowledge she turned him on so much.

Carter kicked off his boots and shucked off his jeans, keeping a hand on her hips, then reached to undo her pants and help her out of them.

She struggled to get out of her shoes but finally managed it and kicked her way out of her jeans, as well. When he unhooked her bra, she shrugged it away, loving the feeling of the soft warm breeze on her bare skin.

As Carter palmed her breasts, she leaned back against him, caught in the sensation of his touch. Craving more, she tugged at his briefs until he pulled them off. Now he was hot and hard against her back. He slid a hand into her panties and found her ready for him. He made short work of getting them off her.

Amanda found she didn't even want socks between her and the world. She balanced on one leg and then the other, awkwardly sliding them from her feet. With her bare toes in the rough soil, the breeze playing over her skin and the scent of pine in the air, joy filled her. She'd never made love outdoors before she met Carter.

Now it was her favorite thing in the world.

Carter guided her forward and lifted her hands to brace them against the trunk of a nearby tree. He used a knee to spread her legs, his hands sweeping over her skin before dipping between her thighs, his fingers touching her in all the right places.

A moment later he slid inside her as Amanda gasped, the sensation threatening to overcome her. She stood on tiptoe, her feet resting on his as Carter settled his hands on her hips and pushed farther inside.

She let out a ragged breath as he filled her, pulled out and pushed inside again. He rocked her against him, pushing deep, setting a slow, steady pace that made her want to beg for more.

When he slid a hand up to cup one breast, pleasure spiked through her, and her fingers dug into the tree's bark as she tried to keep in control.

Carter wasn't having that, though. He moved inside her, increasing his pace, lifting her with each thrust, then tugging her back against him, every rocking motion bringing her closer to the edge.

"Carter," she breathed. It was all she could do to hang on. When he released her breast and tangled a hand in her hair, arching her back as he thrust into her, Amanda went over the edge with a cry, sensation exploding inside her as he bucked against her, sounding his own release.

Amanda clung to the tree, her cries and Carter's guttural sounds mixing until she was wrung dry. When it was over, he pulled out slowly, turned her around and caught her tight against him. His kisses were hard. Still hungry. Searing her as if he wanted to make sure she never forgot him.

As if she could.

Still in possession of her mouth, he bent down, grabbed their clothes, spread them on the ground and lowered her down to them.

And then he made love to her all over again while above them the trees swayed against a crystal-blue sky.

Amanda didn't think she could move when he was done. Thoroughly sated, her legs as wobbly as a new calf's, she let him help her to her feet and leaned on Carter's chest as he dressed her, putting her back into her clothes far more slowly than he'd taken her out of them.

"So much for waiting," she teased him. He growled low in his chest, and she laughed.

"Outside doesn't count," he reminded her, stealing another deep, soul-stirring kiss.

"Outside doesn't count," she agreed happily, wondering how she'd manage when they were indoors tonight. "If it's meant to be, waiting for inside privileges will be worth it," she assured him—and herself.

He hooked his fingers into the belt loops of her jeans and tugged her closer. "I know that, too."

CHAPTER 8

A FTER ANOTHER SLOW, scorching kiss, Carter made himself let Amanda go. He took her hand, and together they picked their way down the slope, past the mine and straight to the settlement rather than taking the road.

He liked the feel of Amanda's hand in his. It emphasized the connection between them, assured him she was still close by his side. They stopped in number twenty-three to clean up, then wandered the streets of the settlement, commenting on the different houses.

"They're all so unique. I would have thought a company town would have picked one floor plan and made them all the same."

"The oldest ones are like that." They made their way to the northeast corner of the town, where he showed her several streets of boxy, one-story homes perched on the slope above the town hall. "The newer houses were built one at a time as the mine got more productive. Everyone who moved here was handy. There was no shortage of men to help construct a house in off-hours."

"Did people have off-hours?"

"Men worked hard, but my family wanted the town to prosper. I think my great-grandfather, in particular, was interested in architecture. He liked to draw up plans and passed on the hobby to my grandfather. When the mine closed and the mill started up, there was plenty of lumber to be had."

"It's an interesting place."

He took her for a quick look at the mill and showed her the hulking wrecks of old vehicles and equipment parked nearby.

"That's the graveyard," he said. "I know it looks awful, but it's more like a supply cabinet than a pile of junk. Dad loved going to auctions to buy the castoffs from larger lumber operations, and Lincoln always had the knack of getting them to work. He'll cannibalize one piece of equipment to get another one up and running."

"That's a handy skill."

Carter strolled with her to the town hall again and led the way inside. "I'll show you something else interesting. You've seen the east wing, but you haven't seen the west wing." He opened the double doors on the left side of the foyer and ushered her into a large room. When he flicked a light switch, Amanda gasped.

"No way." She stepped in and turned around, sweeping her gaze around the large room. "You've got a library?"

"Yep. I had a feeling you'd like it."

"Libraries have always been my safe place."

Safe from what? he wanted to ask but didn't want to ruin the moment. "Of course, no books have been added since we left," he said instead.

It was small, but Carter had been to towns five times as big with smaller libraries. There were no computer terminals or anything like that. Just rows and rows of books and a counter where you checked them out. A small collection of DVDs and a bigger one of VHS tapes. He knew there was even a shelf or two of old vinyl records back there somewhere.

"This is wonderful." Amanda moved to the first row and ran her fingers down the spines. It was the start of the fiction section, mostly paperbacks, with hardcovers interspersed among them. "Why aren't they dusty?"

"Dennis," Carter said succinctly. "He must run a feather duster over them periodically. He takes great pride in caring for Elliott Ridge."

"I haven't seen him since I got here."

"He's around," Carter assured her. Dennis liked to stay in the background. When Carter was a child, sometimes when he and his brothers got sick of playing baseball or hide and seek, they made it a game to find him. Often, they couldn't.

Amanda pulled out a book. Moved a few others over and put it in a new place. She frowned and moved another one. "These aren't in order."

"Mom kept the library up and running. She didn't have time to alphabetize. She made sure things were basically in the right section, though. No one seemed to mind."

Amanda moved another book. And another.

Carter tried not to smile, but he knew he was failing. "Bothers you, huh?"

"Yes," she said firmly. She stepped back and looked at the whole length of the shelf. "None of these are in order. She just stuck all the fiction on here in groups. This is mystery. That's science fiction." She pointed.

"Sounds about right from what I remember."

Amanda turned to him helplessly. "I could sort this out in no time. It's not like I have anything better to do while you're at the mill."

His heart warmed. She depended on him for entertainment. And she really liked the library. Maybe giving her the task of organizing it would make her feel needed here. He had a sense she'd left some problems back in California. His mother used to count pennies when she got stressed out. When their mounting bills overwhelmed her and she couldn't sleep, she'd get up, find the change jar and sort it into rolls she could take to the bank. Would getting the library in order comfort Amanda?

"It's yours," he said.

"What's mine?" She glanced up at him.

"The job. You're now Elliott Ridge's librarian, if you want to be."

"Are you for real?"

"Yep."

She smiled, and Carter's heart did something funny in his chest. She had a beautiful smile. Knowing he'd made her happy felt… pretty great.

"I definitely want to be Elliott Ridge's librarian," Amanda said. "I can whip this place into shape in no time. It's got all the elements: shelves, furniture, windows—even window seats," she added, moving toward one. "It just needs a thorough cleaning and some reorganization, and it'll be a fantastic place to spend time."

"I'll leave you to it, then. I have some work I can do on the house. I'll be back at lunchtime—with a bunch of other hungry men," he reminded her.

"Mm-hmm." She was already at work, clearing an armful of books from the top shelf and reaching for more. Carter decided he'd better come early. If Amanda forgot to cook, he could whip up sandwiches.

It seemed like he'd accidentally created a whole blueprint for luring a woman to Elliott Ridge.

Offer her a house for a buck. Create jobs for her to take ownership of so she felt part of the place.

Fall in love with her.

Carter's step hitched as he let himself out of the building and made his way to number twenty-three.

Was he in love with Amanda?

Yeah, he decided. He was.

SHE DIDN'T KNOW when the snacks appeared.

Amanda came around the corner of a shelf unit to find a plate with a sandwich, an apple, a couple of store-bought cookies and a can of soda placed on top of one of the stacks of books she'd left in the open area between the shelves and the main counter of the library.

The fiction section covered ten sets of shelves. She'd pulled all the books out and was arranging them first in categories and then in alphabetical order by author, stacking them on the floor until she could give the shelf units a good scrub.

The nonfiction section was almost as large; she'd have to tackle that another day. Even though Dennis had done a good job dusting the books over the years, she was pretty grimy. She used the small bathroom near the counter end of the room to wash up before she ate.

Only then did she remember it was her job to make lunch.

Why hadn't Carter come to fetch her?

Amanda hurried to the door, crossed the foyer and peeped in through the glass insert in one of the doors to the cafeteria. The men were just sitting down to their meal, the dull roar of their conversations audible from here. That meant Carter and his brothers had taken charge of lunch, and he had probably left the snack for her in the past five minutes or so. Breathing a sigh of relief, Amanda retraced her steps to the library. As she reached for her sandwich, however, it struck her this was the perfect time to move the painting. It was Saturday, which meant everyone would probably linger over their food. Could she get out the main door without them seeing her?

Amanda realized she didn't have to. There was a door in the side of the library room that led directly outside. She tested it and found it opened easily.

They'd never know she was gone if she moved quickly enough.

Amanda set the snack down, slipped out the door and dashed through the settlement to number twenty-three, where she grabbed the bag with the painting in it from her bathroom. Back outside, she circled through the settlement until she found the track she and Carter had used after they made love. Going up it took longer than it had to come down, and she was out of breath, her heart racing from her exertions by the time she approached the rotting outbuildings.

Amanda poked her head into two of them and retreated quickly before she discovered the third was in slightly better condition than the others. The first two seemed like storage sheds, but this one must have been an office at some point. Just inside its door, an old-fashioned desk was built into the wall. With a lot of effort, she was able to open its drawer, stow the bag inside and jam it shut, but the warped wood made such a squealing noise as the drawer slid open and closed, her heart sped even more as she waited for someone to come running to see what she was doing.

There was no one anywhere near her, she assured herself after several long moments, but she wasn't sure that was true. Carter, his brothers and the mill workers might be in the cafeteria, but what about Dennis? She hadn't seen him since her first day. He could be skulking around.

Amanda hesitated, wondering if she was doing the right thing leaving such a valuable painting in a place like this, even for a day or two. It was well wrapped in several layers of plastic, and the building's roof seemed solid. There was no way it could get wet. Besides, Carter would surely find it if she left it in number twenty-three. She was out of time now, anyway. She needed to get back to the library before anyone noticed she was missing. There was nothing for it; the painting would have to stay.

Cutting straight down the slope again, Amanda slowed when she neared the settlement, then worked her way to the side door of the library carefully. Her relief at reaching it vanished, however, when she twisted the handle and it didn't open.

She cursed herself for not considering that it might lock automatically behind her when she left. She had no choice but to go around to the front. Holding her breath, she walked quickly around, sure she'd meet up with Carter or one of his brothers at any moment. She prepared a story. She'd gotten hot after moving all those books and decided to take a walk.

It didn't matter; no one was around.

She slipped inside the main door and was happy to hear voices in the cafeteria but soon realized the dull roar had subsided to something closer to a murmur. A peek in the window told her the mill workers had already left. She was grateful she hadn't crossed any-one's path. The Elliott brothers sat around one of the tables. Her stomach was growling, and she couldn't wait to get her hands on the sandwich Carter had left her, but she figured she'd better see if everything was okay first. She pushed the door open and crossed the room.

"There she is," Lincoln called out when he spotted her. "Heard you're our new librarian."

"That's me." She joined them, taking a seat next to Hudson, across from Carter. She didn't think they'd noticed she'd slipped out for a jaunt up the Ridge.

"Did you find your rations?" Carter asked.

"I did. Thank you." She couldn't wait to eat them. All that exercise had made her hungry.

"Wasn't sure I could get your attention, you were working so hard."

"I appreciate you letting me get on with it."

"You shouldn't work too hard, though," Nate said. "It's a gorgeous day. Perfect for a swim."

"Already had my swim," Gage said complacently.

"He's up at five-thirty a.m. everyday to cross the lake and back," Lincoln informed her. "And he needs everyone to know it."

"Shove it," Gage said.

"You shove it. If you're up that early, you could be helping us at the mill. What are you doing all day, anyway?" Carter asked him.

"This and that."

"This morning he was prepping Mom and Dad's bedroom to paint it," Lincoln said.

Carter leaned forward. "I thought you said this whole enterprise was a waste of time."

"Mom and Dad might come to visit next spring, whatever happens."

Amanda let their conversation wash over her. Interesting that Gage was anticipating a visit from their parents. She began wondering how all these independent-minded men would act with their mom and dad around.

"The men missed you at lunch," Carter said when there was a lull in the conversation. "I missed you, too."

"I lost track of time, but I won't miss dinner. I feel like I'm playing truant," she confessed. "Messing around with books all day." And going for long, illicit hikes.

"I like the idea of having the library all cleaned up before we start getting other people to move in."

Gage let out a sigh.

"They're going to move in," Carter told him. "That's why we're here, right?"

"I'm looking forward to the place being a bit livelier," Lincoln said.

"A lot livelier," Hudson said.

"I'm willing to work full-time at the mill," Nate said to Gage. "That ought to tell you how much I believe in this endeavor, right?"

Gage just shrugged.

"Has anyone smoothed things over with Megan Lawrence yet?" Amanda asked.

The table fell silent. Amanda wondered if she'd put her foot in it, but if Gage had made the young woman a promise and then reneged on it, and no one else was working to fix the situation, that would tell her a lot about the Elliotts.

"I haven't," Gage said gruffly.

"You should," Lincoln told him. "You promised her

listings. It's not fair to go back on that."

"Dad always said if you make a mess, you clean it up," Carter put in.

Gage stood up abruptly and stalked off.

"Should one of us get in touch with her?" Nate asked, watching him go.

"He'll do it," Carter said. "He might not want to, but he will in the end."

"When are you going to list some of the houses?" Amanda asked.

"When the subdivision approval comes through. Besides, we should get your place done first," Carter said. "Then we can use it like a model home to demonstrate what the rest of them could look like. That would be better than showing people a bunch of abandoned houses, don't you think?"

"I guess so."

"One step at a time," Carter said. "We'll get there in the end."

Amanda hoped he was right.

AN HOUR LATER, after Carter dropped Amanda off at the library and returned to number twenty-three to work on the renovation, Hudson came to find him.

"Warrington is here. You'd better come hear what he has to say."

Carter swore and followed him to his parents' old house, where he found the rest of his brothers clustered in the driveway. Warrington's luxury truck sat parked outside, the black F-450 so new and shiny Carter was surprised Warrington dared drive it on their dusty old roads. The man himself leaned against it, his arms folded across his chest. Carter wondered why he'd bothered to come. Warrington would get his shot at buying the town a year from now if they couldn't pay off their loan. Gage should have run him off the minute the man drove up.

"What's going on?" Carter asked.

Gage looked to Warrington. "Tell him."

"I'm here to raise my offer." He named a number, leaned back and lifted his chin smugly. "You'd be fools to turn me down, so I figure we can cut the crap and sign the paperwork this week."

"Like hell," Carter said. "You're barking up the wrong tree, Warrington. If you want to expand your resort, you need to go in the other direction."

"There's no lake in the other direction. I need Elliott Lake. I want it," he corrected himself, leaning forward now. "And I'm making you an extremely fair offer for it."

"It's a lot of money," Gage said conversationally.

Carter exchanged a look with Lincoln, who he considered his staunchest supporter. Did money matter to Gage? "It's nothing to what we could earn if we subdivide and sell every house individually. We've already started getting interest in our community. The only way you're getting your hands on this property is if we fail to make a go of it, and we're not going to fail."

"I don't see any buyers flocking around the place."

"We've already got our first new resident." Carter

knew he should shut up, but somehow he couldn't. He wanted to wipe that smirk off Warrington's face.

It worked. Warrington straightened. "You sold a house?"

"That's right." He knew what the man was thinking. If people started buying lots, it would be way harder for him to develop the rest of the property the way he wanted to—if he ever got his hands on it. "And we're going to sell more."

"I don't believe you. You haven't even got approval on your subdivision."

"How do you know that?" Nate asked.

"I know everything about Elliott Ridge. I'm staking my future on this place."

"The minute we get approval, that house is sold. It's a done deal."

"Oh, I'm not so sure about that," Warrington said. "My offer is bound to give some of you second thoughts." He nodded at Gage. "I can be patient." He named the number again, a sum large enough that it gave Carter a qualm to think of turning it down. Warrington turned and opened the door to his truck. "I'll be back," he assured them and climbed in. Carter expected him to drive off in a huff, like Megan had, but instead he simply sat there, pulled out a phone, tapped at it for a moment and lifted it to his ear.

Gage rolled his eyes. "Let's go where we won't be overheard." He led the way through their parents' house and onto the back deck, where they could look out over the lake—and be alone. He gestured to the chairs arranged in a semicircle, and everyone sat. Gage disappeared inside and returned with a six-pack of beer.

"Why did you even let that snake in here?" Carter asked him, taking the drink Gage offered him. He was too restless to be comfortable in a chair, but he forced himself not to stand up and pace.

"Might as well hear what he has to say." Gage handed bottles around to the others and sat down.

"What would Dad think?"

"Maybe Dad would be interested in that money."

"He wants the Ridge back to what it used to be," Carter said.

"That's the problem; it'll never be what it was. We could stock the whole place with people, but they wouldn't be Mom and Dad's old friends. Those people are long gone. The ones we do get will be young. Most of them will be single."

Carter couldn't think of a thing to say to that, because it was true.

"I guess we could try to recruit some older people, too," he said doubtfully. "A community should have people of all ages, right?"

"People move off the Ridge when they get old," Gage said. "Mom and Dad would have had to deal with that in their own circle if they'd stayed here much longer."

"The only reason Grandma moved was because Grandpa passed," he reminded Gage.

"I don't know if it would be the same for Mom and Dad without their friends," Gage said. "What would

Dad even do here if he wasn't the boss anymore?"

Carter didn't have an answer for that.

"If we start having kids, Mom's going to want to be close to them," Lincoln said firmly. "She wants to be close to us now. Dad will have to adjust to not running the place, but sooner or later he'll find projects of his own to do. This is a big place. There are a lot of possibilities."

"Gage has a point, though. There are more doctors and hospitals in South Carolina," Nate said. "More support for older people. Less driving on snowy roads."

"It's not like all of their friends are gone," Hudson said. "Plenty of people moved into town when they left the Ridge. They could still get together."

Carter was glad they were having the conversation, but it also made him uneasy. The kind of money Warrington was offering could tear his family apart if they didn't keep their heads on straight.

"I think Dad's been waiting twelve years to come home. We're not selling," he said and wondered how many more times he'd have to assert it before they were done. Amanda was right; they needed to get more buyers here. More women.

Now.

WHEN SHE NEEDED a break, Amanda stepped out of the town hall with the intention of ducking to number twenty-three, but as she headed around the Circle toward Center Street, she noticed a truck she didn't recognize parked in front of number one. Her heart beat a little faster, and she picked up her pace.

Was Buck in that vehicle?

It wasn't likely, but Amanda wished she'd stayed in the library, where it was safe. Neither Carter nor his brothers were anywhere in sight. When the truck's engine roared to life, Amanda gasped and walked faster. It caught up easily, slowing when it reached her. The passenger window rolled down, and a stranger peered out.

She wasn't sure whether or not to be relieved when she realized it wasn't Buck in the driver's seat. After all, he could have hired someone to track her down.

"Let me guess," the stranger drawled. "You're the new resident in town?"

He had a hawklike face, his sharp nose just on the verge of being too long, his blue eyes too piercing for comfort. His hair was dark and short under his black cowboy hat. He wore a crisp white shirt, making it easy to see he hadn't done any physical work today, unlike Carter and his brothers.

"Who wants to know?" She was proud she managed to keep her voice from shaking.

"I'm Blake Warrington. I'm your neighbor from the other side of the ridge. Pleased to meet you."

The one making a golf course? Thank god. Amanda let out a shaky breath. He wasn't affiliated with Buck, at least. "Nice to meet you," she managed.

He cocked his head. "And you are?" he asked, a faintly mocking tone to his voice.

"Amanda." She bit the word off and didn't offer a

surname, even though he waited for one. After an uncomfortable pause, he went on.

"Well, *Amanda*, I just came to call on the Elliotts. Seems I'll have to come and call on you soon, too."

She wasn't sure what he meant by that. "For what reason?" She wished she could keep walking, high-tail it to number twenty-three and lock herself in, but she wouldn't give him the satisfaction of seeing how he unnerved her. She was angry at herself for letting her guard down. She had to stop doing that.

"I'm the buyer," he said.

"The buyer," she repeated dumbly.

"I'm negotiating with the Elliotts for their property?" He asked it like a question. Like she should know about this.

She remembered Carter had told her Warrington wanted the place. "It's not for sale," she said.

"Everything is for sale. I've been negotiating with the Elliotts for a while now. They're driving a hard bargain." He shrugged. "I'm afraid they're using you to get a better price out of me, but that's okay. Let them play their games. I'll win in the end. I always do. Guess I'll be buying you out, too, before all is said and done. I've got big plans for the place, and they don't include a bunch of tacky little houses." He touched the brim of his hat. "Nice to meet you, Amanda. Be back real soon to talk to you some more." He rolled up the window and drove away in the direction of town.

Amanda watched him go, a hollow ache settling in her stomach now that the fear was gone. That couldn't be true, could it? Were Carter and his brothers using her for leverage to get a better price from him?

The sound of faint male laughter made Amanda look around. Were Carter and his brothers at their parents' house? Maybe on the back deck? She circled the house, caught sight of them and quickly climbed the flight of stairs to confront them. She couldn't stand the idea that Carter would lie to her. If he was that kind of man, she needed to know it right now.

"Are you selling the Ridge to Blake Warrington?"

The brothers fell silent.

"No," Carter said. He set down the beer he was holding and came to meet her. "What did he say to you?"

"He said you were using me to jack up the price but that you'd sell to him in the end."

He let out a sigh. "You happy now?" he asked Gage before taking her arm and guiding her down the steps, leaving his drink behind. "I'm sorry Warrington bothered you. I'll tell him not to talk to you again."

"Is it true?"

"No. Believe me, that's the last thing we want. Even Gage hates the man. All we were doing was letting him state his case, and if I had my way we wouldn't even have done that."

"The five of you aren't on the same page." Amanda walked with him to the beach, but she wasn't ready to drop the subject.

"We are when it comes to Warrington. We're not going to let someone turn our town into a resort."

She wanted to believe him, but she knew how the idea of money could make people do all kinds of things.

Carter stopped and faced her. "Amanda, no matter what happens, I swear you won't regret deciding to stay."

"How can you promise something like that? You don't know what's coming."

"You're right. I don't. But I know how I feel about you. I know how I feel about this place. Just… trust me, okay?"

Trust him?

An hour ago she would have said she already did, but Warrington reminded her of Buck—and of her father, too, if she was honest. She was tired of men who refused to play by the rules and felt the world owed them anything they thought they wanted. Was she allowing herself to be drawn into yet another situation guaranteed to get her hurt in the end?

She was already falling in love with this place. If she kept fixing up the library, taking charge of feeding the small army of men who lived here and renovating number twenty-three with Carter, she was going to grow so attached it would break her heart to lose it all.

Here at Elliott Ridge, life felt vibrant in a way it never had in LA. She didn't want to go back.

Didn't want to lose Carter, either. He might think they could be a couple whether or not they held on to Elliott Ridge, but she'd seen enough to know what this place meant to him. Would he be bitter if he lost it in the end?

Bitter men could do a world of damage to the people they loved.

"Amanda?"

She tilted her head and looked up at him. He was waiting for her answer.

"I trust you as far as I know you," she said honestly. "But I don't know you very well, do I?"

The muscles in his jaw tightened. "I don't know you all that well, either, but that's not holding me back."

She'd hit a nerve, and she was sorry for it. "I'm not sure I know myself," she said dispiritedly. If she did, she'd be able to explain how much she wanted everything he was offering—and how afraid she was to lose it.

"Do you wish you hadn't left LA?"

"No. Not at all."

"Why did you come to Chance Creek?" he asked softly.

Amanda looked out at the lake where the breeze was ruffling the tops of the waves. It was so tempting to tell him the truth, but she knew there was no such thing as a secret if you shared it with anyone. People passed on information as a matter of course. He'd talk to his brothers, and his brothers would tell other people. Sooner or later, word would reach Buck Bronson.

What could she say to him? She wanted as few secrets as possible between them. "I needed a change. My life there wasn't working anymore." Buck's reappearance had made that clear to her.

It took her a moment to realize Carter had gone

very still. He was looking down at her, an expression she couldn't read on his face.

"There's more to it than that, isn't there? Something you don't want to tell me." He shifted away from her.

Amanda's breath caught in her throat. If he knew she was lying, who else had seen through her facade—and what would they do about it?

She didn't want to lose him. Didn't want to lose her place here.

"I…" She couldn't find the words to smooth things over. To convince him he had it wrong. To make him come closer again.

"It's okay. You can keep your secret. Someday I hope you'll trust me enough to tell me the truth." Regret tinged Carter's voice. "I'll listen, whenever you're ready."

"Thanks."

"That's all right. It's not like you're a spy, are you?" He bumped her shoulder with his, clearly wanting to lighten the moment.

"No." Amanda relaxed a little. "I'm not a spy."

"On the run for committing federal crimes?"

"No." The word came out more sharply than she intended. Amanda stepped away from him. "What do we do… to keep Warrington from getting Elliott Ridge?" That was a far safer topic. As much as she wanted to spill everything, she simply couldn't. Not yet.

"We need to get your house repaired and spread the word about our little town. We need to find the kind of people who aren't afraid to take a chance on a new place. Pioneers."

"I bet Megan would know how to find people like that."

Carter was watching her, and she had a feeling he wasn't buying any of this. He knew she was hiding something. It would be so easy for him to get it out of her.

She braced for him to resume his questions, but he didn't.

"Maybe you're right" was all he said.

CHAPTER 9

AN UNEASY FEELING settled in Carter's gut as he faced Amanda. She hadn't liked the question he asked her, but she'd answered it. He thought she was telling the truth. She hadn't committed any *federal* crimes.

Had she committed some other kind?

He remembered Dennis's accusations the day he'd brought Amanda to the Ridge. Had the old man seen something in her face he'd missed?

Had he experienced the kind of premonition he'd had before the crash?

Carter shrugged off the nagging questions. Nothing about Amanda suggested she was a law-breaker, but it was clear if he kept pressing her, she might walk away from him. He couldn't let Dennis's accusations goad him into being suspicious of her. He had to trust that Amanda would tell him everything when she was good and ready.

Meanwhile, she was right; they should be renovating something, but that was hard enough when you were in a good mood. Amanda was out of sorts. Before they tackled number twenty-three, he wanted to get things back on solid ground between them.

Carter bridged the distance between them and twined his fingers with hers.

"If we're going to get Megan involved, why don't we walk through some of the other houses in the subdivision and make a to-do list of what it will take to get them ready to show." That was an easy task they could do together. "We just need to grab the keys."

"All right."

Her willingness cheered him up a little. They returned to the deck, where his brothers were still talking, and Carter explained his plan to them.

"That sounds like a good idea," Nate said.

"I'm going to take the master key ring."

"Just bring it back when you're done," Gage said.

Exactly what their father would have said if he was here. Carter ignored him and led the way through the house. He pocketed the large ring of keys from the top drawer of the hall table on their way out the front door. Outside, he brought Amanda to the section of houses flanked by Elliott Way and Center Street. Number twenty-three stood in the middle of this section, but he started at number nineteen, a small white bungalow on First Street with large front windows and a tidy aspect to it.

"This one is nice," Amanda said, but when Carter opened the door and they went inside, she wrinkled her nose. "What's that smell?"

He went to investigate, following the musty odor to a back room, and pointed to a corner. "Something got in here and made a nest." He'd have to go over the house to see where the animal had entered. "I don't think it's been here for a while, though."

"So Dennis isn't infallible."

"Guess not." He surveyed the rest of the room. "Needs a coat of paint, at the very least. We should pull out the carpeting."

"It's in rough shape," she agreed.

"Let's check out the kitchen."

"Do those appliances even work?" she asked when they walked into the small space.

"Don't know." The electricity wasn't turned on in the uninhabited houses. "We can't afford to buy new appliances for everyone, though. People will have to do that for themselves. I think our basic plan should be to gut the houses, clean them, put a coat of primer on the walls and then let the buyers have at it."

"Not every house comes with a Navy SEAL renovator?" she teased.

Carter shook his head. "Yours is special."

"It is." She smiled up at him, and he couldn't help leaning in to steal a kiss. When she met him willingly, her mouth soft and delicious under his, he followed it up with another, tugging her closer and taking his time. This was more like it. The tension between them disappeared. Amanda seemed as eager as he was to be close.

"We could survey the houses some other time," he

suggested when they parted.

"We just told your brothers we were doing it now." She pulled back and looked around. "We need to take notes about what has to be done. Then we can make a checklist."

"How can you even think about checklists?" He drew her close and wrapped his arms around her. Rested his chin on the top of her head. "You feel good."

"You feel good, too, but we can't spend all day messing around."

"I don't know why not," he grumbled.

"Because we're reviving a town for us to live in, and that takes time. Besides, I want to do this right. I want to get to know you—and I want you to know me."

He stopped himself from making a joke about getting to know her in the Biblical sense. Instead, he pulled out his phone, tapped on a notes app and jotted down a few specifications for what needed to be done to prepare number nineteen for sale before they moved on to the next one.

After a while they fell into a rhythm that allowed them to evaluate the homes quickly. By the time they made it to number twenty-four, where he'd bunked the first night Amanda was in town, Carter felt he could estimate what the remaining homes would need. Many of the houses were in better condition than number nineteen, but almost all of them needed new flooring, fixtures and appliances.

The uneasy feeling in his gut relaxed a little as they

worked together. Amanda was too conscientious and hardworking to have done anything really wrong. She'd said she'd tell him her secrets soon. He'd asked her to trust him. He needed to trust her, too.

After all, how much trouble could one woman get up to?

"I'm going to get my brothers over here," he told her, deciding to let it go for now. He messaged Lincoln, Hudson and Nate. When they assembled a few minutes later, he said, "Here's the thing. If we're going to get Elliott Ridge ready for people to settle here, we have to treat this like a mission. A year-long mission. Which means we need to start at the beginning, set goals, break them down and implement them."

"I'm good at plans." Amanda pressed her lips together. "Sorry," she added. "That popped out, but it's true. I'm the only one in my department who could see a big project through from beginning to end." She looked from one to the other of them. "What?" she asked. Carter wasn't the only one chuckling.

Lincoln grinned. "Between us we've got over forty years in the military." He pointed to each of his brothers in turn. "Completing missions is what we did for a living before we came here."

"You don't need my help. Got it." Amanda looked down at her hands.

"No, that's not what I meant." Lincoln rubbed the back of his head. "Hell, guess it came out that way. Just—all of us are good at planning, which means we should be able to pull this off."

"Unless it's too many cooks in the kitchen," Amanda said.

Carter let out a laugh. "You've got us there. Could turn out that way," he admitted. "It's been a long time since we worked together, and we weren't always very good at that, were we?"

His brothers shook their heads.

"We're older now. Don't need to prove ourselves to anyone," Hudson said. "We've done all right at the mill so far."

"We're not at each other's throats this time," Nate said.

Carter knew what he meant. The last couple of years before they left Elliott Ridge, they'd bickered and fought like wildcats caged together. There'd been so much work. So few hands to get it done. Each of them had taken on more and more responsibility until it seemed like it would crush them—if it didn't kill their father first.

"Anyway, we need to get these houses cleaned up— fast. We won't renovate them; the buyers will have to do that. We'll just pull out old carpeting. Give them a coat of primer. That kind of thing. Not counting number twenty-three, there are twenty-nine houses in this part of town. That's seven for each of us and one left over."

"What about Gage?" Nate asked. "Why didn't you call him over here?"

"He's made it clear he's waiting to see what the rest of us do," Carter told him. "I'm not going to hold my breath for him to help."

"I'm happy to lend a hand," Amanda said.

"I'm counting on that," Carter told her.

"I still think we need to get Megan Lawrence on our side," Lincoln said. "Gage still hasn't called her, and he should."

Carter shrugged. "Nate, why don't you work on that?"

"Why me?"

"Why not you?"

"I'll talk to her," Amanda announced, surprising all of them. "Next time I go for the mail and groceries, I'll pop in and see her at her office. I bet she'll listen to me."

"You think so?" Lincoln asked doubtfully.

"I know so. I didn't renege on a deal with her like the rest of you did. She and I have something in common. We've both been taken in by Elliott men."

Uh oh, Carter thought. She must still be upset by what Warrington said.

She smiled at him gently. "I'm kidding. But it is true you lured me here under false pretences. You claimed to have a plan, when the reality is you didn't. Like you said, you've been making all this up as you go along. That's what I'll tell her. I'll say she'd better come talk to you while you're still in the planning stage. That way she can put in her two cents." She paused. "There's something going on between her and Gage, right?"

All of them straightened. "How can you possibly know that?" Carter asked.

"I've got eyes. I saw the two of them together the

other day," she said. "Maybe I'm not some hot-shit military hero, but I've got skills of my own."

"I guess you do," Carter said. "Gage danced with Megan at a wedding last month."

"And kissed her," Hudson spoke up. "I saw him."

That got Nate's attention. "Gage kissed Megan Lawrence?"

"That's right," Lincoln said.

"Then we'd better get her involved," Nate said with a grin.

"I'll do my best to persuade her," Amanda said. "And now I'm going to get back to the library. If I'm going to start helping you clean houses as well as cook two meals a day, shop, run errands and renovate number twenty-three, I won't have much time to get the books in order."

Carter and his brothers watched her walk to the town hall.

"You did good bringing her here," Nate said.

Carter thought he had, despite the mysteries that swirled around her.

"Now all we need is a few hundred more people to fill up this place," Lincoln said.

"HI, MOM, IT'S me. I've got a new number," Amanda said two days later as she sat in Carter's truck outside Carmichael Realty. She'd put off this call as long as possible, since she didn't want to explain everything that had happened since the last time they talked, but if she waited any longer, her mother would try to call her and panic when she couldn't get through to her old number. At least here in town, neither Carter nor his brothers could overhear her conversation. The truck doors were locked and the windows barely cracked. Amanda scanned the street again. It seemed impossible that Buck could have traced her this far, but she wanted to be careful.

She'd already stopped and bought an air mattress for Carter. After her meeting with Megan, she planned to grab a few groceries and check the mailbox before returning to the Ridge. She hadn't made any progress figuring out what to do with the painting. Alone in the library on Saturday afternoon, she'd done some research online but had come up empty on ideas. She'd spent all of Sunday painting the other two bedrooms in number twenty-three. Carter said he'd finish the master bedroom soon and then the second story would be done.

"Hi, honey. Thanks for letting me know. I'll save it to my contacts. What are you up to today?"

Amanda was grateful her mother accepted the news without concern and didn't press her for explanations. Sooner or later she'd need to confess she'd taken her father in and been dragged into the middle of a crime, but she wasn't ready for that yet.

"Just running some errands. What are you doing?"

"Heading out to lunch."

"Where are you going to eat?" Normally her mother stayed at her desk on workdays, claiming she was much too busy to leave it. Amanda knew it was an excuse. Years ago, her mother had been active in many facets of their community in Dallas, but she'd kept a low profile since moving to Houston, just like Amanda had done before coming here.

"One of the neighbor ladies invited me to try a new place."

"Really?" Amanda tried not to sound too surprised. Since when did her mother talk to her neighbors? "What type of food does it serve?"

"Vietnamese. Linda says it's wonderful."

"How did you two meet?" It was getting warm in the truck's cab. Amanda wished she'd found a shadier place to park.

"I was washing my front windows one day, and she stopped to talk to me. She lives at the Eastman."

Amanda tried to picture that meeting. Had her mother been pleasantly surprised, or had she felt overexposed, the way Amanda used to when someone new tried to strike up a friendship? The Eastman was a condo complex a couple of blocks away from her mother's small house.

"She invited me to join her book club. Now we get together every week to do something."

Book club? Amanda blinked. Was this her mother? "I didn't know you joined a book club."

"What else am I supposed to do when neither of my daughters live near me?" her mother asked defensively.

"I'm glad you're finding things to do. A book club sounds great."

"You could try doing things, too. I worry about you. You know that job of yours isn't very challenging. You never go on dates. What do you do when you come home at night? Watch TV?"

As far as Amanda knew, that's what her mother had done for years up until now. "I try to keep busy."

"You need to do more than try. You need to build a life for yourself. Build a community."

Amanda wanted to protest that she'd been following her mother's example, but instead she said, "That sounds like good advice."

There was a long silence on the end of the line. "I thought you'd have some smart answer," her mom said. "You always do when I invite you here."

She was right. Maybe it was time to be more truthful about how she felt. They were always dancing around the subject of the past and never actually talking about it. "I'd like to see you more, Mom. It's hard for me to go back to Texas, though. I'm uncomfortable there."

"It's not like I'm still living in Dallas, where all the bad things happened. I thought you liked Houston."

"I did. For a while, at least." Amanda hesitated, unsure whether she wanted to dredge up the past. "I guess it's because of Erik and Maddy." The two names felt strange in her mouth since it had been so long since she'd spoken them. She barely let herself think about her old boyfriend and best friend anymore. Amanda scanned the street again to make sure Buck Bronson wasn't sneaking up on her, but it was talking about the past that was making her feel vulnerable rather than any real fear Buck might be around.

Her mother hesitated again. "I know they hurt you a

lot."

"That's an understatement." Maddy had been her best friend for years. Erik had been her first love.

Neither were in her life anymore.

"Maddy and Erik did what was right for them and their careers," her mother said gently. "That doesn't mean you can't move on, too."

She knew that now. Her flight from LA had shaken her out of her lethargy, and these days she felt more alive than she had in ages, but that didn't explain why her mother had suddenly changed her way of life.

"How come you're ready to move on all of a sudden?" Amanda asked her.

"I've... been going to counseling," her mother admitted in a rush. "Linda pushed me to do it when she saw how sad I got around Christmas. She kept bugging me until I finally tried it." Her mother sighed. "I should have done this years ago. I owe you an apology, Amanda. I've been a rotten example for you. I've been stewing in the past—in the unfairness of it all. I got stuck when your father did what he did. I couldn't forgive him. I couldn't forgive anyone—especially after the fire."

"I don't blame you. I've been feeling stuck, too."

"I blame me." Her mother sighed. "I acted like there was nothing left when your father went away. Like my career and my girls meant nothing. I know," she added when Amanda began to protest. "At first I was shocked because of the trial and the fire. Of course I struggled. But even after I moved to Houston, I refused to get on with living. No wonder Melissa ran away. No wonder you left, too. I must have seemed so pitiful, holding on to the past like that."

"It sounds like you're making changes now," Amanda made herself say. She wasn't sure why her mother's sudden revelations felt like a betrayal, but they did. Maybe because she'd used her mother's inability to move on to justify her own lack of progress? If so, she was the one who should be in counseling. At least she was working on creating a new life for herself.

"I am. I was wondering if you'd visit soon, actually. I'm going to sell this place and start over. I'm moving to the Gulf. I could use some help."

"You're moving to the Gulf?" Amanda couldn't believe what she was hearing.

"I've always loved the ocean. Why shouldn't I move there?"

It had been hard enough for her to leave Dallas—even after Buck attempted to burn their house to the ground. "You won't miss your book club? Linda?"

There was another pause. "Linda has a house on the Gulf in addition to her condo here in town," her mother admitted. "I could do that, too. I could have the best of both worlds."

"That sounds great, Mom. I'll figure out when I can come and see you soon." Amanda's mind was spinning. How had her mother kept her new social life a secret for so long? And why had she done so?

"You don't think it's strange for me to change after all this time? I thought maybe you'd be angry. That I should make sure you're all right before I think about myself."

"Mom, I'm twenty-six." Was her mom afraid she wouldn't approve of her new choices? "You can't worry about me all the time. Besides, I'm thinking of making some changes, too. When I know more, I'll tell you all about it."

"I can't wait." Her mother sounded thrilled.

"Love you, Mom." The ache in her chest was still there—they'd both endured so much—but it wasn't as sharp anymore. Her mom was moving on from the past, and so was she.

"I love you, too, honey."

"Let me think about visiting. I'll call you when I have some dates in mind."

"Sounds good. Talk soon."

"Bye."

Amanda's head was still spinning when she ducked inside Carmichael Realty, and she forced herself to put what she'd learned aside and focus. "I'm looking for Megan Lawrence," she said to a middle-aged woman working near the front of the small office. Megan popped her head around a cubicle wall.

"Amanda? What are you doing here?"

"Looking for you," Amanda said brightly. "Want to grab a coffee?"

"Sure. I could use a break. There's a good place a couple of doors down." Megan gathered her purse and came to join her. She was wearing a cute green dress with sensible pumps, but the work outfit served only to make her look younger than Amanda knew she was. It had to be hard to break into real estate in a town where everyone knew everyone else. Amanda supposed the old-timers in the business probably had their fingers in a lot of pies.

Grateful they wouldn't have to walk far, she kept pace with Megan, looking around once more to see if Buck had found her. Talking to her mother had made the threat of him seem more real.

She didn't see anything out of the ordinary, though, and soon they were seated at a small table at Linda's Diner. They ordered a banana walnut muffin to share along with their coffees. Once the waitress had delivered everything, Amanda got down to business.

"I don't blame you for being angry at the Elliotts. They weren't forthcoming with me, either," she began. "But I think their hearts are in the right place. Carter has admitted to me they've been short on plans and long on ambition."

"They'd better start making plans, or all that ambition won't mean a thing. I can't believe they sold you a house for a dollar."

"Carter figures once one woman lives on the Ridge, others will be more comfortable moving there."

Megan shrugged. "I hope it works out for you."

She was still mad. Amanda wondered how to ease her mind. "Did you know Carter and his brothers want to bring their folks back to the Ridge?" she asked.

Megan shifted in her chair. "No, I didn't."

"I thought you should. They're serious about making this all work. I think Carter and his brothers miss their mom and dad a lot."

Megan looked down. "I sure miss my parents."

Amanda reached across the table to touch her hand. "I'm sorry for your loss. Carter told me about it."

"I never thought I'd lose them so early," Megan said. "It was just the three of us, so we were never a big family, but my parents were full of fun. We used to play cards all the time. Sunday was pizza night, even after I grew up. They knew I'd go out with friends on Fridays and Saturdays and wanted to be sure they got some time with me. If I'd known they'd be gone so soon, I would have stayed home the rest of the week, too."

Amanda could tell she was close to tears. "Do you have other family in town?"

Megan shook her head. "They're in Bozeman, so I see my aunts and uncles now and then. I've got cousins scattered around. It's just not the same."

"I can imagine. I don't have a big family, either, and we're scattered all over the place. That's one thing I like about Elliott Ridge. I feel like it's going to be a real community, you know? Before I came here, I lived in a big city. I barely knew my neighbors at all."

"You like the Ridge that much, huh?"

"I do," Amanda said honestly. "Did you know they've got a library up there?" She laughed at herself. "I'm probably the only one who gets excited about things like that, but I'm cleaning and organizing it. They basically gave it to me."

Megan looked intrigued. "That's cool. I like libraries."

"You do?"

Megan nodded. "What else is up there? I didn't really get to look around."

"There's a mill. Right now there are twenty temporary workers who are staying in three bunkhouses. I haven't been inside those. They come to eat with the Elliotts in the town hall cafeteria for lunch and dinner. I'm in charge of that, too." Amanda rolled her eyes.

"How'd that happen?"

"Gage assigned the chore to me. He was trying to scare me off."

"He's good at that," Megan said sourly.

"But you still like him."

Megan put her cup down with a thump. "How did you guess?"

"I think he likes you, too, if that helps." She didn't bother to answer Megan's question. It had been obvious.

"Sure has a funny way of showing it."

"Anyway," Amanda pushed on. "There's this one area of the Ridge that's being subdivided. Carter calls it the downslope."

Megan shook her head. "It's actually called Lucy's Corner, because Lucy Greenley lived there in the 1950s. She did laundry for the single men in the community."

"Really? How do you know that?"

"I looked up all the information I could find after talking to Gage at Cindy Glendale's wedding. Total waste of time," she added.

Amanda hurried on. "Carter wants to sell those houses first. We're all helping to clean them up—and we're trying to fix up number twenty-three, where I live, so people can see what's possible if they buy in."

"And I suppose he'll sell those for a dollar, too!"

"I don't think so."

Megan sighed. "Sorry. I'm not mad at you. None of this is your fault."

"You're mad at Gage, aren't you?" It was the heart of the problem. It seemed best to face it head on.

"Did you see the way he treated me?"

"I did."

"I thought he liked me," Megan said. "The morning of Cindy's wedding, my boss confronted me. She said if I didn't bring in a new listing by the end of the night, I might as well quit. I was Cindy's maid of honor. It was supposed to be a special day."

Amanda swallowed a sip of coffee and made a face. "That's awful. Your boss really expected you to work at your friend's wedding?"

Megan nodded. "I did it, too. Asked everyone there if they planned to sell a property soon. Made a complete ass of myself. Blake Warrington hit on me." She broke off. "You probably don't know him."

"I met him a couple of days ago, actually."

"He's a piece of work."

"He is," Amanda agreed. "I didn't like him one bit, and I certainly don't want him to end up with Elliott Ridge. So he hit on you. Then what happened?"

"Gage came to my rescue. Danced with me. Kissed

me," she said defiantly, as if Amanda would deny it.

"Hudson said he saw Gage do that."

Megan looked surprised but quickly recovered. "He said he'd hire me to sell something—either the individual houses or the whole parcel. He told my boss he was going to come in and sign paperwork, then he never did. He never called me. It's been weeks. Now my boss is threatening to fire me again."

Amanda's heart sank. "No wonder you're mad. Gage is a fool."

"I'm the fool, thinking someone like him would be interested in someone like me."

"What's that supposed to mean?" Amanda asked. "Why wouldn't he be interested in you?"

"I'm a boring, small-town girl with a boring, small-town life," Megan said. "Men go after women like you—mysterious strangers who turn up and set their hearts fluttering."

"I don't think I've ever set anyone's heart fluttering." Amanda took a bite of her half of the muffin and groaned. "This is really good. That's real butter in it, isn't it?"

"Probably," Megan said, taking a bite of hers. "But don't try to change the subject. I'm pretty sure Carter's fallen for you. He couldn't stay close enough to you the whole time I was there."

"We've definitely got chemistry," Amanda admitted. It felt good to have someone to share that with. "He's pretty hot."

"He is."

"So is Gage." Not her type with all his brooding, but she didn't need to say that.

"Gage is definitely hot. But he's a lost cause," Megan said.

"Isn't that the best kind?" Amanda finished her half of the muffin and wished she'd ordered a whole one for herself.

"You really think so?" Megan laughed for the first time. "I don't usually go looking for lost causes."

"I don't think it's a matter of looking for them," Amanda joked.

"I should forget the whole thing and walk away," Megan said.

"I think you should jump on the chance to work with the Elliotts. I think they're on to something. Besides, it's way too soon to give up on Gage. Let the man brood awhile. He'll come around eventually."

A smile tugged at Megan's mouth again. "He does seem to be the brooding type, doesn't he?"

"He's very gothic," Amanda agreed. "All smoldering passions and furrowed brows."

Megan laughed out loud. "Enough. I won't be able to look at him with a straight face next time I see him. Besides, if he was interested, he would have called by now."

"Not necessarily. Gage strikes me as the kind of guy who'll shoot himself in the foot to avoid confronting a problem. Maybe there's a reason he's afraid to pursue a relationship with you right now. That doesn't mean he isn't interested."

"Maybe." Megan didn't seem convinced. "What really matters is getting a listing or two. My boss is putting the pressure on me." She seemed to be thinking it over as she took another bite.

"Tell her you're meeting the Elliotts again in a day or two and you're close to working out an agreement."

"Am I close?"

"Definitely."

"WHAT'S GOING ON out there?" Carter's father barked into the phone when Carter took his call.

"Hi to you, too, Dad." His father called about once a week to check in. Every time he did, Carter felt like he hadn't done nearly enough to satisfy him.

"Well? Give me an update."

"Things are moving along." He'd just gotten a message from Amanda that she was at Linda's Diner with Megan and they were almost done. "No one has quit at the mill in the past twenty-four hours. I ducked out to finish painting the master bedroom of number twenty-three. Pretty soon we'll start gutting the other houses in the subdivision to get them ready for sale."

"Did you get the approval yet?"

"Not yet." Carter had been sure they'd have it by now, but so far it hadn't come.

"Better make some phone calls. Everything that can go wrong, will go wrong. You know that."

"You sound like Gage."

His dad was quiet. "Well, worrying runs in the family, I guess."

"Ready for your surgery next month?"

"Ready as I'll ever be," his father said dryly. "Getting old is for the birds, I'll tell you that."

"Hang in there, Pop. We'll have you out at the Ridge in no time." Carter thought about what Gage said the other day. "Do you worry it won't be the same if you moved back here?"

His father hmphed. "I know it won't be the same. But it's still the Ridge. That land is in my blood."

"You won't miss your friends?"

"That's why it's your job to get all the houses filled. So we can make new ones! Make sure you get some people there for your mother. You know the type she likes. The busy ones. Always chattering."

"You can count on me, Dad. If it's possible to get this town up and running again, I'll do it."

"Hmm."

Carter wasn't sure what to make of that noncommittal sound.

"Shouldn't you be at the mill instead of painting?"

"I'm almost done, and then I'll walk over to the town hall, actually. Amanda's on her way back with groceries." He'd meant to keep quiet about her, but his dad's reaction had stung, and Carter wanted him to know someone believed in him. Besides, it would give his parents something to talk about other than the surgery he knew was weighing on his dad's mind.

"Who's Amanda?" his father asked, right on cue.

"Our first buyer. As soon as the subdivision approval comes through, she'll own number twenty-three.

I'm helping her repair it."

"She works at the mill?"

"No, Dad. She's been cleaning up the library. She runs errands for us in town. Cooks lunch and dinner for the whole crowd, too."

"Sounds like a busy woman."

"She's pretty great."

Another pause. "I see."

"This one might be serious, Pop." As soon as he said it, he wished he hadn't. If things didn't go his way, his father would have another excuse to ride his ass.

"Well, that's more like it. About time you boys started to settle down."

"Settle down?" his mother's voice trailed over the line. There was a scuffle, and her voice came louder. "Are you going to settle down, Carter?"

"Not yet, Mom. Be patient, okay? I've got to run now, but I'll call you again next week and tell you all about it."

"You'd better," his mother said. "Send photos, too. Don't keep me in suspense!"

He still wasn't sure whether or not he'd made a mistake telling them about Amanda when she drove up and parked outside the town hall. She was pensive as they unloaded the groceries, so Carter kept his conversation light, updating her on their progress at the mill. He'd let her discover on her own that the master bedroom was done.

"Any luck?" he finally asked her when the groceries were put away and they'd returned to the foyer so she could sort the small pile of mail she'd picked up into the correct boxes. "You know, it'd be faster to just hand that around to folks."

"Start as you mean to go on, right? I'm following protocol."

"Elliott Ridge has protocols?"

"It does now. I'll write down that first rule, put it in a binder and keep adding to it. A few of these are for workers at the mill. Did you hand out keys to them yet?"

"I'll do that today."

"As for Megan, I talked to her, if that's what you mean."

"Is she willing to help us?"

"She is… but you guys stepped on her toes. I told her you'll be selling more houses in Lucy's Corner soon."

"Lucy's Corner?" He smiled to hear the name. "We haven't called it that since I was a kid. Dad always called it the downslope, even back then. I think he thought the name was kind of silly."

"I like it. It celebrates Elliott Ridge's history."

"Lucy's Corner it is."

"Anyway, Megan is struggling right now. Did you know Gage promised to hire her in front of her boss and then never did? She's afraid she's going to lose her job."

"Because Gage broke his word?"

"Exactly. She was depending on him. We need to get her some listings, fast."

"Guess we'd better get those houses cleaned up."

Amanda handed him a few envelopes. "Here's your mail."

"Thanks." He flipped through them.

"I'd better get lunch going." She moved toward the cafeteria.

"I'll help."

WITH CARTER PITCHING in, it wasn't hard to whip together a huge batch of tacos and set up the food buffet-style, so the men could serve themselves as many as they wanted. When she'd taken a seat with the Elliotts, Carter brought up the topic of Megan.

"You should talk to her boss," he told Gage. "It's the least you can do."

"What do I tell her?"

"We'll have a few dozen houses for sale soon." He didn't back down even when Gage scowled at him.

"Fine. I'll go talk to Lainie Carmichael."

"Today."

Gage nodded, finished his meal and left.

"Good job," Amanda said softly when the meal was over. "I'm sure that will help."

"I hope so. Wish I could spend all day with you," he added as they brought their dishes to the kitchen.

"I know. I'll see you later?"

"I'll come back a little early. We can go for a swim before dinner and then I'll help you get the meal on."

"Your brothers won't get mad if you keep slipping away like that?"

Carter shrugged. "I'll make it up to them."

Amanda spent the afternoon in the library, working swiftly to clean the shelves, sort the books and put them in order. She still had a long way to go when the afternoon waned and Carter found her there, but she was satisfied with her progress.

She checked the time when he appeared at her elbow and stole a kiss as she slid a novel onto one of the shelves. "I'm not sure I have time for a swim. We'll be cutting it close."

"Just a quick dip. You'll feel much better afterward. It's hot in here."

"You're right. Okay," she conceded. "Meet you down there?"

"Sure thing."

Ten minutes later, she tossed her towel on the sand and joined him at the edge of the water in the scarlet bikini Storm Hall had convinced her to buy when she went shopping for new clothes. Carter looked her over appreciatively.

"I suppose that water is still ice cold?" she asked.

"That's half the fun of it. Come on." Carter charged right into the lake up to his thighs, dove under the water and reappeared with a happy shout. Amanda dipped a toe in tentatively and shuddered.

"It's freezing!"

"Just jump right in," he encouraged her, taking a stroke or two, then turning onto his back. "You'll get used to it. You were fine last time."

Last time she'd been hot and disheveled after making love in a canoe. She edged in another inch.

"Amanda. Get in the water."

"I will when I'm ready," she said primly. She put a foot in deeper and pulled it out. The Pacific Ocean was never exactly warm, but it wasn't anywhere near this cold.

"We don't have all day." He rolled back to his stomach and came toward her, his powerful arms slicing through the water.

"Don't you dare, Carter. Stay away from me," she cried when he surged to his feet and splashed her way.

"I can throw you in, if you like. Get it over with."

"You'd better not!" Afraid he'd make good on his threat, Amanda charged past him and dove into the water, coming up with a scream. "That is freaking cold!"

"Of course it is." Carter stood with his hands on his hips and laughed at her. "This lake was completely iced over three months ago."

The sliding glass door at the back of his folks' place opened with a rumble. Gage stuck his head out. "What the hell is going on out there?"

"Sorry," Amanda called back when she'd recovered from the shock of his sudden appearance. She hadn't thought anyone was around. "The water is cold."

"The water is cold?" Gage repeated, coming all the way out on the deck. "That's why you're hollering like a banshee?"

Heat rising in her cheeks, she lifted her chin. "Carter was being annoying."

To her surprise, Gage laughed at that. "Fair enough.

Sometimes he makes me want to scream, too."

"Hey!" Carter said. "You're supposed to take my side!"

Gage shrugged.

"Did you talk to Lainie Carmichael?"

"I did. Turned on the Elliott charm. Megan's got nothing to worry about."

"Did you see Megan while you were there?" Amanda asked.

Gage shook his head and went back inside.

Amanda was disappointed on Megan's behalf, but she turned to Carter. "I'm not used to having the calvary come running whenever I'm in distress."

"That's what men are for. Didn't you have a boyfriend in LA?" Carter asked her, wading deeper into the water again.

"Nope." She didn't want to talk about old boyfriends.

"Why does your past seem like such a blank slate?" He swam with her as she pushed off and took a stroke or two.

Amanda wondered how best to answer that. "I haven't done much with my life so far. I've played it really safe."

"You took a chance coming here."

"You're right, I did." She swam a few more strokes. "And I'm becoming passionate about Elliott Ridge." Passionate about him, too. She supposed he knew that.

"Oh yeah? What parts of it?"

"Number twenty-three, for one thing. I already feel

like it's mine."

"It is," he assured her.

"The library. I have a vision for how to make it into a place where people love to spend time."

"I'm sure you will."

"The forest, too. I didn't know I'd like living in the woods, but I do. I like the way it smells here. I like all the birds."

"I know what you mean. When I came home, I took one deep breath and felt myself relax in a way I hadn't in over a decade."

"Being a SEAL must be pretty tough." She swam parallel to the shore. Carter swam beside her.

"There's a lot of training. A lot of boredom. Then moments of pure adrenaline. I'm proud of the job I did, though."

"Your parents must be really proud, too—of all of you."

"They are. My mom worried about us, of course. And Dad… well, Dad had mixed feelings."

"Why?" It was easy to talk as they glided along. There was no wind today, and the lake was as smooth as glass. Now she was used to the water, it wasn't that bad.

"He wasn't ready for us to leave the Ridge. Wasn't ready to leave it himself."

"You miss him."

"Don't you miss your father?"

"I miss who he should have been." Amanda ducked under the surface and swam away, unwilling to talk about that. She struck out in a big loop, ending up back where they'd started. On the beach, she grabbed her towel. They walked to number twenty-three together when they'd dried off.

"Meet you in the kitchen in a few minutes?" he asked.

"See you there." She hesitated, wishing he would kiss her.

He must have read her mind. Touching her hip, he moved in close and bent down to brush his mouth over hers. His skin was cool against hers. She was shivering even though she was wrapped in her towel. Still, it was hard to pull away.

"See you in a minute," he reiterated.

Amanda nodded. "See you."

As she made her way into the house, she wondered why she felt so unsettled. She had every right to be here with Carter. Had every right to fall for him.

Still, when he kissed her, she felt like she was living on borrowed time. Like she needed to get back to something she'd left undone.

Probably because of the precious artwork hidden away in the building by the mine. She still had no idea how to return it without being caught. And at some point she needed to deal with her apartment in LA. Her rent would be deducted from her bank account automatically, so she had time, but she shuddered to think of the food going rotten in her refrigerator. She was afraid to ask anyone to go empty it, even though a work acquaintance had a spare key. What if Buck was watching her place?

Buck.

Sometimes she managed to forget about him for hours at a time, but whenever she remembered, fear flooded her, leaving her feeling sick. Amanda shut the door behind her and fought against an urge to lock it, aware Carter would hear it if she did and probably read her intentions wrong.

She went upstairs, changed out of her wet things, showered and dressed in clean, dry clothes but had to put a hand on the dresser to steady herself as memories of the night she left LA overwhelmed her.

What would have happened if she hadn't texted her father at the moment she did? If Buck had broken in before she managed to get away?

Would he have hurt her?

Killed her?

Amanda shook the thoughts from her head. Carter was waiting for her to join him at the town hall kitchen. She had to keep moving.

Tomorrow she'd figure out what to do with the painting, she told herself with a sigh. Right now she'd make dinner and enjoy Carter's company.

"There you are," Carter said when she made her way to the town hall. Amanda's heart warmed. He'd been waiting for her, just like he promised. So far, he'd never let her down.

He was the only person in her life who hadn't.

An hour later she was deep in preparations for dinner. She'd just made the biggest batch of meatloaf imaginable, and potatoes were boiling in an enormous pot on the stove.

"Now that Gage has smoothed the way with Lainie Carmichael, when do you think you can get Megan here to talk shop?" Carter asked.

"When do you want her to come?" Amanda chopped vegetables for a salad.

"As soon as possible. We should show her the homes we're cleaning up and get her input on how much to do before we advertise them."

"I'll call her and see."

"I'd appreciate that."

They worked together in a companionable silence after that, busy with their own thoughts.

"I like it here," Amanda told him when the meatloaf was ready, the potatoes mashed and they could hear Carter's brothers and the mill workers coming into the cafeteria. "I like having people around to talk to and a whole crowd for meals."

"Who knew accosting a strange woman at the airport could turn out so well?" he joked. "Maybe I should write a how-to book."

"I'm not sure I'd go that far."

"It was a damn good thing I didn't overthink asking you to come to the Ridge. Where would we be if I'd chickened out?"

Amanda shrugged, her good mood slipping away. She'd be holed up in a motel or vacation rental and probably wouldn't have slept a wink, terrified of every sound outside at night. Gratitude swept through her that she'd stumbled across such a good man when she needed one.

She couldn't tell Carter any of that, though. Instead, she slipped mitts on her hands and lifted the meatloaf out of the oven. "Let's eat," she said.

"I'm always ready for that."

CHAPTER 10

THE NEXT MORNING Amanda came downstairs wearing jeans and a shirt he hadn't seen before, one of the new items she must have picked up in town. Its forest green color highlighted her blonde hair, making him want to touch her.

He'd slept in the living room again, but at least the air mattress made it more comfortable. Someday he'd get back into a real bed. Amanda's bed, hopefully. He could be patient, though.

They hadn't been together again since they'd climbed up the Ridge. Ever since he'd questioned her about her past, Amanda kept him at a distance. They spent time together. They kissed.

Nothing more.

He promised himself he'd find a way to heat things up between them again. Meanwhile, there was plenty of work to do.

"Ready to tackle number nineteen?" he asked her when they walked to the town hall for breakfast. "If you help me this morning before I go to the mill, tonight I'll get on with renovating your house."

"Sounds like the perfect day."

"Really?" He took her hand and squeezed it. "You're not missing your corporate job?"

Amanda snorted. "Not at all. Like I said, I kind of fell into that line of work. My sister is the one who had a real calling. I keep waiting for something to draw me in the way dancing consumes her, but nothing ever has so far." She grew pensive. "When I was in college, I wanted to go into finance."

"You still could."

"I'm not sure I'm interested in that anymore." She made a face. "You know what's funny? When I was a girl, I wanted to be a librarian. Guess dreams really do come true."

"Why didn't you study that in college?"

"It never occurred to me that mere mortals could become librarians."

Carter laughed. "Mere mortals can become anything."

"I know that now. I'm a librarian, head chef and postmistress. What am I going to be next? Mayor?"

Not a bad idea, Carter thought. They were going to need a mayor. He didn't say anything out loud, though. He'd made enough unilateral moves; he'd better consult the others before he gave her another job.

"Anyway," Amanda said. "I like the variety of my days here. I like how active I am."

"I like that, too." He wasn't missing Navy life half as much as he'd thought he might.

"I'm enjoying the company," she added.

Carter focused on Amanda. That was good news. He stopped and wrapped her in his arms, cupped her chin and kissed her. "I'm enjoying it quite a bit myself," he said. He wanted to feel all of her again and wanted her to feel him, too. He didn't think he was going to be able to keep his distance much longer.

"Amanda," he growled into the nape of her neck when he finished kissing her mouth, jawline and behind her ear.

"I know," she whispered. "I'm trying to keep my head on straight, but it's hard around you."

"I'm glad to hear that." He took her hand again, his whole body buzzing with need as they finished their trek to the town hall.

Inside, surrounded by his brothers, he tried to focus on his breakfast, their conversation—anything except the woman he wanted to take to bed.

"Megan is going to come talk to us this afternoon," he announced when they'd all settled in. "We can show her some of the houses so when they're ready, she'll have the listings all set to go. Amanda and I will work on number nineteen this morning, then I'll head to the mill."

"It's not supposed to rain for the rest of the week," Nate said. "As we strip the houses, we can pile junk in the Circle, so it'll be easy to load and take to the dump."

As they discussed the details of the work, Carter saw Amanda frown. She pulled out her phone, tapped it a few times, read a message and got up from the table.

"I've got to make a call," she said. She crossed the cafeteria, went out through the double doors and into the foyer.

Carter watched her go. He hadn't seen her communicate with anyone before this. Who'd gotten in touch just now? A man or a woman?

Someone important enough to make her jump to call him or her back.

"You know anything about Amanda yet?" Lincoln asked in a low voice.

"Yeah, I've been wondering that, too," Nate said. "She had only one suitcase when she came. What's her story?"

"I'm not sure," he admitted. "She said she's trying to decide what to do with her life." His grasp of her history sounded thin to his own ears. Who had she left behind who might call her?

"Sounds like she could leave at any time," Gage said.

"She's staying," Carter asserted.

"Did she tell you that?" Hudson asked.

"She told all of us, remember? She said she likes it here. She likes me."

Lincoln rubbed the back of his neck. "I don't know, man. I wouldn't get too attached if I were you. Seems like a setup. She could go back where she came from at any time."

"It's not like that." Carter got up and gathered his dishes. For all he knew, it was. She'd acknowledged she was keeping secrets. "I've got it under control."

But as he stalked off to the kitchen, he had to admit that wasn't entirely true.

"WHERE ARE YOU?" Melissa asked, picking up on the first ring when Amanda called her.

"Hello to you, too." Amanda bit back a rush of annoyance as she stepped outside the town hall. Why was Melissa always so rude? She wasn't that way when they were kids. Back then she'd had an outsized personality and loved to perform for anyone who would watch. Most of the time Amanda was her main audience, but their parents would indulge her sometimes, clapping as Melissa twirled and leaped around the living room even before she started formal lessons.

She was so much fun back then, even if she had to be the center of attention. Amanda had been content to play second fiddle most of the time. They'd shared a bedroom and whispered half the night, Melissa telling her wild stories about little girls who ran away to star on Broadway. It was only later, when Buck started coming around, taking up all their father's time, that Melissa's behavior began to go downhill.

"I'm serious, Amanda. Why did I have to email you twice to get an answer? Why is your phone number different all of a sudden? You've had that old one for years."

Typical, Amanda thought. It was like pulling teeth to get Melissa to answer a few texts every six months, but when *Melissa* wanted to talk, Amanda had better be accessible right away.

"I… lost my phone. I had to get a new one."

"You couldn't transfer your number?"

She hadn't wanted to—not when Buck could possibly trace her through it. "Fresh start. Fewer sales calls that way." She wasn't sure how much to tell her sister— or how much Melissa would pay attention if she did. Her sister had a way of cutting her off midsentence and changing the subject if she focused on herself for too long. A couple of times, Amanda had tried to talk to her about how lonely she was in California. How she didn't know what she wanted from life. Melissa had told her to get laid.

"You didn't think to let me know? Or did you not want me to have access to you?"

That was rich. "I was busy."

There was a long silence on the other end of the line. "Where are you again?" Melissa asked.

Amanda wished she felt safe enough to give her that information. "Traveling. Won't be home for a few weeks." Or ever, probably. Already, her life in California seemed like a distant—and not too pleasant—dream.

"Since when do you travel? What the hell is going on, Amanda? Tell me where you are!"

Still trying to have her own way in everything. It had been a long time since Amanda felt the need to jump at Melissa's commands. "I'm in… Montana, okay?" It was a big state, after all. Telling her that much was safe enough.

"Montana? Where in Montana?"

Amanda heard the irritation in Melissa's voice, a reminder of just how little patience her sister had for her these days. She was restless and driven, a dancer who actually made a living from her passion in France, where she'd lived these past few years.

"I can't talk about this on the phone," Amanda said. Maybe it was stupid. Maybe Buck Bronson couldn't possibly hack her phone, but she couldn't shake the feeling he could find her no matter where she went. How far did his reach extend?

"How else can we talk? It's not like we share a bedroom anymore. Come on, Amanda. Where in Montana are you? Billings? Bozeman? Glacier National Park?"

She sounded like she was reading from a list. Had she looked up a map of the state online? Probably, Amanda decided as she suppressed a snort of laughter. Her sister loved drama, but she hated mysteries. It must be killing her that she couldn't pinpoint Amanda's location exactly.

"No, not any of those." She paced away from the town hall's entrance.

"Missoula, Great Falls, Big Sky?"

"Melissa." She was always like this. Silence for months on end and then she had to know everything.

"Whitefish? Butte? Chance Creek?"

Amanda sucked in a breath.

"Chance Creek? Is that the place?"

"Melissa—Dad went back to his old profession." Amanda shut her eyes. She hadn't meant to say that. Melissa got pissed when she criticized their father.

Another long pause. "Okay."

"I mean it. He was staying with me. He stole a painting." She checked to make sure she was still alone.

Melissa didn't answer for a moment. "Amanda, if you're in trouble, I can help," she finally said. "Where are you exactly?"

Her unexpected offer put Amanda off balance. She'd expected a very different reaction. "I'm... safe. Laying low. Stay in Europe, and for god's sake don't get mixed up in this." She thought of the painting in the outbuilding by the old mine. No more putting things off. She had to get it out of here soon.

"How did *you* get mixed up in it? Why didn't you tell me Dad was staying with you?"

She didn't have an answer for that. Amanda supposed she'd wanted him to herself for once.

"I... would have told you, whenever we talked."

"So you hid the fact that Dad was staying at your place, and now you're claiming he stole a painting."

"He did steal it. *Afternoon in Sun and Shadow*. It was part of a traveling exhibit."

"He ran off with it?"

"Not exactly," Amanda admitted. "He had to leave it behind. Buck was after him—he found out about it somehow."

"So where is it now?"

Amanda swallowed. "I... don't know." She wasn't good at lying to her sister. "Buck Bronson came to my apartment. I barely got out of there before he broke in, Melissa. I had to run for my life!" That would throw her off the scent.

The silence drew out so long this time, Amanda wondered if her sister had hung up. Finally, Melissa sighed. "That must have been scary," she said grudgingly.

Amanda relaxed. "It was."

"But you grabbed the painting on your way out, didn't you?"

Amanda clutched her phone and turned to scan her surroundings, terrified someone could somehow hear her sister's words. Her heart banged in her chest.

"Come on, Amanda. There's no way you'd leave a masterpiece lying around for Buck to find. You took it with you, I'm sure you did. You're probably looking at it right now."

"No, I'm not." At least that wasn't a lie.

"What are you going to do with it? Sell it? Keep all that money for yourself?"

"I'm going to give it back." How could her sister think she'd do otherwise?

"Give it back? What are you going to do—call the police? You'll be the one to go to jail this time."

"Not if I do it right."

"Where are you?" Melissa demanded. "You're in too deep to handle this on your own, you know."

Amanda shook her head even though her sister couldn't see her. She wasn't going to tell Melissa where she was, and she needed to get off the phone. Now.

She hung up.

"EVERYTHING OKAY?" CARTER met Amanda as she

came back into the town hall and headed her off so they could talk in private near the mailboxes.

"It's fine." She wouldn't meet his gaze, though, and Carter was pretty sure whatever had happened, it was not fine. Who had she called? A family member?

The boyfriend she claimed not to have?

"Sometimes it helps to talk about it."

"Are you my psychiatrist now?"

Uh oh. Amanda was mad. "I hope I'm your friend." Nate, Lincoln and Gage walked past on their way out the front doors. Amanda moved toward the cafeteria.

"I didn't finish my meal," she told him.

"No rush." He trailed her inside, where they sat down again at the table. Everything except Amanda's plate had already been cleared. Hudson was in the kitchen taking care of cleaning up.

He decided not to take her anger personally. Someone had gotten in touch. Amanda had called him or her back. Whoever it was had made her upset.

Or worried.

"Are you in trouble?" He decided to cut to the chase.

She'd been about to take a sip of juice, but she set the glass on the table and finally looked at him. "Why would you ask me that?"

"Because you came here without much luggage. You won't answer any questions about your past, and you're being mighty secretive right now." A thought occurred to him. "You're not married, are you?"

"Married? No." She laughed, although it wasn't a

happy sound. "I've got problems, I'll admit that, but I'm not running from a marriage. I told you I'm single."

"Yeah, that's what you told me." It was time to put his cards on the table. If she didn't trust him, this relationship was going nowhere.

She lifted her glass again. Took a sip. Buying time, Carter thought. "You don't believe me?" she asked.

"Should I?"

She set her glass down. Looked down at the remains of her food. Pushed her plate away.

"I'm single," she said finally. "My problem is with my family, not some boyfriend. It's my father—and my sister. She's the one who got in touch today."

Carter sat back. Now they were getting somewhere.

"What did they do?"

She thought about that. "Three months ago, I made the mistake of letting my dad back into my life. I thought he'd changed. Turned out he hasn't. I know I'm better off without him, as painful as that is to admit, but my sister can't see that. She still wants to idolize him, and I'm afraid she's going to get hurt."

"In what way?" She was still being awfully cagey.

"My dad pretends he loves us, but when it comes right down to it, the only thing he cares about is money. Melissa doesn't understand that."

She stood up, picked up her plate and glass.

"Amanda."

"Carter, I don't want to talk about it." She took her dishes to the kitchen, where he could hear her chatting with Hudson.

Carter supposed he deserved that. He'd pushed her, and she'd pushed back.

"Do you mind if I skip out on helping you this morning?" she asked when she came out again. "I'm going to get to the library. Books never let you down."

"I'm sorry your father did." Disappointment filled him, but he told himself it was his own damn fault she didn't want his company.

"I am, too," she said. She softened a little. "I love him, despite everything. I wish he cared about that. I wish my sister knew I care about her, too."

"I care about you. You know that, right?"

When Amanda looked away, he stifled a curse. Hell, he'd really lost ground by pressing her for more information at exactly the wrong time. His instructors in counterterrorism would have had a lot to say about his lack of technique. You had to know when to press a source and when to back off. People's lives could depend on it.

Amanda wasn't a source, though. She was someone he cared for deeply, and it was his heart he was risking when he questioned her.

"I want to believe that," she said. "I really do. The problem is, right now I'm having a hard time believing anything."

SHE SHOULDN'T HAVE said that to Carter, Amanda thought when she was alone in the library. So far he'd been a man of his word. If he said he cared about her, she ought to believe him. Everything he'd done to this point backed up his claim. She'd lashed out at him simply because talking to Melissa made her ashamed— of herself and her whole family. What right did she have to fall for a man when she was hiding stolen property— on his land? She could get Carter and his brothers in trouble if she didn't get rid of the painting.

As soon as she was safely ensconced in the library, hiding among the stacks with a clear sightline through the shelves to the door so no one could sneak up on her, she pulled out her phone, struggled to get on the internet and looked up local LA news sites.

There still wasn't any mention of *Afternoon in Sunlight and Shadow*. Amanda wasted precious minutes picturing how her life would be different if her father had turned his artistic prowess into a safer line of work. If he couldn't pay his bills from selling his paintings, couldn't he have turned to art restoration instead of forgery?

If he had, she would never have come to Elliott Ridge, she reminded herself.

She looked up the Chance Creek sheriff's department next, but she knew calling them wasn't an option. For one thing, the sheriff might simply arrest her under suspicion of committing the theft herself. For another, he would definitely go after her father—and this time her dad wouldn't get off with a slap on the wrist. He'd committed the crime, not Buck. He would be the one to pay for it.

While Amanda knew her father probably should suffer the consequences of his actions, there was a third reason she couldn't call the sheriff, and this one had to do with her own safety.

When she was young and Buck came for Sunday dinners at her family's home, he'd made it clear he had friends in law enforcement all over the country. He bragged that he could call them up for a favor any old time, despite being kicked off the force. She had no idea if Buck would have a contact in the Chance Creek sheriff's department, but she told herself she had to assume he did.

Out of curiosity, she brought up the FBI's website next and straightened when she discovered its tip line.

As she read on, she realized it wouldn't be a good idea to use it, even though she doubted a man like Buck would have any connections to a federal agency. When the FBI deemed a tip to be credible, they usually got local law enforcement involved, which meant they'd call the Chance Creek sheriff.

She was back to square one.

Amanda hesitated, then started over again. There had to be a way to return the painting.

One that didn't end up with her in jail.

CHAPTER 11

B Y THE TIME three o'clock rolled around, Carter was having trouble concentrating on anything except Amanda. She'd been preoccupied at lunch, barely participating in their conversation, and returned to the library directly after the meal was over. He was glad for the excuse Megan's visit gave him to see her again midafternoon. Lincoln had appointed one of the workers to take charge for an hour so they all could meet with the realtor, but they arranged to hold their brainstorming session in the mill office, so they'd be on hand if there were any problems. Carter had invited Amanda to join them.

She showed up just before Megan arrived, but he didn't have time to talk to her alone before the meeting started. They all took seats around a rough wooden table that must have been there since before his father was born.

"Thanks for coming back," he said to Megan when everyone was settled in.

"Of course," Megan said guardedly. "You said you

have some houses that will be ready to list soon?"

"That's right. There are twenty-nine empty houses in Lucy's Corner. We've divided them up and begun stripping out the old carpet and appliances, painting the walls with primer and so on. They won't be stunning, but they'll be ready for people to come in and renovate how they see fit."

"How long before they're ready?"

"A few weeks for the first batch, I guess. We're working on them when we're not at the mill. Amanda and I are trying to spiff up number twenty-three. If we can get it done, people can tour it and get ideas for their own renovations."

"How long will that take?"

"A few more weeks? Like I said, we've got to keep the mill running."

"So another month or two at the very least." Megan didn't sound pleased.

"But you can start the paperwork, right? That should keep your boss off your back."

Megan was already shaking her head. "You know, Lainie saw right through you," she said to Gage. "She might have told you what you wanted to hear when you came in, but afterward she came to me and said I was a fool to have anything to do with you. She thinks you'll cut a deal directly with Warrington in the end and won't use an agent at all."

"That's not true," Carter protested.

"You sure about that?" Megan was still looking at Gage.

"We can't guarantee anything," Gage said. He considered her. "You're that desperate for a listing?"

"Lainie's looking for any excuse to fire me." Megan slumped back in her chair, her bravado draining out of her. Carter realized the situation must be dire.

Gage nodded slowly. "Guess I've got a house you can sell."

They all stared at him.

"What house?" Carter demanded. Since when did Gage have a house?

"It's on Randell Street in town. Four bedrooms, two baths."

"Where'd you get that?" Lincoln asked.

Carter could tell neither Nate nor Hudson knew about it, either. Trust Gage to keep a secret that big.

"Bought it a long time ago, in the fall after I graduated from high school. It was in rough shape. Dirt cheap. I had no idea how bad things were about to get here." He looked around at them. "What? I worked in the mill for years before things fell apart. Dad paid all of us well back then, remember? I saved everything I earned. What else was I going to do with it?"

He asked the question defiantly.

None of them answered. They knew what he'd meant to do with those savings. Go to college.

Carter wasn't sure why Gage had turned his back on that plan. He'd graduated two years before the crash. When the time came to start at Montana State, he changed his mind, kept working in the mill full-time—then more than full-time when they began to lose their contracts and workers.

That still didn't explain why he'd bought a house— in town, rather than on the Ridge—and hadn't even lived in it. Had he considered it an investment? Elliotts had been buying real estate in the area for over a hundred years, after all.

"I've been renting it out ever since, but there's no reason to keep the house now. If things work out, I'll live up here. It's your listing if you want it," Gage told Megan.

"That would be great," Megan said uncertainly. "It would get Lainie off my back for a while, anyway."

"I'll be in tomorrow to sign the papers."

She frowned. "You made a bunch of promises last time. How about you follow me to town when this meeting is over, and we get it done today?" She met his gaze again and held it. Gage was the one to look away first.

He nodded.

"That's the plan, then," Carter said, more relieved than he'd thought possible. "Megan, you've got a listing to tide you over. Meanwhile, we'll get these houses cleaned while we wait for the subdivision to be approved. We can list one or two even before I'm done with number twenty-three if we need to, although I don't want to keep Amanda waiting forever. Speaking of which, can you recommend someone who can draw up a contract for my sale to Amanda?" Maybe it would cheer her if they made some progress on that front.

Megan nodded, opened her purse, shuffled through

a few things and drew out a business card. "Andrew Fong is the man to see."

"Thanks."

The meeting split up. Gage followed Megan when she left. Amanda stuck around only long enough to say she'd see him at dinner.

"Are you okay?" he asked as he walked her to the door.

"I'm fine," she said and was gone.

AS AMANDA EXITED the mill, she watched Megan climb into her dusty blue truck.

"I'll wait for you at the Circle. Don't even think of blowing me off, Gage Elliott," Megan called from her open window before driving away.

Gage watched her go, then noticed Amanda's approach.

"She's got me cornered. Can't back out now even if I wanted to," he said, falling into step beside her. They trudged down Center Street together.

"You don't want to sell your house in town?"

"It's not that," Gage said and fell silent.

"You don't want to be alone with Megan?" When he didn't answer, she went on. "If you don't like her, Gage, just tell her. It's not fair to ghost people."

He sighed. "I don't want to ghost her."

"Then man up, get over yourself and ask her out."

He turned a baleful look her way. "Did I ask you for advice?"

"No." He hadn't and she was sticking her nose

where it didn't belong. "I like Megan, and I don't want to see her hurt. I like you, too, by the way. Despite all… this." She gestured at him.

Gage's mouth curved into a half smile. "Some women like 'all this.'"

She could understand that. Like she'd said to Megan before, Gage was handsome in a brooding way. Thank goodness she didn't fall for men like that. She preferred men like Carter who called it like they saw it and didn't leave you guessing about their intentions.

"I could say the same thing, you know," he said when she didn't answer.

"That you like me despite 'all this'?" She struck a pose.

That earned her a chuckle. "No. That I'm worried about Carter. That if you don't like him, you should just tell him."

His concern surprised her a little, but she supposed it shouldn't have. That was Gage's problem, wasn't it? He cared too much. Worried too much, too. It was keeping him from even trying to succeed at the things that were important to him.

"Do I look like I don't like him?"

"No," he admitted. For a few minutes they shared a companionable silence as they walked down the forested road. The peace of this place, despite the whine of saws at the mill from time to time, soothed her. Amanda had always lived in cities and had no idea how pleasant this kind of setting could be. "Just be honest with him, no matter what happens," Gage finally added.

"Carter has been hurt before. Not by women," he qualified.

"By your family?" she guessed. Carter had alluded to it a few times.

Gage nodded. "By me," he admitted, surprising her all over again.

"I think Carter puts family above everything else," she said.

Gage looked her way again. "But if you let him, he'd put you above even us."

SOMETHING WAS REALLY wrong.

If Carter had thought Amanda was reserved at lunchtime, she was downright pensive at dinner. When he suggested a walk afterward, she came willingly, but her mind was clearly elsewhere. They ended up at the beach, where Carter had hoped he might try for a few more kisses as a prelude to a night where he didn't sleep in the living room, but he could tell romance wasn't in the cards.

Instead, he built a fire and his brothers joined them, Hudson, Lincoln and Nate trading stories about their years in the service until even Amanda smiled once or twice. Gage wandered over and sat down but seemed as distracted as Amanda was. That was nothing new, though.

When they finally made their way to number twenty-three, Amanda said good-night and went straight upstairs after giving him a quick peck on the cheek. He heard the patter of her feet across the ceiling, the opening and closing of the bathroom door, the sound of water running in the pipes. He undressed and lay down on his air mattress, but he knew he wouldn't sleep anytime soon.

Two hours later, he could tell she was still awake. He got up and crept to the bottom of the stairs, where he could see that light still spilled from under her bedroom door, creating a dim glow in the upstairs hall. Every once in a while, he heard the tread of her steps across the floor. It was as if she was going from her bed to a window, pausing there to look out and then heading back again.

What was keeping her up?

He didn't bother trying to sleep himself. Half an hour later he was rewarded when he heard her bedroom door open and then the first creak of a stair. Carter got to his feet again, silently pulled on his jeans and waited. He wasn't sure if he should confront her or let her go about her business. She might not like it if she thought he was spying on her.

Another creak.

Another.

He came to stand near the steps. "Amanda? Everything okay?"

She sucked in a surprised breath, then slowly came down the rest of the stairs. "You scared me. I thought you were asleep."

"What's wrong?"

"I was… hungry. I was going to head over to the kitchen. I just can't seem to settle down tonight. This thing with my sister—my family… It's driving me crazy. I didn't eat enough at dinner, and now my stomach is growling so hard it's keeping me up."

"I've got a granola bar around here somewhere. Will that hold you for now?"

She nodded, looking grateful. "Thank you." She sat on the stairs as he dug through his things and pulled out one for each of them, then fetched her a glass of water, one of the few items her kitchen could supply.

"Want to talk about it?"

Amanda sighed. "Not really. You don't know how messed up a family can be," she added.

"Is that what you think?" If only she knew. "I know a lot more about that topic than I'd like to."

"I know you've had problems in the past, but you and your brothers are close. You're all here rebuilding your family's town. And don't start in about Gage. He's cranky, but he's here, and you yourself said he wants you to succeed. I think you're right."

"It took twelve years of us being apart to get back to a place where we could be together." There was nowhere for them to sit comfortably down here, so Carter took her hand and led her up the stairs to her bedroom.

"Are you seriously trying to make a move on me right now?" Amanda asked.

"I'm trying to find somewhere for us to sit and talk. Although I could be persuaded," he admitted, ushering her into the bedroom. He plumped the pillows against the headboard of her bed, took a seat and patted the bedspread beside him.

With a long-suffering sigh, Amanda joined him there. She wore a soft T-shirt-and-shorts combination meant for sleeping in that made Carter miss the tank top and panties she'd worn her first night here. Had she upgraded to something a little less revealing in case of nocturnal conversations like this? If so, it was too bad.

"You really think your sister is worse than my brothers?" he asked to restart the conversation. Maybe the late hour and the warm glow of the small lamp on the bedside table would inspire confidences.

"I know she is. And I'm not buying that the five of you didn't talk for twelve years."

"We talked," Carter admitted. "Now and then. Mostly because Mom demanded it. She set up video calls and group chats and kept after us until we all participated, but if she hadn't done that, I don't know if we would have kept in touch."

"What happened that made you so angry with each other?"

Carter wished they were talking about her family, but he figured he had to give a little to get a little. Maybe if he told her about his past, she'd share more about hers.

"It wasn't so much we were angry," he said slowly. "It's more like we were… ashamed."

The truth of it hit him even as he was saying the words. He'd never stated it so clearly, but now that he had, he was forced to face it.

"Ashamed of what?"

"Being complicit in my father's failure. It… hurt.

Your dad is supposed to be infallible. When you're a boy growing up, you think someday you'll be infallible, too. We watched him lose everything. More than that; we failed right alongside him."

Amanda bit her lip, but she didn't interrupt him. Carter rubbed his palm over his jaw, aware of the tension massed throughout his body.

"We tried," he went on. "All of us gave it everything we had. The collapse of this place didn't happen all at once. First the price of lumber started to slip. We lost a contract or two. Dad had to let a few people go. And then a few more. Gage and Nate went to work with him to pick up the slack. Later, the rest of us joined in. We did school when we could, worked every minute of the day when we got home. More people started to move away."

"That must have been hard."

"After a while, Lincoln, Nate and I were working the mill night and day. Gage shifted over to the logging operation, and he and Hudson were practically running it around the clock. We went from eighty men to sixty to thirty-five to fifteen. Then it was just us. Dad was juggling bills, robbing Peter to pay Paul, maxing out credit cards. You name it."

Carter's voice thickened with the memory. Those days had never seemed to end. The constant work, the skipped meals, the aching muscles—

The mistakes.

He'd never forget the day Nate was nearly crushed when a couple of logs fell off a truck during the unloading process. He'd never heard his father yell so loud. Never seen his brother move so fast, either. They'd all been shaken by the accident and the knowledge that next time they might not be so lucky.

"The work was killing my dad. You could see it happening. We tried to take the burden off his shoulders, but there weren't enough of us. I'd come across him hunched over, rubbing his chest or his arm. His face would get so gray." Carter broke off and shook his head. "It wasn't the workload that was crushing him. It was the failure. He couldn't stand it. Elliott Ridge was supposed to be our legacy."

"When did he give up?"

"He never did. That's the thing." The pain of it filled his chest and burned his throat. This was the hard part to tell. The part no one outside his family knew. The part that filled him with a shame that seared him from the inside out. Putting it into words felt like walking naked onstage in a packed auditorium.

He backtracked, needing to tell her more family history before she could understand how things had ended. He was grateful for the reprieve.

"That library you like so much," he said. "That was Mom's happy place. She was a reader and expected us to be, too. When we were little, she read out loud to us every night. We got books for Christmas."

Amanda nodded, but he could tell she wasn't sure why he'd taken the conversation in this direction.

"Nate got into science fiction. There was this one series he couldn't get enough of, a complicated political saga set on various planets. One thing about it fascinated all of us. Each family dynasty in the series had its own secret language—a sign language they could use in battle situations so enemies couldn't understand what they were saying. We'd seen enough war movies by then to know that soldiers used gestures like that, too, when they needed to communicate silently. We took the idea and ran with it."

"You had a secret language?" A smile curved her mouth.

"Hell, yeah, we did. Drove the other kids in the community nuts. We used it during sports, playing card games, when we were hanging out." He shrugged.

"I would have loved that. My sister and I were close when we were kids, but we never came up with our own language."

"Nate tried to recreate the entire English vocabulary, but the rest of us never mastered it. We ended up paring it down to the most useful signs. Since it was supposed to be secret, we didn't use any gestures that someone else would be able to guess. Like, we didn't use an hourglass motion to mean, 'She's hot.'"

"What did you use?"

Carter made a sideways chopping motion with his right hand twice. She noticed he held his arm straight down, moving only his hand. If you weren't looking for the gesture, you might not even notice it.

"Why'd you pick that?"

"Because it made no sense. That was the point. No one except us could figure out what we were talking about. Anyway, one gesture became the most important one."

"What was it?"

He bunched the fingers of his right hand together, then flicked them wide. "Shut your mouth and open your eyes. In other words, keep quiet, listen to what I'm saying and go along with it—no matter what. It came in handy when one of us was about to get into big trouble and needed the rest of us to back up his alibi. We made a rule about it. You could use it only when there was no other way to get the job done. If you did use it, the rest of us had to go along with it, no questions asked."

"Seems ripe for abuse," Amanda said. "One of you could have completely overplayed it."

"Not as much as you'd think, given how unruly we were in those days." He smiled to remember it. "But we'd mostly grown out of the habit when Gage used it one last time."

"What happened?"

Carter sighed. He couldn't put off the rest of the story anymore.

"It was Gage who ended things," he said. Once again shame unfurled hot tendrils throughout his body, and his voice felt thick with the emotions he wanted to hide. "He'd found Dad curled up in pain on the floor in the mill office the day before. Dad refused to let Gage call an ambulance or even take him to the doctor. He pretended nothing was wrong. Gage couldn't stand it anymore. The next day at breakfast, he stood up and announced he was leaving. He was joining up. We all were."

Carter took a deep breath, remembering the way it all went down. The pancakes going cold on the table. His mother standing in the doorway between the kitchen and dining room. The tears in her eyes. "It was news to the rest of us, let me tell you. You could have heard a pin drop around that table. Hudson opened his mouth to challenge him, but Gage made that sign and stopped him. None of us knew what to do. No one had ever used it in a situation like that. Were we supposed to go along with it? Were we actually supposed to walk out on my dad?"

Amanda was watching him. Carter swallowed against the lump of pain in his throat. He'd never known panic until that day. He'd had seconds to evaluate everything—his future. His family. His loyalty to his father. His duty to save his life even if it broke his father's heart.

"Dad turned to the rest of us. Demanded to know if it was true. If we left, there was no way he could keep the place going himself. Nate was the first to agree with Gage. Then Hudson. Then Lincoln. We all knew what Gage was doing. We knew Dad wouldn't give up—so we had to force his hand. I'll never forget how it felt when Dad turned to me. I'm the baby. His favorite, although he'd never admit it. If I refused to agree with Gage, the game was over. We'd go on just like we had before—until we buried him. It was all up to me."

"What did you do?" Amanda whispered.

"I wanted to say I was staying. I love my father. Going against him felt like stabbing a knife in his chest. But I knew if we stayed, the Ridge would kill him for sure. So I said…" Carter's voice went raspy. He cleared his throat and tried again. "I said I was joining up, too."

He was unprepared for the sorrow that washed over him. The sharpness of his betrayal still stung as bitterly as it had twelve years ago. He hadn't been able to meet his father's gaze. He knew he'd rung the death knell of the home they all loved.

"Dad didn't say a word. He just stood up and left the table. Went to his room and shut the door. He was still there when we drove off a half hour later. Gage said we had to go through with it. We had to leave Elliott Ridge right away, or one of us would cave in and it would all be for nothing. He said it was the only way to save Dad—and Mom, for that matter. He didn't want to make a widow of her to save a patch of forest. 'We have to make our own way now.' That's what Gage said. So we packed our bags. I don't think I've done anything harder in my life."

"You left together. Why didn't you all join the same branch of the military?"

Carter remembered the way they'd stood by their vehicles outside the home they grew up in, Gage arguing for all of them to join the Army.

"I couldn't forgive Gage for making me betray Dad," he said quietly, remembering the rage that had burned through him, leaving him taut with agony. "When he said he was joining the Army, I chose the Navy. I wanted to get as far away from him as I could. I guess Nate and Hudson felt the same. Lincoln was the only one who went with him, but they chose separate paths from there. Gage became a Ranger. Lincoln went into the Special Forces."

"So you all scattered."

"We let him down. My dad. We put an end to everything he'd spent a lifetime building," Carter said. "We couldn't stand to see each other and be reminded of what we'd done."

"Carter." Amanda touched his arm. "I'm sure your father understood."

"I'm not." The more he talked about it, the more his throat threatened to close up. He needed to change the topic. "So now you know my story. What about you? What are you and your sister arguing about, anyway?" He tried to make his tone light, but he was having trouble shaking the pain that still lodged hard in his chest.

Would she finally trust him enough to tell him the truth?

AMANDA HAD SO many questions she wanted to ask Carter, but she could see how hard it had been for him to tell her this much. It wasn't fair to keep him in the hot seat when she was keeping so many secrets herself.

"There's one parallel between my story and yours," she said slowly, trying desperately to decide how much she could share with him. He'd bared his soul to her. By all rights she should do the same, but she couldn't involve him in a criminal matter. That wasn't fair.

She'd waited hours tonight, hoping he'd fall asleep and she'd be able to sneak past him so she could fetch the painting from the outbuildings by the mine. She didn't have a plan yet for what she'd do with it, but she was running out of time and had to do something.

She'd figured she could take the road that curved by the lake before heading up the Ridge. There was a moon out tonight, and she could use her phone as a flashlight. As terrifying as it was to think about the journey there through the dark woods, or the danger of rooting around in an abandoned building past midnight, she was even more afraid to try to retrieve it in the daytime. Someone was always around. Anyone who saw her going to the mine would be sure to ask uncomfortable questions.

"My father is the major player." She cut off. "I haven't told many people about this," she admitted. She wasn't sure she wanted to now.

"You can tell me." Carter covered her hand with his own. She was aware of the strength of him. Of his determination to know what made her tick.

Amanda supposed he was right. She could tell him some of it, as embarrassing as it was. She just had to keep her wits about her and not say too much.

Which hurt, given how honest he'd been with her.

"I was fourteen when my father went to jail—the year before he and Mom officially divorced." Amanda braced herself, but Carter didn't say anything or pull his hand away. She supposed he'd seen a lot during his years of service. Why had she thought he'd be shocked?

"He's an artist. A painter," she went on. "A good one. Very technical. Very correct." She sighed. "He made friends with the wrong people." She still refused to consider that he had been the mastermind of the crime he'd committed when she was a teenager. She needed to believe her father had started out an honest man and been corrupted by Buck.

"He was a good dad. When I was young, he worked in different galleries for his day job, because he couldn't support us through his art. He painted every chance he got, though, and eventually he managed to book some showings of his own work. We were all so proud of him. Mom had a steady job, which helped a lot. We were able to afford a small bungalow in a working-class neighborhood in Dallas. Dad claimed the detached garage as his studio. Melissa and I thought it was a magical place, although we weren't allowed in it much."

He really was a good father to her and her sister back then. He'd taught them to rollerblade and throw a baseball. He'd taken them trick or treating at Halloween. He was funny and did good voices when he read out loud to them. Both her parents worried a lot about money, though.

"When I was thirteen and my sister was twelve, things changed. My dad made a new friend. Buck Bronson." Amanda hadn't meant to mention him, but now that she had, she found she couldn't stop her narrative. There'd never been anyone to tell about what happened. Her mother refused to talk about it, and Melissa still worshipped the ground their father walked on. "They met at one of the galleries where Dad worked. Buck used to be a police officer and picked up security guard shifts there when they held big events. They got to talking, and I guess they hit it off. They started getting together outside of work. Buck praised Dad's paintings to the skies. I think that was heady stuff for my father. He was good at what he did. Very technical, like I said. He wasn't innovative, though, so he still wasn't selling much, despite the shows."

"Was Buck a collector?"

"In a way." Amanda shook her head, wishing she could share her private joke with Carter. Security guards didn't make enough money to collect art in a serious manner; when Buck stole a painting, it wasn't with the intention of keeping it for himself. "He started coming to the house. Mom would invite him to dinner. It became a weekly affair, and soon he was almost a member of our family. He brought Melissa and me little presents. Chocolate, hair clips, magazines. We showed him our report cards and art projects. He was the uncle we never had. After dinner, he and Dad would go to Dad's studio and talk art. Melissa hated that, because we weren't allowed. I guess it bothered me, too."

"What happened?" Carter asked when she was quiet for a long time.

"Buck had an idea for how Dad could make some real money with his painting skills. Melissa and I were getting older. Our bungalow was beginning to feel cramped, I guess. Mom still tried to support Dad's painting, but when I look back now, I see that she was losing faith it ever would come to much. They were probably fighting about money and what they wanted out of life. Mom likes things cut and dried. In her head, things either work out or they don't, and Dad's painting wasn't working as a career. All that time he was spending in his studio was time he could have spent looking for a better job or helping her around the house."

"What was the idea?"

"Buck would get work as a security guard for one of the major art galleries in the city. Dad would create a forgery of one of the paintings showcased there. Buck would make the switch after hours and find a buyer for the original through his connections. He'd worked for the Dallas police for eighteen years. We found out later he left the force to avoid being kicked off it. He was a man who made friends—lots of them—on both sides of the law. I think he knew someone who knew the kind of collector that would buy stolen art."

"Your dad went along with it?"

"He did," Amanda said quietly. That part always shocked her. Was Buck that persuasive, or had her father always been comfortable with cutting corners? "Turned out he was good at forging a painting. Buck was less good at swapping it for the real thing." She suppressed a shiver at how wrong it had all gone.

"He got caught?"

"Another employee walked in on him." She took a deep breath. "Buck killed him."

Carter's hand tightened around hers.

Amanda found it hard to keep her voice steady after

that. The moment Buck shot the other security guard was the moment he'd ruined all their lives.

"I guess he thought he had a better chance of getting away with it if he fingered someone else for the murder, so he planted evidence that led the police to my father and skipped town. My dad panicked the minute they showed up at our house and told them everything. They caught up with Buck before he made it too far." She'd never forget that night. The lights of the police cars swirling in their driveway. She and Melissa hiding terrified in their bedroom while uniformed strangers shouted and crashed around in their house. The way her mother held them as her father was arrested. Melissa had screamed and screamed as her father was dragged away and put in a squad car.

"So his connections on the force didn't keep Buck out of trouble? Something tells me he wasn't too happy about that."

"He managed to get the charge down to voluntary manslaughter. He was sentenced to eleven years in jail. In the end, Dad wasn't convicted. He created the painting with the intent to profit off stealing the original, but the switch wasn't successful, and he wasn't present when Buck killed the other guard. He was locked up pending arraignment, though. That's when Buck got his revenge."

Carter waited patiently as Amanda stared at her hands tangled in her lap. She liked to believe the world was a fair place and that most people were good, but when she had to remember what happened to her father, she wasn't so sure that was true.

"Three days into his time in jail, my father was badly beaten by another inmate, who let Dad know he'd been paid for his trouble. Dad ended up in the hospital. He was the prosecution's star witness against Buck, but the minute the trial was over, he disappeared from our lives. I guess he thought that was the only way to get beyond Buck's reach."

"Wait. He left you behind?" Carter frowned. "After Buck proved what he could do even from jail?" She could tell he was trying to bite back what he really wanted to say—the same thing she'd thought a thousand times.

Her father had taken the coward's way out.

"He didn't think Buck would go after us. He thought if he was gone, we'd be fine."

That's what she told herself, anyway. Believing the alternative—that he'd gambled with their lives to save his own—was too awful.

"Was he right?"

Amanda's breath caught. No one had ever asked that question. Now that he had, she couldn't lie to him.

"No." The word came out a whisper.

"Amanda."

"I mean, I don't know," she backtracked. "Something happened. Maybe Buck didn't have anything to do with it. Nothing was ever proven."

Carter waited, his gaze locked on hers.

"Our house. It caught on fire."

He still said nothing. Amanda's words spilled over

each other to get out. She'd never told this story to anyone.

"The flames started in the garage. Right outside the bedroom I shared with my sister. We woke up to alarms. Smoke so thick we couldn't see a thing. I don't know how we got out."

She remembered running barefoot into the street. Clinging to Melissa, both of them hollering at the top of their lungs for help. She remembered sirens. Someone pulling her out of the way as a firetruck veered to a stop outside her house.

"Mom—" She stopped and fought to control her voice. "She'd taken a sleeping pill—"

Carter's grip on her hand was firm. Amanda clung to it.

"When they dragged her out, I thought she was dead. She wasn't moving."

"But she was okay?" Carter prompted when she couldn't go on.

Amanda forced her emotions down. Kept going. "We all spent a night in the hospital. Then we went home."

Carter stiffened. "You went back to the place Buck nearly burned down around you?"

Amanda nodded, swallowing against the terror of the memory. "Melissa and I slept in the living room for months. They had to rebuild a whole wall to make our bedroom habitable again. The night it was ready, Melissa ran away."

"She was afraid?"

"Probably. Angry, too. She'd already decided everything that had ever gone wrong was Mom's fault." Amanda had said that before, but Carter needed to understand where things stood.

"She left you alone with your mother. In that house."

"She was found and brought back, of course. She did it a few more times over the next couple of years. Mom finally gave up and moved us to Houston. I guess she realized that even though she fixed our house, she couldn't recapture the past. I was happy to move. No one there knew anything about my dad or what he did. Melissa was still angry, though. She met a guy, and six months later, she ran away again. This time Mom let her go—like I told you before. Melissa lived with his family until she graduated. Meanwhile, I finished school. Went to Rice University for college. Studied business. I nearly had a perfect GPA." She didn't say that studying was her go-to way to stop the memories from crowding in her mind. That she'd decided if she was perfect—if her grades were perfect—she'd be safe.

"So everything was all right in the end?"

Hardly.

Carter leaned in closer. "Something else happened." It was a statement, not a question.

In for a penny, in for a pound, she supposed. He might as well know the rest.

"I made a new best friend in high school in Houston. Got a boyfriend, too. We were like the Three Musketeers and all went to Rice University for our business degrees. We had most of our classes together. Studied together. Went out together. You get the picture. All of us were near the top of our class." She'd been the closest. "When we graduated, we applied for an entry-level training program together at a prestigious international company. We were positive we'd get accepted. I was a shoo-in for sure." She took a steadying breath. "That's when my dad's crime made it to *Prominent Cases*." She named a popular national true crime show.

Carter's hand tightened around hers.

"They sensationalized the whole story. Included the fire and everything. We'd refused to be interviewed for the show, so they got actors to play us. Everyone I met after that wanted to know all about it—including the man who conducted my follow-up interview for the training program. I didn't get accepted, of course. Maddy and Erik did."

Carter was watching her with concern. "They went ahead without you?"

Amanda nodded. "As they should have. Last I heard they're still together. Married. One kid. Probably another on the way by now."

"Amanda."

The pity in his voice felt like razer blades scraping her skin. She fought the urge to get up and walk right out of the room. She decided it was better to say it all once and then never talk about it again.

"I took the first job I was offered. Moved to California. Los Angeles. Went to work. Came home. Kept busy however I could. Made some nice acquaintances that never quite became friends. Saved my money. It was like... I went to sleep and couldn't wake up. Like I couldn't figure out a reason to keep trying for happiness. I didn't want to lose any more pieces of my heart."

"That's understandable. It's how I felt after we left the Ridge—like I didn't want to get attached to anything." Carter shrugged. "That served me well while I was with the SEALs. You get moved around. Your situation changes all the time. There's no such thing as continuity. But then you get to wondering what you're doing it all for. There was no one waiting for me when I finished a mission."

She nodded. "Exactly. I worked hard all day and came home at night to an empty apartment. What was the point of it all? I kept thinking something would happen. I'd get a sign that it was time to come back to life."

"Did you get one?" he prompted when she fell silent again.

"I thought I did. My dad showed up three months ago. Said he wanted to make up for lost time. He wanted to start over. Despite everything, I wanted that, too." She looked up at Carter. "I was a fool, wasn't I? He nearly got my mom, my sister and me killed, and there I was inviting him into my home. I was so sure he'd learned his lesson, but now that I think about it, he never even apologized for what he did before."

"He's still your dad."

"I lied to Mom—by omission." She was ashamed of

that. "I never told her or Melissa I let him move in with me."

"He moved in?"

She nodded. "He painted all day while I was at the office. Said he'd rekindled his love for it while he was away. After dinner he spent the evenings with me. It seemed like he finally wanted to be the father he hadn't been since I was a kid. And then—" Amanda stopped short, realizing how close she was to spilling everything. She couldn't tell him her father had committed another crime. "He… left."

Carter waited, as if he knew there was more.

"Suddenly he was gone," she repeated. "He never made me any promises, so I shouldn't have been so surprised, but I was. It really hurt that he thought he could blow in and out of my life that way after everything else he'd done. I felt used. Tricked. I just… couldn't face carrying on like everything was business as usual. I needed to get out of LA. I needed a change."

It pained her to twist the truth after telling him all the rest.

"What made you pick Chance Creek?"

"Pure luck," she said and forced herself to smile at him. "And it really was lucky, because that's where I met you." Amanda made up her mind. Tomorrow she would figure out what to do with the painting if it killed her. She would get it into the right hands and get out of this mess. Then she'd tell him everything.

"I feel lucky, too."

He leaned in. Amanda met his kiss gratefully. He'd

listened to her in a way no one else had. In a matter of days, when she was able to tell him the rest, she thought he'd be able to understand that, too. She felt better than she had since the day she escaped out the back window of her apartment. She had Carter on her side, and that meant she could handle anything.

When he eased her down onto the bed, she let him, warming to his kisses, free of worry for once. Carter gave her all the time in the world to push him away, but now that they were past the hard part—now he knew what her father was and still cared for her—she didn't want to hold back any longer.

She wanted this man. Cared for him. Wanted to stay here in Elliott Ridge with him and forget all about the past—and the future. For tonight, the present was enough. She was hungry for closeness—for love. Wanted to be with Carter all the way.

Carter sat up, pulled his shirt over his head, then tossed it aside. Straddling her, he reached to help her dispose of hers, but Amanda was ahead of him. She arched her back, tugged her T-shirt over her head and shoved it away. She wrapped her arms around his neck, pulled him down and delighted in the feel of him as he allowed his weight to settle on top of her.

"You okay with this?" he asked. "We're inside. This time it counts."

"I want it to." She wanted whatever Carter was willing to give. It wasn't fair, since she hadn't told him everything yet, but Amanda couldn't wait anymore to let him know how she felt. She was his, if he'd have her.

She couldn't pretend anymore that she could hold back.

As he bent to explore her, brushing kisses over her mouth, cheeks and neck, Amanda ran her hands over his wide shoulders and back. He was all muscle, his scars rough under her fingers.

When his explorations took him lower, Amanda helped him unclasp her bra and gasped when his mouth covered one newly freed nipple. She gave herself up to sensation then, clinging to Carter, moaning inarticulately each time he gave his attention to another part of her anatomy.

Carter took his time reacquainting himself with her body, and only when she was burning with desire for him did he shuck off his boxer-briefs and settle himself between her legs again, his hardness evidence of how much he wanted her, too. He flexed his hips and slowly pushed inside her in the most delicious way possible. Amanda opened to him with a sigh and tilted her head to meet him as he lowered his mouth to hers. As Carter possessed her fully, she melted into him, every nerve ending lit up at the electricity of his touch.

As he moved within her, Amanda joined his rhythm, knowing she'd always remember this moment. She'd shared with Carter things about her family that had caused her shame, and he hadn't blinked. He still wanted to be with her.

She pushed away any worry about the secrets she still kept. He was hers and she was his, which was exactly what she wanted.

She could have picked any flight, Amanda thought

suddenly, clinging to Carter as he picked up speed. She could have gone anywhere. It was pure luck that had brought her to Chance Creek. Pure luck that had her in Carter's arms right now.

Or fate.

Maybe all this was meant to be.

Maybe Carter was the man she'd waited her whole life to meet. Maybe this was why her days had felt so empty in Los Angeles. Because the man she was supposed to love belonged in Montana.

Love.

Amanda wrapped her arms tighter around Carter's broad shoulders, met every thrust of his body against hers with a tilt of her hips. She wanted all of him. Wanted everything he could give her. Wanted to never let him go.

She was in love with this Navy SEAL. This man who'd welcomed her at first sight. Who'd offered a new way to live. Who was making her dreams come true.

She loved Carter.

His next thrust brought her over the edge. Wave after wave of sensation crashed through her. All Amanda could do was ride it out as Carter reached his limit, too, pounding his own release into her with thrusts that threatened to push her against the headboard.

When he finally collapsed on top of her, Amanda felt like she'd been wrung dry. He kissed her neck, rolled over and brought her with him, tucking her under his arm as he lay on his back, breathing hard.

"You're wonderful," he growled into her hair, holding her tightly against the length of his body.

"So are you." She couldn't remember ever feeling like this. Carter was... perfect.

As his hand brushed over her skin, curving around her bottom and sliding up to the small of her back, Amanda could tell he was already recovering.

Already wanting more.

She wanted more, too. "I can't believe I found you," she murmured against his shoulder.

"I'm so glad you did."

CHAPTER 12

THE PATTER OF rain on the windowsill when he woke couldn't dampen Carter's good mood. He'd slept in a real bed, had a beautiful woman in his arms and the prospect of a shared goal to challenge them. He couldn't wait to get up and get started—after he showed Amanda how happy he was to find himself next to her.

He pressed kisses along her neck and bare shoulder until she sighed and stretched.

"Is it morning already?"

"It is," he confirmed. "Another beautiful day."

"It doesn't sound beautiful," she murmured, but she didn't push him away or move to get out of bed. It was some time before they actually got up.

"Hope someone else got breakfast on the table," Carter said when they were finally ready to trek to the town hall.

They entered the cafeteria to find Nate had taken charge of the meal today. The others were already eating. Carter's stomach rumbled as he helped Amanda into her seat.

"I've got some news," Nate said. "I ran into Carolyn Snyder last night in town. Remember her?"

"Of course. She's married to Dustin. He drove logging trucks for years for Dad. How are they? I didn't realize they were still in Chance Creek."

"Carolyn looks well, but Dustin passed away last year."

The news made Carter's gut twist. "He couldn't have been more than sixty-five."

Nate nodded. "Heart attack. One minute he was here, the next gone, according to Carolyn."

"What a shame."

"Anyway, she's interested in buying their old house. It's in the subdivision. I got her up to date on what's happening and warned her we can't guarantee we'll be able to keep the Ridge. She doesn't care. She misses her old home."

"I bet. They raised three kids there."

"Who are grown and scattered around the country now. She doesn't know if any of them intend to move back."

Carter thought about that as Amanda passed the platter to him and he heaped four pancakes onto his plate. "Won't she be lonely up here?"

"For now, but if Mom and Dad ever move back, she'll be thrilled. They always were close."

"I guess." He filed the idea away to think about later. "We should have her up to see the old place before she makes any decisions. It's pretty rough around the edges."

"Doubt that will put her off," Lincoln said. "The Snyders were pillars of the community."

Carter nodded. "While we're talking about the future—I was thinking. We need a mayor. Someone to take charge of the town's finances. A point person for enquiries and decisions. Someone organized and conscientious."

"I suppose you're nominating yourself," Hudson drawled.

"Actually, I nominate Amanda."

Amanda, who'd been about to pluck a piece of bacon from a serving dish with tongs, dropped it. "Me?"

"Yes, you." He spoke to his brothers. "If any of us is mayor, the rest of us will resent him, right? It'll cause a rift in the family, and that's the last thing we want. Amanda is a neutral party."

"Is she, though?" Hudson asked. "You're sleeping in her house. Which used to be *your* house. That doesn't sound very neutral."

"I was just renovating it, that's all." Carter sent his brother a hard look to remind him to keep his mouth shut. "And she's not an Elliott, no matter what my relationship is to her."

"Your *relationship*?" Lincoln emphasized the word. "Are you two having a relationship?"

Carter suppressed the urge to toss a pancake at his face. "None of your business." He wasn't going to let any of his brothers get to him after the morning he'd had with Amanda. "All of us are busy with the mill and cleaning houses. Amanda has already proved how organized she is. Why shouldn't she take the position?"

"Do you even want to be mayor?" Nate asked her. "You're already doing a number of jobs."

"It would be an honor," Amanda said slowly. "Unfortunately, I need to find a paying job soon. I'm not sure if I can handle the shopping, the mail, making lunch and dinner, running the library, being mayor *and* working full-time."

She was right; that was asking the impossible. And once again, he'd taken a step without consulting his brothers, despite what he told them last time. Carter thought it over. Could they afford to pay Amanda a salary? He should have looked into it before bringing this up.

"Elliott Ridge never had a mayor before," Lincoln pointed out.

"That's because it's not an incorporated town," Gage spoke up. "It's a company town. We own it, and we run it. That's the way it's always been. We can't have a mayor."

"So what can we have?" Carter asked. "Someone needs to stay on top of things."

"A manager?" Lincoln suggested. "In a way this town is an extension of our business. Amanda could work for us."

"We could give her a contract that lasts until next June," Nate said. "At that point, we'll know where we stand as far as moving forward. If we pay her a salary, she won't have to get another job. It won't be much," he told Amanda, "but it will be something."

"It doesn't need to be much," Amanda said. "You're already feeding me. If you keep that up, I just need to be able to buy clothes, personal supplies, a few extras—and still have a dollar left over to buy my house when the subdivision is approved." She grinned.

"You can help us figure out how to structure the town in the future, if we manage to pay off our loans," Lincoln said.

"I can do that," Amanda said. "And if I can't, I'll ask for help."

"Hell, that already makes you a better candidate than any of us," Nate said. "Just try getting an Elliott to admit he doesn't know something."

Even Gage nodded at that. "I'm good with Amanda being town manager," he said. "Once she's pulled all the information together about governing the Ridge when part of it is subdivided, you'll see it's a lot more compli-cated than you think."

"Dude, cheer up," Carter said. "It's okay to be hap-py once in a while."

"Meanwhile, we're not going to pay off our loans if we don't get our logging operation running again," Gage went on, ignoring him. He turned to Hudson. "Are you making any plans?"

"Me? Why should I make plans?"

"Because you're the logger in the family."

"You had a hand in it before it all went south," Hudson said.

"Only because things were desperate. Better get on that."

"If you need help figuring out how to start that part of the business up again, let me know," Carter said. Hudson didn't look too pleased with his new assignment. Carter thought he knew why. Hudson was a doer, not a pencil-and-paper guy. Give him a chainsaw, and he'd lay a tree down nice and easy, wherever you wanted it to fall. Give him a laptop and ask him to create a spreadsheet, and he'd probably throw it at you.

"Whatever," Hudson said. "Is Amanda going to run this town or what?"

"Let's vote," Nate said. "All in favor of making Amanda town manager?"

"Aye."

"Aye."

"Aye."

"Aye." Carter, Lincoln, Hudson and Gage chimed in without hesitation.

"Aye," Nate said. "Amanda, congratulations. You're hired."

"My first order of business is going to be to make all future votes confidential," Amanda said. "What if one of you had wanted to vote no?"

"I would have thumped him," Carter said cheerfully. "Eat up. I want to start gutting your kitchen this morning. Can you guys do without me at the mill for a couple of hours?" he asked Lincoln.

"Yeah, I think we can make that work today. We need to talk about securing another contract and hiring some more men soon, though."

"Sounds good."

When the meal was over, they returned through the rain to number twenty-three, where they peeled off their wet outer things and surveyed the kitchen and dining room. Carter had already taken down the wall between the two rooms and with the help of his brothers had wrestled the old appliances outside. Now there remained a mess of cabinets and countertops to tackle. He fetched his crowbar and a pair of gloves for each of them.

Soon they fell into a rhythm of work. Carter pulled the cabinets and countertops out from the wall, and Amanda lugged the pieces outside to the Circle, where they were accumulating trash for a dump run. An hour or so later, the rain tapered off to a fine mist, and they were down to one stubborn corner cupboard.

"I'm going to run upstairs a minute and freshen up," Amanda said. "Be right back."

"Sure thing." Carter kissed her before turning back to his task. A few moments later, when he heard a buzz of a phone, he looked around to locate it. He had his own on vibrate in his pocket, but he spotted Amanda's on a nearby windowsill. Someone named Melissa was calling, but as he moved toward it the call cut off.

Melissa. Wasn't that her sister?

Now a text appeared on the screen. Carter picked up the phone. It was locked, but he could read the texts as they flashed across it.

What's your new address again?
Hello?
Address, Amanda!

Sending you a present.

Stop playing hard to get.

A cute emoji followed that last text.

Carter thought about what he knew of the sisters' relationship. It had been damaged by their father's actions and Melissa's tendency to blame everything on their mother, but Amanda had said she wished they were closer. It seemed like a good sign that Melissa wanted to send a present.

The phone buzzed, surprising him. Melissa was calling again.

Carter answered it. Amanda would be back from the bathroom soon, and he knew she wouldn't want to miss her.

"Hello?"

"Hello?" a woman's voice said. "Who's this?"

"This is Carter, Amanda's friend. She'll be back in a minute. Can you hold on?"

There was a silence, then, "Hi, Carter," the woman said. "I'm Melissa, Amanda's sister."

"She's told me about you."

Another pause. "I hope it was all good things." She sounded like she thought it might not have been.

"She said she misses you."

"Really?"

"That's right. Like I said, she'll be back in just a minute." He could still hear her moving around upstairs.

"Look, I've been in Paris these last few years. I'm trying to send her a present and don't have her current address. Could you give it to me?"

"Sure thing." Carter gave the address of the PO box in town, since mail wasn't delivered directly to the Ridge.

"I was hoping for a street address," Melissa said when he was done.

"We're forty-five minutes out of town. No one delivers here," he explained.

"Is that still Chance Creek?"

"Elliott Ridge, actually, but we're in Chance Creek County."

"Sounds like heaven."

Carter wasn't sure if she was being sarcastic. Had an edge crept into her voice? "I think I hear Amanda. Just a second."

"You know what, Carter? I've got to run, but I'll call her again soon. Thanks for the address."

"But—" The call cut off. Melissa was gone.

"What are you doing?" Amanda demanded, coming into the room behind him.

"Carter? Why do you have my phone?" Panic propelled Amanda across the floor to snatch it out of his hand.

"I…"

She swiped at the screen and looked at her messages. "You were talking to Melissa?"

"Your phone kept buzzing. I saw it was Melissa and remembered her name. I thought you'd be back any second, so I answered it." He shoved his hands in his pockets and shrugged.

"What did she want?"

"Just to know your mailing address so she could get a package delivered… Amanda, are you all right?"

He stepped toward her, but she stepped back, one hand outstretched to stop him. She'd had time now to read the texts herself, and she felt dizzy.

"You told her the address here?"

"The PO box in town."

So Melissa still didn't know exactly where she was, but anyone at the post office could clear up the matter and tell her—or Buck, if he had listened in on that call somehow—where she actually lived.

"Amanda," Carter said again. "What is it?"

"I… I'm not on good terms with Melissa at the moment. I wish you hadn't talked to her behind my back."

"I wasn't trying to talk to her behind your back," Carter said reasonably. "You told me you rarely heard from her, and it seemed like Melissa was trying to fix that."

Amanda told herself to stop overreacting before he got suspicious and started asking questions she didn't want to answer. Melissa was in Paris, after all. Buck didn't have any access to her—or her phone.

"You're right," she managed to say. "I'd better call her. I'm sorry I snapped at you." She went up on tiptoe and kissed his cheek. "My family is complicated."

"Isn't everyone's?"

She nearly sighed with relief when he accepted her apology and returned to work. "I'll be back in a minute," she called to him and went out on the front porch. She put the call through, but Melissa didn't answer, so when her voice mail came on, Amanda said, "Don't you dare tell Dad where I am if you hear from him. Don't tell *anyone* where I am. Got it?"

She hung up, more frustrated than she could say, determined to get rid of the painting as soon as humanly possible. How on earth could she fetch it without Carter knowing? And how could she take it anywhere when she didn't have a car of her own?

Maybe it was time to tell Carter everything.

Amanda thought it over but decided against it. If Carter didn't know about the painting, he couldn't be accused of being an accomplice if she was caught with it. After all, it was stolen property.

She was on her own as far as returning it was concerned, and that was nothing new, she told herself. She was used to being on her own.

When she went back inside, Carter was finishing up.

"Finally," he said, lifting the corner cabinet off the wall. "I thought I'd never get this one down. I'll haul it out to the Circle and keep going to the mill. I'm already late. Meet you at the town hall for lunch?"

"Sure thing. I'm going to grab a shower and then I'll head over to prepare the meal."

"Are you still mad?" he asked. "I shouldn't have answered your phone."

She could tell he wanted to reach for her, but she was glad when he didn't. She was too wound up to be close to anyone right now. "It's okay," she assured him, even if she wasn't sure it was. If her father contacted Melissa, she knew her sister would pass along what she'd learned.

How often did they talk these days?

Amanda didn't know. During the time her father lived with her, she'd never heard him talking on the phone with Melissa. She supposed they might have texted each other. The subject of her sister simply hadn't come up.

Amanda was ashamed to admit she'd never broached it. She supposed she hadn't wanted to share him once she'd had him to herself. If Melissa had called during the time he lived with her, of course she would have passed the phone to him so the two could talk. Melissa hadn't called, though, and her father hadn't asked about her.

Had the two been in touch since she left LA?

Her thoughts spun in circles as Carter edged past her with the cabinet. Once he was gone, she climbed the stairs slowly and undressed in the bathroom. The hot water soothed her a little, but she didn't come up with any answers and was still tense when she walked to the town hall.

She let herself into the building, veered left instead of right and slipped into the library, needing to breathe in the quiet peace of the place before she got to work preparing the meal. She walked among the half-empty stacks, wishing she could bury herself in cleaning and organizing the books. Libraries were places where sanity won out. You could trust librarians.

Amanda stilled.

Librarians.

She drew out her phone and brought up a search engine. The Chance Creek library was too small for her purposes, but the Billings library looked like a large, modern building, the kind of place where you could easily blend in. She could make up a reason to take Carter's truck to Billings tomorrow. On her way she could stop and walk up the Ridge from the far side of the settlement. That way she'd be able to fetch the painting and scoot back down to the truck with no one the wiser.

Amanda crossed quickly to the counter at the far end of the room. She'd often wondered if Carter's mother made her patrons check books in and out. There were drawers there with old office supplies in them, including an old-fashioned date stamp and ink pad that had long gone dry. Rummaging around, she found a roll of packing tape and a faded bubble mailer big enough to contain the painting. She tested several permanent markers until she found one that still wrote and added a pair of scissors to the pile for good measure. Now when she secured the painting, she could package it up in the mailer, label it with the Billings head librarian's name, drive to the Billings library and leave it somewhere near the circulation desk or back office where it would be easily found.

She'd include written instructions asking the librarian to report the stolen painting to the FBI tip line. As long as no one saw her leave the package, no one would be able to trace the painting to her. She'd have to look for cameras and be a little sneaky, but she was sure she could pull it off. Any librarian worth her salt would contact the authorities immediately and get the painting back where it belonged. Librarians believed in the public good. They knew right from wrong. Once the painting was in its rightful place, Buck wouldn't have any reason to come after her.

And it would be safely out of her father's hands, too.

It was the best she could come up with.

"Amanda."

She whirled to find Gage had entered the library and shut the door behind him.

"Y-yes?" She put a hand to her heart. "You scared me. Can I help you? Need a book?" she added. She checked the time. "I'll be getting lunch ready in a minute."

"Lincoln needs a manual."

"A manual? For what?"

He crossed the room to a shelf unit she hadn't tackled yet. Amanda came out from behind the counter and followed him, leaving the little pile of supplies she'd gathered behind.

"Here's his collection." The stack of tattered volumes had been shoved any which way onto the shelf instead of organized. "Mom made him keep them here because he kept throwing them out, then complaining when he couldn't find the information online. Some of the vehicles and machinery in the graveyard are pretty old."

"I didn't even know what those were."

Gage rifled through them and pulled one out. "Here it is. Didn't believe him when he said it would be."

"You make a habit of that, don't you? Not believing your brothers." Amanda shut her mouth with a snap. That wasn't any of her business.

"Because I'm not cheering them on about resurrecting the town?"

"That's right. You don't think Carter can do it."

"You're right, I don't. And now I've got to spend the rest of the year watching him bust his ass for a lost cause."

"Or you could help." She held her ground when he turned to level a sharp look in her direction. "You're here anyway, right? A year is a year whether you're sitting on your butt doing nothing or accomplishing something worthwhile. Why not pitch in? You'd get to spend time with your brothers. Or don't you want to do that?"

His expression darkened. "You don't know what you're talking about." He walked out of the library, and the door swung shut behind him with a decided click.

"SHOULD I SLEEP upstairs or downstairs tonight?" Carter asked Amanda later that evening.

"Upstairs."

Carter bit back a smile. Good. She'd seemed pretty ticked off about him answering her phone earlier. He was afraid he'd be back on the living room floor.

"Carter," she said and stopped, as if not sure how to proceed with what she wanted to say. She trudged up the stairs.

"Yeah? Everything all right?" he asked as he followed her, turning into the bedroom when they reached the top.

"You're going to think I'm such a girl." She opened a drawer in the dresser and busied herself with tidying clothes that were already tidy as far as Carter could tell.

"I like that you're a girl." He came to put his hands on her shoulders and gave her a little massage.

"But tomorrow you're going to regret it."

"Am I?" He doubted that. He swept his hands down to rest on her waist, appreciating the curvy wonderfulness of her.

"I need to go to Billings."

He paused. "Why?" It was a workday, and he'd already spent too much time away from the mill. He wasn't sure he was comfortable taking a whole day off.

"Because I need to get my hair done. I'm sorry—I like this whole ghost-town way of life, but there aren't any salons in Chance Creek County that I'd trust with this." She twisted a strand of her hair.

Carter hadn't expected she would be so particular, but then women could be funny about that kind of thing. "I'll talk to Lincoln, I guess. See if he minds me skipping out on them again." He didn't want to set a bad example for the mill workers. They were all supposed to be working together to make sure they hit their deadlines.

"Oh, no. No, no, no." She turned and wagged a finger at him, dislodging his hands from her waist. "You are not coming along for salon day. I'm going to get my nails done and enjoy myself. I'll be home at the end of the afternoon, and I swear I won't go back for a month."

She was going to Billings once a month? For a haircut? "O-okay." Seemed like a lot of fuss to him.

"Don't look at me like that. You think this whole package just happens naturally? Well, it doesn't. It takes a lot of work."

"If you say so." Carter gathered her close again. "I'll miss you," he grumbled into her hair. "I like having you around."

"I'll miss you, too."

"You can take the truck."

"Thanks. I was hoping you'd say that. I need to look around soon for one of my own."

"I'll put some feelers out, but you can use mine for as long as you like. Now go get ready and come to bed."

He crawled under the covers with her a few minutes later and groaned with satisfaction when she burrowed against him, fitting her curves to the hard planes of his body. Losing himself in exploring her, he made love to Amanda more than once before they collapsed together, breathing hard, gloriously spent. He didn't know when he fell asleep, but by the time he woke up, Amanda was dressed and ready for her trip to Billings. She bent over the bed to give him a long, slow kiss, which served as a reminder of all the fun they'd had the night before.

"I'll be home in time to make dinner," Amanda said. "Can you handle lunch? I left several shepherd's pies in the refrigerator and instructions on how to heat them."

"Sure thing. Have a good time." He sat up and stretched.

"I will." She waved and headed downstairs. A minute later, he heard the engine of his truck fire up. He got out of bed and crossed to a window to watch it trundle down the road and disappear around the bend. The house seemed empty without her cheerful presence. As he looked around the master bedroom, he wondered how he ever thought he'd be happy living here by himself. Number twenty-three was Amanda's house now, but he hoped like hell someday it would be his again, too.

He was getting ahead of himself, though.

He took a shower and rustled up some clean clothes, then walked to the town hall and found Lincoln in the kitchen.

"Heard your truck a little while ago," Lincoln said. "Thought you went out somewhere."

"Amanda went to Billings. Hair, nails and stuff." He opened the refrigerator and checked out the pies. A note on the door told him how long to heat them and the temperature to set the oven. He'd just have to nip back from the mill early so they were ready when everyone else got here.

"I had a girlfriend like that once. High maintenance."

"I didn't think Amanda was like that, but maybe she

is. Maybe I don't know her enough to predict what she'll do."

"You're getting to know her pretty well, seems like."

Carter heard what he didn't say. That maybe he was moving too fast. He'd brought a stranger home to the Ridge, moved her into a house and started renovating, and now he was sleeping with her. Of course, Lincoln didn't know he was sleeping with Amanda, but Carter had a feeling his brothers had guessed as much.

"I like her," he announced. "She's a good one, Lincoln, even if she wants to get her hair done at a particular salon."

"Sounds serious," Lincoln joked.

"I think it might be," Carter said, surprising himself. He thought he'd wanted to keep that to himself. "I can picture her in my life long term. I can imagine having a family with her. That's why I offered her the deal for my house in the first place." He pulled a carton of eggs out of the refrigerator and shut the door, feeling overexposed. He hadn't meant to divulge any of that.

"That is serious." Lincoln leaned against the counter. "But why shouldn't you be thinking about starting a family? You're in your thirties. If you're going to settle down, now is the time for it."

"What about you? You ever think about a wife? Kids?"

"Sure, I do. Now that I'm home, I think about it a lot. I just need to find someone." Lincoln put a pan on the stove and took the eggs from Carter's hands. "Why don't you start some toast?"

"I've got a hot tip for you." Carter went to fetch the bread. "If you want a woman, go to the airport." Someone snorted behind him. Gage had entered the kitchen. "Breakfast won't be ready for a while," Carter told him.

"Thought I'd get a head start this morning. Did you have any luck with that edger?" Gage asked Lincoln.

"Not yet," Lincoln said. "I'll try again today."

"Need a second pair of hands?"

Lincoln's eyebrows shot up at Gage's unexpected offer. "Definitely. That would be great. Carter, can you take the lead at the mill this morning while Gage and I fix that piece of equipment?"

"Of course." Why was Gage offering to help all of a sudden? Carter knew better than to ask. So, apparently, did Lincoln. The three of them finished preparing the meal and brought it out to the table without saying another word.

Hudson and Nate joined them, and they all dug into their food. Carter's phone buzzed in his pocket. He pulled it out and saw he'd received an email from Matt Wren, who worked at the county office.

"Oh, hell," Carter said when he read the message.

"What is it?" Gage asked. All of his brothers tensed, ready for action.

"The subdivision request. Matt says it looks like it's going to be denied." He held up a hand to forestall their comments and called the man, grateful he'd made a friend in the office. Otherwise, he wouldn't have known about the outcome until it was a done deal. "Matt?" he said when the man picked up. "What's going on?"

"Hang on," Matt said tersely. All Carter could hear was his breathing for thirty seconds or so. Then sounds of traffic filtered through the line. "Okay, I'm outside now. I shouldn't be talking to you."

"What's happening?"

"Everything was lined up to go. Rod Stevenson was all ready to sign off on your request. You guys did a good job with all the paperwork and reports."

"Thanks."

"Then Blake Warrington came in for an appointment."

"With Rod?" Carter couldn't believe it. "Do those two know each other?"

"Rod worked with Warrington quite a bit when he first arrived in town. Helped walk him through the approval process for getting infrastructure extended to his resort. Wouldn't have called them friends before now, but they were pretty chummy when Warrington left Rod's office yesterday."

"What do you think happened?"

Matt didn't answer his question right away. "I can't say much, Carter, because my job is on the line, but if you have any influence, now's the time to use it." He hung up.

Carter swore and shoved his phone into his pocket.

"What did he say?" Nate asked.

"Warrington got to Rod Stevenson at the planning office. Rod's going to turn us down."

"He can't do that," Lincoln said. "What did Warrington do? Bribe him?"

"Matt wouldn't say, but something like that." An idea occurred to him. "Maybe Rod decided to invest in Warrington's resort."

"So what do we do?"

"I don't know. Matt said we should use our influence."

"What influence?" Lincoln asked.

"That's the million-dollar question, isn't it?" Carter asked.

DRIVING OFF WITH Carter's truck for the day had been easy. Fetching the painting was turning out to be a nightmare.

After driving down Elliott Way and turning onto the county highway, Amanda kept going until she estimated she was past the settlement, then parked the truck by the side of the road like she'd planned. In a perfect scenario, she'd have found somewhere to hide it, but there weren't any side roads nearby and she didn't know the terrain well enough to think of an alternative. Besides, she needed to move fast. The men would all be at breakfast and then would go to the mill, except Gage, who seemed to keep to his parents' place most of the time. She needed to scurry up the Ridge to the mine, grab the painting and race down before anyone was the wiser.

If only it were that easy.

It had rained overnight again. The forest was soaking wet, the loamy ground sodden underfoot. The day wasn't exactly hot, but it was humid, and between the dripping trees and the damp terrain, she was getting wetter by the minute as she trudged uphill.

Even though she was far past the area where the mill and bunkhouses lay, she was still afraid someone might take a notion to go for a walk out this way. She'd never been over on this part of the ridge before and spent so little time with the mill workers, she didn't know their habits. All she could do was hope she wouldn't run into anyone and keep going.

A half hour later, she was cursing the day she'd decided to move the painting out of her house. If she'd left it in her bathroom, it would have been easy enough to collect it this morning, hop in the truck and be on her merry way. The briars that dotted the slope lower down thickened out to blanket it up here, and thorns tore at her clothing as she tried to push her way through them. Each time she thought the going might get easier, it seemed to get worse, but she felt confident she must be high enough on the Ridge that the mine should be somewhere around here.

All she had to do was find it.

Amanda took a break, leaned against the side of a pine tree and caught her breath. She was sweaty, and her T-shirt was streaked with dirt in several places. Thorns had scratched her bare arms, drawing blood. She'd have to clean up somewhere in Billings before going to the library or she'd attract attention to herself no matter how big it was. She let out a sigh and closed her eyes, willing her heart to slow down.

Now that she wasn't thrashing through the under-brush, she realized how quiet it was up here. Birds calling to each other brought a smile to her lips. Oh, to be one of them with nothing more pressing on her mind than finding her next meal.

A rustle behind her startled Amanda. She opened her eyes and spun around, grabbing the pine tree's trunk to steady herself. She ducked down, keeping one arm around it, and scanned the hillside. Was someone else up here? Had Carter followed her somehow?

Was it Dennis?

Amanda straightened. She didn't have to be afraid of an old man.

Another rustle sounded, and she dug her fingers into the pine's bark. "Dennis?" she called softly. "Is that you?"

She held her breath, heart beating hard. After a long moment, the noise came again from a thicket of bushes about twenty feet away.

"Carter?" Amanda asked, her voice coming out more like a croak. When there still wasn't an answer, anger boiled up inside her. Someone was playing tricks, and she didn't like it.

She stooped, grabbed a rotting chunk of wood from the ground nearby and hurled it at the bushes. It would serve whoever was hiding there right if she hit him.

A black bear exploded from the thicket, its massive body a blur as it hurtled past her and disappeared down the slope. Amanda shrieked and dropped to her knees. Cowering behind the tree trunk, she panted for air until she realized the danger was past and the bear was gone.

Still, she clung to the tree for long minutes afterward, searching for the strength to stand.

Carter had mentioned bears, but she never thought she'd actually see one.

Now Amanda realized how stupid that was. Where did she think bears hung out, if not in the woods?

When she finally was able to get to her feet again, she braced herself against the trunk for a few more minutes before pushing off and cutting sideways across the ridge. Alert to every noise, she pressed on, telling herself the bear had to be far down the slope by now.

She was beginning to fear she'd never find the mine and would have to return to the settlement with some lame excuse for why she hadn't gone to Billings after all, when she stumbled into the clearing where it was located. Amanda blinked back tears of relief as she hurried to the outbuildings, which seemed to have slumped farther into the foliage since the last time she visited.

Poking her head gingerly into the last of them, she spotted the old desk and murmured a prayer of thanks that it was still standing. It must have expanded with the dampness of the air, however, because the drawer was stuck shut, and she had to apply all her strength before she could budge it an inch. Its squeal of protest made her let go and cower back, as if someone down in the settlement could hear her all the way up here. Laughing at her own timidity, she grabbed hold of the handle again and tugged.

It was stuck.

Amanda swore under her breath. She was losing precious time. She still had to get down the slope, package up the painting, drive all the way to Billings and find the library. After she left it there, she had to find a salon and get her hair and nails done before she could drive home.

She planted her feet on the rotting wooden floor and pulled with all her might. The drawer squealed again as it finally let go, opening enough for her to see the plastic bag in which she'd stored the painting.

Thank goodness it was still here.

She slid it out carefully, tucked it under her arm and shoved the drawer back in. It protested even louder this time, but she muscled it into place and checked the desk over to make sure she hadn't left any traces of her presence here. Satisfied, she turned to go.

She'd done the hard part, she told herself. From now on, everything would be smooth sailing. She had to hurry, though.

Amanda picked up speed as she went out the door—

And crashed into a man's arms.

CHAPTER 13

I F THEY COULDN'T sell the houses in the subdivision, they were sunk.

Carter pushed his breakfast around his plate until it went cold, then stood up, no longer hungry. He needed to go somewhere he could think. How on earth could he pressure Rod Stevenson to take their side?

"Meet you at the mill," he told the others. "I'm going to take a walk to clear my head."

"I'll meet you there later, too," Gage said. "Need to do something first."

"I thought you were going to help me with that edger," Lincoln protested.

"I will. Won't be long."

"Guess I'll clean up," Hudson said. He went into the kitchen.

"Don't you think you should stay so we can figure this out?" Lincoln asked Carter. "Sounds like we don't have much time."

"I think better on my feet. I'll find you at the mill in a half hour."

"All right." Lincoln grabbed his dishes and Carter's, too, to bring into the kitchen.

Carter went outside, his feet automatically taking him down the road past the lake to where it curved up the ridge. Three-quarters of the way up, he struck off on the path that went even higher to his favorite lookout. Last time he was here, Amanda was with him. He wished she was here now.

He took a seat on the edge of a ledge that overlooked the town. His dad used to find him here when he was young. They'd sit together companionably, surveying their kingdom, as his father had called it.

"Someday this will all be yours," his dad would say with a flourish. The thought of it had filled Carter with pride.

Now his chances to revitalize it and bring his parents home were slipping away. Selling houses in Lucy's Corner would have given them a quick way to raise the cash they'd need to make the balloon payment at the end of their loan. It might be possible to earn enough from collecting rent and fulfilling lumber contracts, but it wasn't a slam dunk. They might struggle to attract anyone to settle here if all they had were rental homes to offer. People would come and go rather than forming a stable community. Renting had worked when the mill employed everyone, but he wanted a more diverse economic base for the town now.

Should they offer Rod a piece of the Ridge? Was that how deals got done these days?

"Don't fall off."

"Hell!" Carter nearly did before he caught himself, lurched to his feet and moved away from the edge. "Dennis, what are you doing here?"

"Need to show you something."

"Show me what?" His close call made him angry, and it bugged him that anyone could sneak up on him without him knowing. When he was serving in the military, that could have gotten him killed.

Dennis led the way down a path Carter quickly recognized. He hadn't been to the old tree fort since he came home. Curiosity won out as his anger ebbed away. He should have shown it to Amanda when they'd taken their tour of the Ridge. He bet she'd like it.

"Is the fort still here?" he asked. The elements might have destroyed it over the years.

Dennis merely grunted. He kept going, Carter following him.

"Look."

Carter's anticipation at seeing one of his childhood haunts fell away as he took in the sight ahead of him. The fort was still there, but that wasn't what stopped him in his tracks.

"Someone's been sleeping here."

"That's right." Dennis nodded.

"Who?"

The older man shrugged. "Thought you should know."

"Definitely. I'm glad you told me about it." Carter moved forward to take a closer look. The old tree fort consisted of several levels, the lowest boxed in to form a little covered room. The other levels were open-air lookouts. To a child, the closed-in room had seemed high up in the air, but as a grown man, he could see right through the open doorway to where a sleeping bag was bunched in one corner along with a couple of water bottles and empty food wrappers. "Could that have been here before we came home?"

Dennis shook his head. "Wasn't here last week. It's recent. I'd bet someone slept here last night."

Prickles of awareness danced across Carter's neck and shoulders. "Where is he now?"

"That's the question, isn't it?" Dennis said.

Carter's phone buzzed in his pocket. He pulled it out and answered it.

"Why's your truck parked here on the highway?" Gage asked.

"What?"

"Your truck. It's on the side of the road about a quarter mile from Elliott Way."

"Where's Amanda?"

"Not in it."

Fear shot through him. "Someone's been sleeping at the ridge. In the old fort." He filled in Gage on what Dennis had found.

"You think they're connected?"

"I don't know, but I don't like it. Amanda is supposed to be in Billings." He'd told his brothers that at breakfast time.

"She didn't get far. Question is, did she plan to go at all?"

A new fear twisted Carter's gut. Could Amanda have lied about why she was here all along? Had she been playing him for some reason?

No. He couldn't believe that of her, and besides, it didn't make sense. What could she possibly gain by sneaking around at the Ridge? She couldn't run off with an empty house. Couldn't steal lumber when the mill was full of workers. There wasn't any silver left in the mine.

"Maybe she needed a pit stop and just ducked into the woods," he said, but that didn't ring true. Amanda was a city girl. She'd have turned around and driven back if she needed a bathroom.

"Maybe whoever was camped in the fort flagged her down and lured her out of the truck," Gage said.

Carter swallowed. He didn't like that idea.

"I'll start walking up the ridge from here," Gage said.

"I'll cut over and come down," Carter said. "Call the others. Tell them to come and look, too."

"You carrying?"

Carter knew Gage was asking if he was armed. "No," he said, cursing himself. "Didn't think I needed to."

"I'm not, either," Gage said.

"Tell the others," Carter said again. "I'm going to look for her." Nate, Lincoln and Hudson could stop at their parents' house to fetch weapons from the gun safe. There'd never been a reason to be armed growing up at the Ridge. Not unless they were heading out for a hunting trip.

"Amanda was going to Billings, but she stopped a quarter mile down the road," he relayed to Dennis. "We're going to look for her."

Dennis lifted the edge of the dusty shirt he wore and drew a Glock out of his shoulder holster. "Take this."

Carter tried to hide his shock.

"Been out here alone for over a decade." Dennis's voice grew rough. "I've seen things on the Ridge. I ain't stupid."

"Guess not." Carter took the pistol gratefully and set out at a loping run.

"Check the mine," Dennis called after him.

Carter slowed again. "The mine?"

"Only reason to climb the Ridge."

He was right, Carter supposed, but why the hell would Amanda want to go there? There was nothing of value left in it or in the nearby outbuildings, if that was where she was going.

His mind went to Blake Warrington. Could she be working for him in some capacity? Could she be headed straight up and over the ridge to his property?

That didn't make sense, either. If she wanted to report to him, she could simply call him—or drive around to his side. There was no reason to hike over rough terrain.

He continued to scan the woods around him as he raced onward. He'd nearly reached the edge of the clearing where the mine was located when he felt the vibration of his phone in his pocket again. He pulled it out, slowing his pace as the trees thinned. It was Nate this time—he'd sent a message to all of them.

Went by the lake. Didn't see anything. Heading for the mine.

Carter stopped at the edge of the trees and sussed out the situation. Nothing was moving that he could see.

His phone vibrated again.

Walking straight up from town hall, Lincoln texted. *Nearly to the mine.*

No one's seen Amanda at the mill. I'm halfway up the ridge now, Hudson texted.

Near the top, Gage told them. *No sign of her here.*

She had to be up here somewhere, Carter thought. Where else could she have gone? He could see the mine, but there was no sign of Amanda.

He eased to his left, staying within the treeline, edging toward the entrance to the mine and the nearby outbuildings. Was Amanda exploring them? Making use of them in some way?

He'd told her how dangerous those buildings were.

A screeching wail sounded from one of the buildings stopped Carter in his tracks, giving him shivers up and down his spine. It wasn't a human sound. At first he thought it might be a wounded animal, but as his brain tried to make sense of it, he realized he'd heard it before. Humidity could swell doors and windows in old houses. When you tried to open them, they made the most unearthly noises.

A rustle in the bushes nearby announced someone approaching.

"What the hell was that?" Lincoln hissed, picking his way quickly toward him through the scrub.

"Not sure," he whispered back. "Something in one of the outbuildings, I think." Maybe Amanda was in there after all.

They both thought a moment, Carter trying to remember what was in those places. He hadn't been in any of the outbuildings since he was a teenager.

"That desk," Lincoln said. "In the overseer's building. Nate wanted to bring it down to the house and fix it, remember?"

Carter did vaguely remember that. They'd been adolescents, Nate proud of his growing abilities in their grandfather's woodworking shop. He'd been crestfallen when their father pointed out the desk was built right into the wall. There was no way to rescue it without destroying it.

"Maybe someone's trying to open a drawer," Lincoln said.

Carter craned his neck but couldn't see anything inside the building. "I'm going to get closer. Tell the others what we heard and where we are."

Lincoln got busy with his phone. "What if Amanda is just exploring?" he asked. "We're all going to feel like assholes if we scare her to death."

"Then we'll apologize and have a good laugh about it. Don't forget, there's someone else up here. Whoever slept in the tree fort last night." They were talking too much. "We'd better stick to hand signals from now on. Text the others and let them know."

Lincoln nodded. Carter passed him and kept going as quietly as possible, which meant his trek through the edge of the forest took longer than he wanted it to.

A second groan came from the outbuilding, an almost comically loud sound. Now that he had remembered the desk, he could almost picture Amanda struggling to open its drawer. What did she hope to find in there?

A treasure map? Sprinkles of silver?

Carter struggled not to laugh, the whole situation suddenly striking him as absurd. There were five highly trained military men ranged around this clearing, ready to charge in and tackle an enemy. Lincoln was right; they were going to look pretty dumb when it turned out Amanda was just satisfying her curiosity about the place.

Of course, that didn't account for the stranger who'd slept in their tree fort last night.

Carter hesitated. Should he cut straight across the clearing and confront Amanda? Or would he scare her to death?

He decided to stick with his first plan. He kept moving quietly, picking his way around until he made it to the far side of the outbuilding. From this angle, nothing blocked his view of the front door. As soon as Amanda emerged, he could step forward, and she'd see him, too.

"Finally," he heard someone say distinctly. That was definitely Amanda in the building. The squealing sound came again. Was she closing the drawer?

Carter tensed. Time to show himself—

Hell.

Who was *that*?

Carter stilled again just in time to avoid revealing his presence.

A man stepped out of the shadowy interior of the next building. Amanda emerged blinking into the sunlight.

Right into his arms.

"WHERE'S MY PAINTING?"

"Dad?" Amanda struggled to understand how her father had tracked her to an abandoned silver mine on Elliott Ridge.

"Is that it?" He grabbed for the plastic shopping bag that held *Afternoon in Sunshine and Shadow*, but she snatched it back.

"What are you doing here?"

"What the hell do you think I'm doing here?" There was no trace of the amiable man who'd sponged off her for three months in Los Angeles. Her father was furious.

"I thought you were on the run! I was worried about you!"

Her father's face twisted into a scornful sneer. "Not worried enough to call me." He took a step toward her.

"I thought Buck might be able to trace a call." Amanda stepped back. "You told me to get out of there! You said he was after me."

"I didn't tell you to take the painting!"

Amanda stared at him. Had Melissa ratted her out? "The painting? Is that all you care about? Buck nearly got me, Dad! He was breaking in. I had to climb out a window to escape." When her father rolled his eyes, she lost control. "He could have killed me!"

"Buck Bronson is in jail, Amanda. Where he's been for the last eleven years. You know that."

"But…" She gaped at him. "You said he was free!" She couldn't take in what she was hearing. He'd lied to her?

"Do you always believe everything you hear? You're a grown woman, Amanda. You should know better."

"You're my father!"

"And I told you what you needed to hear to get you out of that apartment. You shouldn't have come home early. Another ten minutes and I'd have been gone. Everything would have worked just fine if you weren't such an interfering brat. Give me the painting."

"No." She didn't understand what was going on, but she knew better than to do that. Her father couldn't be trusted with it.

"Amanda," he warned.

"No!"

"Oh, for god's sake." He reached behind his back and pulled out a pistol. Pointed it at her. "I don't have time for games. Hand it over. Now."

CARTER WAS SURPRISED to hear Amanda call the stranger "Dad." But when the man pulled a Springfield XD out of the waistband of his pants, you could have knocked him over with a feather. Amanda had confessed her father was an art forger, but from her story, it was her dad's partner who was the violent one. She'd made her father sound like a victim, not the kind of stone-cold criminal who could point a weapon at his own daughter.

He heard a soft footstep beside him. "It's me," Lincoln murmured. "That's her dad? Now what do we do?"

Carter wasn't sure. Normally he'd say take the shot when it came, but even if one of them could target the stranger without hurting Amanda, he couldn't fathom doing so in front of her like that.

"Whatever it takes to get Amanda out of this," he whispered back. She came first in all his calculations. Her shock and fear were apparent, and it took all his strength to stay where he was. He couldn't move without giving himself away, but Dennis's Glock was in his hand, and he was ready to do what it took to save her.

A glance over his shoulder told him Lincoln had edged away. He knew without being told that his other brothers were fanning out around them, hidden for now among the trees and buildings. They were trained for this, he told himself. It was five against one. Nate or Hudson would have handed Gage a weapon by now. Amanda's father had the upper hand at present—he was standing too close to her for any of them to get a clear shot—but he'd make a mistake sooner or later. That's when they would get him.

Please, he found himself praying, to what or whom,

he didn't know. *Please keep her safe.*

If anything happened to the woman he loved, he didn't know what he'd do.

THIS TIME WHEN her father grabbed for the painting, Amanda let him take it. What else could she do with a gun pointed at her forehead?

She was shaking, choking down the nausea that threatened to overwhelm her.

Her father—

He had a gun—

He was pointing it at her.

When he grabbed her arm, she shrieked. He spun her around, tugged her wrists together and bound them with something she couldn't see. Something plastic and sharp-edged.

A zip tie?

Had he come prepared for this?

He gripped her bicep. Amanda dug in her heels as he tried to drag her into the forest.

"Take the damn painting. You don't need me." He'd never needed her. He'd made that crystal clear. He'd come to LA in the first place only because she was useful to him. She'd saved him three months' rent, and in exchange he'd tangled her up in a crime. She could have been home right now, living her life, safe and happy—

No, not happy.

She hadn't been happy until she came here.

Amanda struggled again. Tried to break free.

"Quit it. You're my insurance policy to get out of here." Her father pressed the gun to her temple with his free hand and reached to fish in her pants pockets, the plastic bag dangling from his wrist. He found her phone and tossed it away. Found Carter's keys.

"Handy you brought me a getaway vehicle."

Amanda wondered how he'd gotten here. Had he hitched a ride? Walked all the way from town?

She tried again. "If you leave me here, you'll be able to move faster."

"Shut up. We're going to move fast." As if to prove his point, he shoved her forward, past the other outbuildings and straight into the forest. Amanda stumbled along, trying to keep on her feet, not wanting to cooperate but afraid of what would happen if she didn't. Dying was bad enough. Being shot by her own father—

The edge of the pistol's barrel grazed her temple every few steps as they covered the rough ground together. As they began their descent, she tried to come up with a plan to get away. She imagined tripping her dad and running away through the woods, but with her hands tied behind her back, she knew she'd fall flat on her face.

Would he kill her?

Amanda didn't know, and that was worse than anything else.

This snarling stranger wasn't someone she recognized. He seemed pressed to his limit, almost feverish in his talk and actions. She'd never dreamed she'd fear violence from her father, but there was something off about the way he was behaving. A brittleness to him she hadn't seen before.

She had to keep her wits about her and wait for the right opportunity, she told herself, but the farther they went down the hillside, the more her terror grew. Her dad was moving quickly, slipping and sliding down the steep slope, dragging her along with him. The minute he had her in Carter's truck, she'd be lost.

Amanda tried to slow their pace, but her father yanked her inexorably forward. She stumbled and went down hard on her knees, nearly pulling him down with her. He let go to keep his balance, and for one brief moment, she thought she had a chance. She surged to her feet again, darted forward two steps, tripped and went head over heels. Her father was on her in a moment, pulling her upright again, swearing up a storm.

His hand gripped her bicep hard as he marched her downhill, striding so fast Amanda ran to keep up. She tripped again, and her father swore.

"Get moving, Amanda."

"I'm trying!"

The next time she stumbled, her father struck his pistol against her head. The blow sent her staggering, woozy with pain and fear. Something warm and wet trickled down her forehead, puddling into her left eye. Blood, Amanda realized, trying unsuccessfully to blink it away.

"Dad!"

"Stop whining, or I'll give you something to cry about."

"Why are you doing this?" Worse than the pain was her shock at the casual way he'd hit her.

"Because I had one chance to get the life I deserve and you screwed it up, like you always do."

Like she always did? "What do you mean?"

"Why the hell do you think I got married in the first place? Because I loved your mother? Jesus, Amanda. Did you ever get a look at the two of us? You think we were meant to last anything more than a couple of weeks?"

They kept going, deep in the brambles now. As her father dragged her, thorns tore at her clothes and skin, her vision was clouded and she could barely keep her feet. They were moving so fast she could hardly think, let alone understand what he was saying. Her father was destroying her sense of herself as thoroughly as the briars were shredding her clothes.

"Your mom and I met on spring break. We had a good time. That was all it was supposed to be. We'd already gone our separate ways when she called me. Pregnant. I thought it was a joke."

"Dad!"

"Oh, I gave it my best shot. Marriage. Fatherhood." He made it sound like a joke. "The three of you always wanting more, more, more. What chance did I have to become the artist I knew I could be when I had to work all the damn time?"

"But—"

"Then Buck came along with his idea. I would have been rich if he wasn't so damn trigger happy. At least I had an excuse to disappear."

"He tried to kill us!"

"You survived." He brushed that off. "And I got a second chance. Or so I thought. Still had to pay the damn bills, even without you three. Still had to work. Got a job painting houses. Can you imagine that? Me, painting houses?"

"Work is work," she said. His grip was hard on her arm. She didn't know how she could stop their headlong flight down the Ridge.

"Work is work until you fall off a ladder and break your back."

Suddenly several things fell into place she hadn't allowed herself to see before. Her father's gauntness. The way he could paint for only a short period at a time.

All those vitamins.

Had they been vitamins at all?

They broke free of the brush. She knew they had to be getting close to the highway.

Had those pills been something else? Something stronger?

Something that might explain what was happening right now?

"Amanda Elizabeth Stakewell, move your ass!" her father bellowed, giving her a shove that nearly knocked her over. When she stumbled, he bashed the gun against her temple again, and she cried out. Tears blinded her along with the blood, but she could make out the highway now.

And there was Carter's truck. Her father would toss

her inside and drive her away.

Who knew what would happen then? He was out of his mind. High on something. Would they crash?

Would he dump her somewhere to die?

If she got into that vehicle, she'd never make it back to Elliott Ridge alive. She'd never see Carter again. Never know what might have happened—

In desperation, Amanda dug in her heels and ducked to avoid another blow. She twisted straight out of her father's grip. Raced away from him blindly toward a stand of trees. She needed a barrier between her back and his gun.

When the ground dropped beneath her, she stumbled straight into another thicket and cried out as thorny branches clutched at her clothes.

"Get back here!" Her father came after her.

Amanda fought her way through the brambles, heedless of the thorns ripping her skin. She had to get away. She needed to—

Amanda screamed when a huge black shape reared up onto its hind legs in front of her. She screamed again when an ear-splitting sound roared behind her and hot pain creased her scalp. The ground raced up to meet her, knocking the air right out of her lungs. She thrashed in the bushes. Where was the bear?

Where was her dad?

Which of them would kill her first?

Sounds crashed overhead, and Amanda fought to decipher them. Men shouting. Gunfire ringing out.

She huddled in the dirt, thorns scraping her scalp

and shoulders. Her hands were still tied behind her. Blood streamed into her eyes. Nausea filled her throat.

Her dad was going to get her.

Or the bear—

Amanda fought to keep conscious. Fought to push herself away from the commotion raging overhead.

As the world began to spin, she thought of Carter.

She would have liked to have more time with him.

Would have liked—

Everything went dark.

CHAPTER 14

C ARTER SAW RED the first time Amanda's father pistol-whipped her, but he kept her so close it was impossible to get a clear shot without possibly hitting her, too. Carter refused to take any chances where she was concerned, but sooner or later he was going to have to try something.

He'd followed as closely behind them as he dared as they slipped and slid down the hill toward the county highway. He knew his brothers were spread out around him, all of them waiting for the opportunity to take down the man who had Amanda hostage.

He'd seen her father take the plastic bag she'd brought out of the outbuilding. What the hell could that bag contain?

Drugs?

Cash?

And how had the man known where Amanda was, or that she'd go to the mine today?

More questions than answers.

One thing Carter knew: Amanda's dad had the look

of a man pushed to the edge. He was hopped up on something. Not in his right mind. Carter couldn't allow him to get Amanda into his truck. He edged closer but stilled when her father slowed again and looked over his shoulder. This wasn't the time to blow his cover, but the time was coming soon. As a last resort they'd have to confront the guy and hope their superior numbers convinced him to give her up.

But a desperate man could take desperate measures. Carter didn't want to risk that.

He lifted his pistol. Sighted on the man, but Amanda's father kept moving, and Amanda kept moving with him.

When she tripped and nearly pulled him down with her, then broke free for an instant, Carter dropped to one knee and took aim.

Before he could take the shot, her father lunged after Amanda and snatched her off the ground.

Carter lowered his weapon, stifling a curse.

Then they were on the move again.

He caught sight of Lincoln thirty feet away. His brother made the wavy motion with one hand that meant "better luck next time" and kept going. Where were the rest of his brothers?

Close by, he figured.

Carter tracked the stranger and Amanda, trying to get even closer. He risked being seen, but time was running out. They'd nearly reached the bottom of the ridge. His truck was parked on the road nearby. Amanda had his keys, which meant her father probably had them now. No way was he letting that man drive away with the woman he loved.

He caught sight of Lincoln again when his brother dropped to one knee and went still.

What had he seen—or heard?

Carter stopped, too, all senses alert.

After a moment that dragged out far too long, Lincoln relaxed. Got to his feet again.

What? Carter asked him with a gesture when his brother looked his way.

Lincoln gestured back with a sign Carter didn't remember.

What?

Lincoln signed again. Carter still didn't understand. Lincoln pointed at Amanda, as if to say that's where they needed to focus. Carter decided he was right. Whatever Lincoln had seen wasn't worrying him anymore. Carter didn't need to worry about it, either.

Come on, he willed Amanda's father as he edged closer. *Make a mistake, would you?* They were damn close to the highway.

Lincoln sighted on the man but pulled back a moment later, shaking his head with frustration. Her father still had Amanda hugged too closely to his body. And the damn trees were always in the way. Carter could feel himself losing concentration, and he couldn't allow that to happen.

Not now.

Not when Amanda's life counted on him getting this right.

"Amanda Elizabeth Stakewell, move your ass!" her father bellowed.

Amanda stopped, ducked and twisted straight out of his grip. Dashed toward a stand of trees. Carter's heart leaped as he lifted his pistol. She might just get away, he thought as he got her father in his sights. Hudson and Gage had to be over there somewhere.

Amanda screamed, lurching forward in the periphery of his vision.

Carter's finger rested on the trigger as he tracked the man racing after her.

"Get back here!" her father roared.

Almost had him…

Amanda screamed again.

A huge black shape reared up onto its hind legs in front of her. Carter jolted in surprise, then cursed himself. *Bear.* That's what Lincoln had been signing. Her father backpedaled, discharging his pistol wildly. Amanda pitched sideways.

Carter took his shot as gunfire rang out from several directions. The black bear roared its fury and confusion, fell back to all fours and galloped away.

"Hold your fire!" Gage shouted.

Carter was already on his feet. He raced toward the thicket where he'd seen Amanda last, thrashed through the bushes and found her tucked into a ball. Her face and shirt were drenched with blood, her clothing torn, her hair caught in the brambles.

"Amanda!"

He heard footsteps. His brothers running toward

him from all sides.

"You got him!" Hudson shouted. "He's down."

Carter barely heard him. Amanda's eyes were closed. Her face pale. She wasn't moving.

His heart plunged into his gut. "She's hit!" Carter felt for a pulse, found one, but it was ragged. "Call 911! Hurry!" He was dimly aware of Lincoln yelling into his phone.

"Elliott Ridge. You'll see a truck a quarter mile before the turnout. We're right in the trees—she's been shot!"

Lincoln dropped to his knees beside Carter. Tugged his T-shirt over his head, balled it up and pressed it to Amanda's scalp.

"Amanda." Carter cupped her chin. Wiped the blood off her temple and cheek as best he could. "Amanda, stay with me, honey. Stay with me."

She didn't respond.

Carter bent closer. "Amanda?"

"Ambulance is on the way," Hudson said.

Carter prayed it would come in time.

CHAPTER 15

S OMEONE HAD BEATEN her with a tire iron. Or a golf club. Or a baseball bat.

Amanda tried to swallow but found her tongue thick and her throat aching nearly as much as her head and shoulder did. She tried to open her eyes but immediately closed them again when the light caused her temples to throb.

"Hey, take it easy. It's okay," someone said.

A man.

A man—there'd been a man—her dad. He'd had a gun—

Hands restrained her when Amanda scrambled to get up off the ground. Her dad was going to shoot her—he was going to kill her.

"Shh. Amanda, it's okay. You're okay."

She finally got her eyes open enough to take in a clinical, white space. Medical equipment. Carter bending over her, trying to keep her in her bed.

"You're in the hospital," he confirmed. "You've been shot."

Shot?

Amanda's mind reeled, but she let him ease her back onto her pillows, grateful to see him. If Carter was here, she was safe.

"What happened?" she tried to say, but it came out an indeterminate sound.

"Bullet creased your scalp. You got lucky. A half inch lower, and you'd be done for. I'm sorry, honey. None of us could get a clear shot at your dad until the very end."

She'd been running, Amanda remembered. There'd been a bear—

No. That couldn't be right. But she couldn't martial her thoughts into any kind of order. She had glimpses of the forest. Thick trees. Brambles tearing at her clothes. Her dad forcing her ever onward toward Carter's truck.

"Dad?" she breathed. Was he still alive? Would he come after her again? All her terror came flooding back, and suddenly she couldn't find her voice.

"The sheriff has him."

Tears welled from her eyes and slid down her cheeks. She'd thought she was going to die. She'd thought she'd never see Carter again.

"Shh, it's all right," Carter said softly, smoothing her hair from her forehead. "I'm here with you." He took her hand, and Amanda clung to it.

"Don't leave," she managed to say. "Please don't leave. I'm sorry."

"Sorry?" Carter repeated. "Why should you be sorry?"

Because she'd brought danger to his door. Because her father could have killed him and his brothers. Why had she ever thought it was okay to stay at Elliott Ridge? She'd been so selfish.

"Selfish?" Carter asked, and she realized she must have said the word out loud. "Honey, you weren't the one running around the Ridge taking people hostage. I wish you'd come to me if you were in trouble, though. I would have helped you, no matter what you were mixed up in. You know that, right?"

Amanda felt the warmth of his tone and heard the care in his voice, but her brain stuck on that one phrase. *No matter what you were mixed up in.*

What did he think had happened back there at the Ridge?

And how had he known to find her there? How had he known she needed help?

"I didn't steal it." She tried to get up again, but Carter restrained her. "I swear. I didn't take it. My dad…" She snapped her mouth shut. Even now she found it hard to expose her father. They must have given her pain medication or maybe it was her throbbing head making it hard to keep her thoughts straight.

"Maybe that's my cue to enter this conversation," a man's voice said.

Amanda opened her eyes again. Who was that?

"I'm Cab Johnson, sheriff of Chance Creek County." A tall, barrel-chested man moved into view through the doorway. "Mind if I ask you a few questions?"

"She just woke up. She's too weak," Carter protested.

But Amanda knew there was no getting out of this now. "It's okay," she said faintly. She'd tried to do things her way. Had tried to undo a crime after it was committed, as if you could erase the past. Now it was time to pay the piper. To do things right. If she didn't, she'd keep putting Carter in danger.

As the sheriff positioned himself at the side of her bed, she pulled herself together, accepting a sip of water when Carter offered her a cup and allowing him to plump the pillows behind her.

"Do you know the man who assaulted you?"

"My father? Yes. Of course." She nodded and winced. It was becoming easier to form words, but it still hurt to move.

"Do you know why he was after you?"

"I had something he wanted." She wished she had more strength. Just forming the sentence took more energy than she seemed to possess, and her voice was so thin it was barely above a whisper.

"We found a painting in a bag at the scene. Was that what he was after?"

"*Afternoon in Sunshine and Shadow.* Yes." Was this really happening? Was she being questioned by a sheriff because her father had tried to kill her? Shame welled from deep inside her, a feeling that was all too familiar, but it was worse than it had ever been before. This time her father's crime felt personal. He'd lied to her. Used her. Come after her. Pointed a gun at her head.

She heard Carter expel a breath and knew he had to

be putting it all together. She'd told him her father had forged a painting once before.

"Does it belong to you?"

She shook her head, more gingerly this time. "It's part of a traveling exhibit. A Deloitte. It's worth a lot of money."

"Did you take it?"

She shook her head.

"Your father did?"

Amanda closed her eyes, and a tear slid down her cheek. She'd never again be able to pretend her father was a good man, the way she'd always done until now. She'd told herself it was Buck's fault her father had been involved with forgery. She'd thought he'd stayed away to try to keep his wife and daughters safe. That wasn't the case, though. He'd welcomed an excuse to get away from them—all of them.

He'd never even wanted her in the first place.

"How did you end up with the painting?"

"I found it among my father's things one night in LA, when I came home from a party much earlier than he expected me to. I called him to find out why it was there, and he told me…" She trailed off. How could she explain the twisted history that made her believe his threats about Buck? "He's done this before." She had to make them understand.

Amanda told the sheriff about the first time her father forged a painting. About his partnership with Buck and how it had all gone wrong when Buck shot the security guard.

"After Buck's attack on my father, and the fire at our house, I was terrified of him. I've always been afraid he'd get out of jail and come after us again. Dad guessed that. So when I called and told him I'd found the painting, he made up a story to get me out of my apartment long enough so he could come and get it. He said Buck was coming for it—for me. He told me to get out of there and then he hung up. He wanted me to run and leave the painting behind. I believed him, so when I heard someone at the front door, I did run. But I grabbed the painting first." She hung her head at her foolishness. "I didn't want Buck to get his hands on that masterpiece. I wanted to return it to the gallery before my dad got in trouble."

Cab made a note. "What made you come to Chance Creek?"

"I left my car at the airport in Las Vegas, then flew to several different places. I was afraid Buck could get access to my credit card statements somehow. I didn't think my flight destinations would show up there, but every time I rented a motel, I knew the location would show up on my bill. I thought if I could fly to some small town no one had ever heard of, I could find a rental situation where I could pay cash. I was in Wyoming by then. One of the flights I could book from there came to Chance Creek. I'd never heard of it. I figured no one would think to look for me here."

"But then your father showed up."

"Turns out Buck is still in jail," Amanda said dully. "Dad lied—about everything. The night I came home early from the party, he'd meant to leave without telling me. He must have run out to grab something from the store, thinking he had plenty of time, but I got home before he did. When I found the painting and called him, he did the only thing he could do—tried to scare me out of there so he could come back, take the painting and make his getaway."

"You said someone was at the door," Carter pointed out.

Amanda thought about it. What had she heard? The doorknob jiggling? Could it have been her father trying to scare her away?

"Maybe it was him," she said. "He told me if I'd come home ten minutes later, he'd already have been gone."

"I should tell you we looked into this Buck Bronson person when we found out your dad was tied to a previous art theft attempt. Turns out Buck was due to get out of jail this year, but he was killed by another inmate a few weeks ago."

"Did my dad have anything to do with that?"

Cab was already shaking his head. "Purely a prison dispute. Seems like Buck made some enemies over the years."

Amanda tried to take that in. She'd never have to worry about Buck coming after her—or anyone else in her family—again. Somehow she didn't feel relieved. She just felt… sad. She couldn't understand why he'd made the choices he had.

Carter leaned forward. "Yesterday, when Melissa

called, I told her where you were. Did she tell your father? Is that how he found you? He must have hopped on a plane right away."

Cab shook his head. "Amanda's father checked in to the Evergreen Motel two nights ago. He made a bit of a nuisance of himself asking around about you yesterday."

"How did he know you were in the area?" Carter asked.

"I called Melissa at breakfast two days ago—after she emailed. She got it out of me that I was in Chance Creek County. She just didn't know where I was staying," Amanda admitted. "She must have told Dad right away, and he got straight on a plane. When he couldn't track me down, he must have had her call back with that ruse about the present."

"Which I fell for," Carter said. "She asked for a street address, but I said no one delivered here. I gave her our PO box number instead." He thought a moment. "But I told her we were at Elliott Ridge. That's easy enough to look up."

Before Amanda could assure him none of this was his fault, Cab cleared his throat. "I should tell you that we have Melissa in custody, too."

"Melissa—in custody? Where? In Paris?" Amanda asked.

"At the Chance Creek County Sheriff's office."

"I don't understand. Melissa is in France."

"She told me she was calling from Paris," Carter echoed, then stopped. Shook his head. "Actually, what she said was that she'd spent the last few years there.

She didn't say she was there at the time."

"She arrived in Los Angeles about a month ago to take on a new job," Cab said. "Assistant event coordinator for the Warden Gallery."

Amanda gaped at him. "She... what?"

"Your dad needed someone on the inside to make the switch."

"But..." Words failed her. Melissa had participated in their father's crime?

She was shocked, but then she wondered if she should be. After all, Melissa had always taken her father's side when the past came up. Maybe she wasn't satisfied with the life she'd created any more than he was. Dancing careers tended to be short-lived.

"Sounds like your dad planned to follow her back to Europe as soon as they pulled off the heist." A wry smile tugged at Cab's mouth. "Your dad isn't talking much, but once your sister got going, she couldn't seem to stop. She told us she made the switch after hours, when she was supposed to be preparing for an upcoming event. She hid the original in a supply closet very few people used other than her. The next day during normal work hours, she ordered pizza and shared it around. When she took home the leftovers..."

"She smuggled the painting out in a pizza box? She could have damaged it!" Amanda was shocked all over again. Of course, she was one to talk; she'd carried *Afternoon in Sunshine and Shadow* halfway across the country in her carry-on bag.

"Your sister brought the painting straight to your

father, who was all packed up and ready to go. They went around the corner to pick up a few last things from the store, thinking they had plenty of time."

"And I came home from my party two hours early."

And ruined everything.

Again, as her father had made so clear.

Her heart gave a pang when she remembered what he'd said. He'd married her mother only because she was pregnant. He'd never wanted her.

"I should have known my sister was involved," she said dispiritedly, thinking about their first conversation after she arrived on Elliott Ridge. "She pretended to guess that I'd taken the painting. She said she knew me—I wouldn't leave a masterpiece behind for Buck to get. She had me completely fooled. I thought I was the one telling her that Dad was up to his old tricks again. She knew all along." And all that pretending about the present. It made Amanda's stomach twist to think of her sister trying to get her address.

Carter squeezed her hand as if he could read her thoughts.

Amanda turned her attention back to Cab. "Melissa found out about Elliott Ridge yesterday. Why didn't Dad show up then?"

"He did. He slept in our old treehouse last night," Carter said. "Dennis found his things this morning and came to find me. Then Gage came across my truck parked on the road. That's how we knew where to look for you."

"Thank God you did." She shuddered to think of

the gun in her father's hands. "He must have been waiting to catch me alone. If you hadn't stayed with me last night, he might have come for me then."

"You left without me in the morning," Carter said. "He saw his chance and took it."

"That's something I don't understand," Cab said. "Amanda, you took Carter's truck, drove off down the highway, parked just a little way down the road and went up the Ridge on foot. Why?"

"To get the painting." She figured he actually did know that but wanted her to say it in her own words. "I hid it in one of the outbuildings near the mine. I didn't want Carter or anyone else to see me going to get it."

"Even if Amanda's father saw her drive off, how'd he know to go to the mine to intercept her?" Carter asked.

"We found his rental car a mile or so down the road from where Amanda parked. It was tucked behind some trees on the side of the highway. You wouldn't have noticed it if you weren't looking," Cab told them. "Let's assume he parked it there and walked the rest of the way to the Ridge yesterday so you wouldn't spot him. Reconnoitered the place and then holed up overnight in your treehouse. Got up early to keep casing the joint. When he saw Amanda drive off this morning, he would have assumed she was going to town. Maybe he took off running after her thinking he could get to his car, follow the highway and catch up with her before she even reached it. For all he knew, she had the painting with her."

"If he was running after me, he might have seen me pull off the road, even from a distance," Amanda said. "At the very least, he would have come across the truck within a few minutes of me parking it."

"And then he followed you up the Ridge," Carter said.

"I never even heard him tracking me." Amanda stared up at the ceiling, utterly exhausted. "I did everything wrong."

"You didn't do anything wrong." Carter leaned closer. "Your father and sister are the ones who screwed up."

Shame overcame her as she realized soon everyone would know about the stolen painting. The news would spread just like it did the first time her father committed a crime. Chance Creek was a small town. Every time she went to the store or post office, people would stare and retell the story. They'd point and laugh. Or shift away when she came near.

Worse, she couldn't pretend anymore that Buck was the one who'd destroyed her happy childhood. Her father had chosen a life of crime—twice over.

He'd used her for cover—for a free place to stay. Put her in danger. Come after her to get his prize back.

And her sister—

Amanda found it even harder to believe what Melissa did. She'd conspired with their father to steal a masterpiece. She'd helped him track her down to take it back.

Had either of them ever cared about her at all?

Amanda turned away from Carter and curled up on her side, burying her face in her hands. The IV line tugged against her bandages, but she ignored it. She wanted to sink into the hospital bed and disappear.

"Amanda." Carter's fingers stroked her hair as her tears flowed silently. "It's okay. Everything's going to be all right."

She didn't know how he could say that. Her own family thought she was worthless. Disposable. All she'd wanted was a place to belong. Somewhere safe and calm. People to love.

What chance did she have for that now?

"That's enough for today," she heard Cab say quietly. "You'll stay with her?"

"I'll stay right by her side."

She heard the door close.

"I should have never told your sister where you were." Carter kept stroking her hair until her tears ran their course.

"It's not your fault," she finally managed to say.

He gently turned her toward him. "It's not yours, either. You tried to set things right, didn't you? Where were you taking the painting? Somewhere in Billings?"

"The library," she croaked, her voice rough from all her crying. She explained how she planned to address it to the head librarian with instructions to turn it over to the FBI. "No one would ever know where it came from," she said. "The painting would be returned, and no one would get hurt."

"I thought I lost you back there." He ran a finger

over her cheek to her chin. "I couldn't have stood that."

She nodded miserably. "I thought I lost you, too."

"I don't ever want to be apart from you again. Amanda, I love you," he said. "And I always will."

She heard his words, but she could barely take in their meaning. He loved her?

But how? She was such a mess.

"I love the way you feel in my arms," he told her, kissing her forehead. "I love the way you understood what I was trying to do with the Ridge and decided to pitch in to help." He kissed one cheek and then the other. "I love the way you saw the possibilities for number twenty-three. I love the way you didn't back down when Gage tried to scare you off. You're the kind of woman I always hoped I'd someday find, and I can't stand the thought of not getting to keep you close." He dropped a kiss on the end of her nose.

"My dad's a thief," she said. "A forger. He's a criminal. So is my sister."

"So we'll leave them off the guest list for the wedding." Carter shrugged. "I'm not in love with your dad—or your sister, Amanda."

Wedding? Amanda held her breath. What was he saying?

"I love you," he said again.

Amanda's heart overflowed with emotion. "I love you, too," she confessed.

"You do?" He cupped her chin and searched her gaze as she nodded, then groaned as he bent to kiss her on her mouth, softly at first and then more deeply.

Amanda wrapped her arms around his neck, wanting to hold him there forever, but he pulled back an inch. "Then I'm going to go ahead and ask you. I know it's crazy. I know it's too soon, but will you marry—"

"Yes!" Amanda surged forward and kissed him again. "Yes, I will." She wasn't going to let this chance at happiness slip away. She'd learned in the past twenty-four hours that you never knew what life was going to throw at you. Some surprises were good. Most weren't.

He wrapped his arms around her and buried his face into her hair. "I didn't even ask the whole question."

"Then ask!" She kissed his neck and the underside of his jaw, loving the taste of him, the feel of him in her arms. She'd thought she'd lost him twice today, once at the Ridge when her father pointed his pistol at her and again when she'd had to confess the sordid story of her family in front of him. Carter didn't care what her family had done, however. He could look past the mess of her life and still love her.

"Amanda Stakewell, will you marry me?"

"Yes," she said again.

Carter pulled back an inch. "There's something I have to tell you."

Amanda didn't think she could take any more bad news—Carter was looking too serious for it to be good. "What?"

"The subdivision was denied. I can't sell you number twenty-three for a dollar."

It took a moment for his words to sink in. "Where... will we live?" She hadn't expected that.

His smile was a little lopsided. "In number twenty-three," he said. "At least we will for as long as we own the Ridge. Don't think of it as losing a house so much as gaining a hundred and twenty more of them, since you'll be an Elliott soon and we'll have to retain ownership of them all. If we can't sell them, we'll just rent them out. It's how we always used to do things."

She nodded slowly.

"We won't let Warrington win," he promised her.

"Of course not."

"But if he does, I might want to move to South Carolina to be close to my folks."

"I can do that."

"You sure?"

"All I want is you. And that eight-foot kitchen island you promised me," she added.

He smiled. "You can have both, wherever we end up." He moved to take her in his arms. By the time a nurse rapped on the door and opened it, he was halfway in the hospital bed with her. Amanda laughed when she saw the look on the woman's face.

"Guess you're feeling better, Amanda." The nurse came to check her pulse as Carter slid back into his bedside chair and composed himself.

"I am." Although it still hurt to think of her father and sister and what they'd tried to do. It hurt to remember what her father had told her. He'd never wanted her—

But Carter wanted her. Amanda resolved to put her father and Melissa out of her mind. From now on, she'd concentrate on the people who did love her. She still had her mother. And Carter's big family. That would have to be enough.

"That's what we like to hear." The nurse moved around the room efficiently and noted something on Amanda's chart. "You're supposed to be resting, you know."

"I'll keep her quiet," Carter said.

And winked at Amanda.

Love surged through her, chased by desire. Amanda couldn't wait to be alone with him again.

There was another knock on the door, and it swung open again. Gage appeared.

"No more visitors. She needs to rest," the nurse admonished him.

"I won't stay long." He held the door until she'd gone. After closing it, he faced them. "Amanda, you doing all right?"

"I've been better," she said, "but I'll be fine."

"Glad to hear that."

"Amanda just agreed to be my wife," Carter said.

"Glad to hear that, too." If Gage was surprised, he hid it well. "I won't keep you long. I imagine you've got a lot to talk about."

Carter smiled at her. Amanda had a feeling there wouldn't be a lot of talking going on once they had the room to themselves.

"Just thought you'd want to know the subdivision has been approved after all."

Carter straightened. "How the hell did you manage

that?"

"Who says I had anything to do with it?"

Carter waited him out.

"I might have had a word with Rod Stevenson this afternoon and reminded him of some unfortunate photos that landed online about a decade ago."

"What photos?"

Gage shrugged. "Amazing what you can find when you go digging. Seems Rod had a bit of a drinking problem when he was away at school. Took his clothes off in public a few times. His friends obliged him by documenting it. I'm sure those pictures wouldn't disturb anyone from the big city, but more than a few people in Chance Creek would be surprised."

"Gage Elliott, you are devious," Amanda said.

"I live to serve. Most people have something in their past they'd like to hide. I figured Rod would, too. That's why I was on my way to town this morning. I needed a better internet connection to do some research on him. That all went to hell when I spotted Carter's truck by the side of the road. As soon as you were safely at the hospital, though, I got back to it and hit up a few friends whose skills are even better than mine. Didn't take us long to find what I needed. I imagine Rod jumped through some hoops at some point to scrub those images off the web."

"Didn't scrub hard enough, though?" Carter asked.

"Not by a long shot."

"I didn't think you cared if the subdivision went through or not."

Gage stilled. "Don't ever assume I don't care," he said quietly. "Night, Amanda. Feel better."

"Thanks. For everything," she called after him as he left.

Carter shook his head when Gage was gone. "I wouldn't have believed it if I didn't hear it for myself." He turned to take her hands. "Guess I can sell you that house after all."

CHAPTER 16

"**A**RE YOU SURE you're up for this?" Carter asked on a late May morning about two weeks later.

"I'm sure," Amanda said.

Once again they were paddling a canoe across Elliott Lake.

"Tell me if you get tired."

"I haven't done a single physical thing in two weeks," she protested. "You're being too protective. My head is fine."

As far as Carter was concerned, he hadn't been protective enough, and that was how Amanda had gotten shot in the first place, but he could maneuver the canoe all on his own if she got tired, so he decided not to argue with her.

"I'm glad you agreed to this," he said instead. "I've been wanting to get back out on the water. I don't mind keeping busy, but we've got work enough to fill every spare minute."

"And I haven't been much help lately. It feels weird resting while everyone else is scurrying around."

"You've helped a lot at the house," he said, propelling them forward with his paddle.

Amanda looked over her shoulder, holding her paddle across her knees. "How? By sitting in a chair?"

"By keeping me company while I renovate and answering questions about how you want things done."

"Well, thanks," Amanda said, "but I'd rather be working myself. I can't wait to get back to the library."

"After your appointment this afternoon, I'm sure you'll get the go-ahead." Carter paddled on, directing them toward a small island a fair distance away from the main beach. Tucked in a cove, you couldn't see it unless you were almost on top of it. Carter escaped here when he really wanted to get away from it all.

"Then I can get back to meal prep, too. I've been feeling like a slacker."

"You needed your rest," Carter said firmly. "Gage has lunch under control today, so don't even worry about it."

"Even guilt wouldn't make me pass up a picnic on a day like this." Amanda looked back over her shoulder at the basket Carter had stowed near his feet.

The journey to the island was uneventful. Carter kept a close watch on Amanda and noticed as they neared the cove, she was resting her paddle on her knees more often. Just as he thought, she was better but maybe not a hundred percent yet.

He angled his paddle to steer them into the cove and was rewarded when he heard Amanda give a small exclamation of surprise.

"It's beautiful here," she said softly. "Is that an island?"

"Sure is."

Carter slowed the canoe with a few backstrokes.
"Before we get there, I've got something I want to say."

Amanda half turned on her seat. "What?"

"Remember the first time we went out on the water
together?"

"Of course."

A glow of satisfaction filled him at her smile. They
wouldn't be trying those kinds of acrobatics today, but
he relished the sparkle in her eye. "The first time I saw
you I knew you were special, but after we made love in
the canoe, I was thoroughly hooked."

Amanda laughed. "That's what sold you on me? My
sexual dexterity?"

"It might have sealed the deal." He grew serious. "I
mean it, Amanda. The minute I saw you get out of your
plane, I wanted to marry you."

"It didn't take me long to want to marry you, either."

Carter pulled a small velvet-covered box out of his
pocket. He'd gone to town the day before to fetch it.
Amanda let out a shaky breath when she saw it. Her
gaze lifted to his, her eyes wide.

"You haven't changed your mind, have you?" he
asked her.

She shook her head quickly. "Have you?"

"I want you more than ever. I want to spend the
rest of my life making you happy. Keeping you safe.

Showing you how much I cherish you."

There was too much distance between them. He set his paddle down carefully and slowly edged forward over the first thwart to the yoke at the center of the boat. Amanda just as carefully made her way to join him.

They knelt, facing each other in the middle of the canoe, the yoke between them, just as they had the first time they went for a paddle.

Carter braced his knees wide to steady the boat. He still held the small box in one hand. With the other he touched her cheek. "Will you marry me?" he asked.

"I already said yes," she reminded him. "Of course I'll marry you."

"You were in the hospital. You'd just been shot. I wanted to give you the chance to change your mind."

"I'm never going to change my mind." Amanda carefully rose on her knees and kissed him. "You are stuck with me, Carter Elliott. I'm not going anywhere."

"I'm not going anywhere, either."

He kissed her back, savoring the taste of her and the knowledge he could share this with her forever. Easing away, he opened the box to show her the ring inside.

"Oh, Carter." Amanda kept still as he lifted it out and put it on her finger.

"Do you like it?" His voice was husky. The act of giving her the ring felt more significant than he'd expected.

"I love it." She lifted her hand to examine the triple diamonds on the band. "I never knew I could be this happy."

He pocketed the box, wanting both hands free to touch his fiancée. As their kiss grew more heated, it was harder to keep the canoe steady.

"We'd better take this to shore," he murmured against her cheek.

Amanda shook her head. "I wish we could stay right here. Do it like last time."

"Not today but someday soon," he promised her. "Stay right there. I'll take us in." He kissed her again, made his way back to the stern and paddled until they reached the island. Once there he scrambled out and dragged the canoe on shore. After helping Amanda out, he fetched their picnic and spread a blanket on the sand. "We can stay here as long as you like."

"This has to be paradise," she said as he took her in his arms.

"I agree."

JUST AS CARTER predicted, the doctor cleared Amanda for all normal activity at her appointment late that afternoon. Back at the Ridge, she shooed Carter out of the town hall kitchen and happily took on the chore of making dinner. It felt good to be active again after her weeks of enforced rest. Thinking about what had happened at the mine could still make her shaky, but that was fading. Her father would remain in custody until his trial, and Cab assured her he'd do jail time for coming after her. She didn't look forward to testifying, but she knew Carter would be with her and that everyone on Elliott Ridge would look out for her from here on in. Even the mill workers had made it a point to check in to see how she was doing these past two weeks. Once or twice, she'd caught sight of Dennis lingering nearby. Carter said the old man was patrolling the Ridge constantly, looking for more invaders, as he called them.

She had put together a big pot of chili and was setting some corn bread in the oven when her phone buzzed.

To Amanda's surprise, Melissa's name showed on its screen.

She didn't know if she wanted to answer the call, but in the end she did. She'd only wonder what her sister wanted to say if she declined it.

"Hello?"

"Amanda? It's me."

"I know," Amanda said shortly. She really had no desire to talk after everything Melissa did.

"I just wanted to say—I'm sorry."

Amanda grabbed another pan of cornbread and put it in the oven, untouched by her sister's sentiment.

"Did you hear me? I said I'm sorry," Melissa repeated.

"I heard you." She just didn't believe her. Melissa had gone out of her way to get her address and give it to their father, knowing full well he meant to come and steal *Afternoon in Sunshine and Shadow.*

"I didn't know he had a gun," Melissa said. "I had no idea he'd hurt you."

"Did you think he'd show up and we'd have tea? You knew I wouldn't give him that painting."

"I don't see why not."

Amanda shut her eyes. The worst of it was that Melissa probably didn't. She'd become so self-centered she thought everyone was the same.

"I'm not a criminal," Amanda said. That was as blunt as she possibly could be.

"You're saying I am?"

"You stole a painting. What would you call it?"

"Making sure I had a future. You think dancers earn a decent living? That's the problem with you, Amanda. You have no idea what it's like to be creative. You're content to be a drudge in an office building. Not all of us are cut out for that."

"You know what? That's not my problem. *You're* not my problem." It felt good to say it. All these years, it had hurt so badly to know her sister hardly thought about her. She'd felt it was some personal failing that caused Melissa to barely remain in touch. Now she knew that wasn't the case. Melissa wasn't capable of a true relationship.

"I'm your sister. And I need a place to stay. I have to stick around until the trial. And my dance company let me go…" She trailed off. Amanda wondered if that was a lie, too. Had her sister quit in anticipation of the millions she thought their father would get for the painting?

Cab had told her Melissa probably wouldn't get jail time because she had no prior record.

"You can't stay with me," Amanda said. She never dreamed she'd say such a thing to the sister she once had adored, but she wasn't a child anymore, and neither was Melissa.

"Why not?"

"Because you can't. Bye, Melissa. I hope you figure it all out."

"But—Amanda!"

Amanda hung up.

She tried to recapture her previous happiness as she finished loading the pans of corn bread into the oven and shut its door, but the day had lost its luster, so when Carter walked into the kitchen, she was happy to see him. He was followed by a beaming woman who looked to be in her late sixties. Gray-haired and thickset, she looked around the kitchen with approval.

"Nothing's changed!"

"You're right, it hasn't. Except Amanda is new," Carter said. "Amanda, this is Carolyn Snyder, an old friend of the family. Carolyn, this is my fiancée, Amanda Stakewell."

"Nice to meet you," Carolyn said. "Welcome to Elliott Ridge."

"Carolyn and her husband and kids used to live in number thirty-one," Carter explained.

"And I'm moving back," Carolyn proclaimed. "Just have to do the paperwork. Imagine, it'll be the first house I've ever owned. We rented back in the day, and I've been renting in town ever since everyone moved away."

"We'll be glad to have you back," Carter said.

"I look forward to having a neighbor," Amanda said, surprised by this turn of events. Carolyn looked like a very comfortable neighbor to have.

"Just one street away. I'm working on my kids, too. Maybe I can convince one or two to move back, as well," Carolyn said.

"We'd love to have them," Carter said. "We'd better keep going, though. I'm giving Carolyn a tour of the place so she can be sure she wants to settle here. It's not quite the same as it was," he explained to Amanda.

"It's good enough for me," Carolyn said. "I've missed the place for twelve years. Wild horses couldn't keep me away. See you soon, neighbor," she said to Amanda.

"See you."

Amanda found herself smiling when they left. Maybe the day wasn't ruined, after all.

"GOOD MORNING," CARTER said when he woke up on his wedding day and found Amanda kissing him. It was the third week of June, and the sun had been up for hours, breaking through the forest canopy to light up their room.

"Morning, sleepyhead. It's time to get up. We've got a busy day ahead of us."

He chuckled. "You're right, we do." He reached for her, but she wriggled away.

"Plus you need to open your present first."

"Present? Now we're talking." Carter pushed onto

one elbow and took the tiny gift-wrapped square Amanda handed him. "What's this?"

"Open it," she urged him.

He undid the elaborate bow and tore open the wrapping. Inside was a dollar bill.

"Never did pay you for this house," she said with an impish grin.

"I suppose now you'll want paperwork saying it's all yours." The lawyer Megan had suggested had been working on that paperwork. Carter had it ready to go downstairs, which Amanda knew. He'd figured they didn't need the formality of exchanging a dollar, but they did need a notary present before they signed on the dotted line.

In the weeks since Amanda was shot, they'd made great strides with their renovation, and eight days ago they'd traveled together to Los Angeles to pack up her apartment and bring her things to Elliott Ridge. Now the house was full of her treasures, but her little bear figurine still sat on the dresser, taking pride of place.

"It really did turn out to be a good-luck charm," she'd told him last night.

Carter supposed it had. If a black bear hadn't scared her father on his wild scramble after Amanda, his shot might not have gone wild. Carter hoped Ian Stakewell would end up in prison for a long, long time. His trial would start soon. Carter meant to do everything he could to see that justice was served.

"Absolutely," Amanda said now. "This is my house. Of course, as soon as the ceremony is over, it'll be yours again, too." She leaned over and kissed him on the nose.

"Do you like your house?" This time when he reached for her, she came willingly. She didn't wear anything to bed these days, complaining he was like a furnace lying next to her, so there was nothing to come between them when their bodies met.

"I love my house," Amanda said. "Almost as much as I love you." She moaned with pleasure as he swept his hands over the curves of her body, molding her closer to him. When she pushed up to straddle him, giving him a full frontal view, Carter found it hard to hold back his appreciation.

"You are so beautiful," he told her as desire curled through him. "Have I told you how much I love you?"

"Once or twice." She leaned forward, her breasts swinging into reach of his mouth. Carter stopped talking then and lavished his attention on them, making sure no inch of her was left out of his worship.

No matter how many times they came together like this, Carter felt like it was the first time. Her skin felt so good under his fingers. His explorations of her only heightened his desire to come to know her more.

When Amanda lifted her hips, Carter shifted into position and entered her smoothly, groaning as he pushed inside her. Amanda arched her back, taking him in, making him feel like he'd found home.

"Amanda," he said, but that was the extent of his ability to express himself with words.

From now on his body would have to tell her what he wanted to say.

SHE TRUSTED HIM.

Perched on top of Carter, letting him fill her and caress her and coax her to new heights of desire, Amanda finally knew what it meant to let another person have full access to her heart.

Carter treasured her in a way no one ever had. She felt safe in his arms, capable of allowing him to push the boundaries of their intimacy to bring them both pleasure. With Carter, she'd learned to love her body—and his—in a way she'd never thought possible, and that capacity for growth extended to their time out of bed, as well.

She had feared people. Amanda had never admitted that to herself, outside of a healthy terror of Buck's potential for violence, but it was true. She was afraid other people might act as erratically as her father and Buck had. Or would abandon her the way Erik and Maddy had. Then she'd met Carter and learned how to trust. Now she was ready to rejoin the world.

Every day she learned something new about what it meant to live with a man who truly wanted the best for her. His smallest gestures sometimes brought her close to tears. The touch at the base of her spine when he ushered her through a door. The fresh flowers that appeared on her bedside table. The way he always joined in when it was her turn to clean up after a meal.

Carter was there for her. He was steady. Strong. Kind. And his body made her come alive. Feeling him inside her, moving with him as one, made her feel so good it was hard not to cry out with it.

He knew exactly how to bring her to the brink, pull back and extend the experience and then bring her to the brink all over again. When she thought she couldn't hold on another moment, Carter gripped her hips, plunged deeper into her and brought her straight over the edge.

Amanda arched back, cried out and rode the waves of her release as they expanded within her. When Carter grunted a moment later, bucking against her in his own release, she wasn't surprised. They were always in sync like this.

She let his love flow through her, riding the storm until it subsided, before easing down onto his broad chest. She snuggled close, pressing her mouth to the corner of his jaw, loving this man so much she thought she couldn't contain it.

His arms wrapped around her, holding her there. "I'm going to get to spend my life with you," Carter said.

"I'm going to get to spend my life with you," she repeated, understanding the wonder in his voice.

He pulled back an inch or two, the better to see her face. "I'm going to be the man you need me to be. I promise."

"You already are."

CHAPTER 17

"**C**ARTER ELLIOTT, YOU must be the handsomest groom I've ever seen," Celia Elliott said as she entered Carter's childhood bedroom and came to straighten his tie. She wore a rose-colored dress and a string of pearls she'd inherited from her mother.

"Don't you think you're biased?"

"It's still true." She dusted an imaginary piece of lint off the shoulder of his jacket. "I'm so happy for you. Still can't believe I'm really here." She looked around the room. "Nothing's changed."

"Some things have," he reminded her. He'd taken her on a tour of number twenty-three when his parents arrived yesterday, and she'd oohed and aahed over every renovation.

"I suppose that's true. I can't believe Carolyn is back in her old house. Makes me wish I was settled in mine."

"I look forward to that day." He was doubly determined to transform Elliott Ridge into the bustling little community it once had been now that he was settling here with his wife. It had lifted all their spirits when

Carolyn moved into her old house two days ago. Carter and his brothers had rushed to repaint it inside and out to her specifications. They'd done whatever else they could to spiff it up given the limited time frame, but it was like stepping back in time whenever he visited number thirty-one.

"I can't believe there was a shootout here." His mother grew serious. "Nothing like that ever happened at Elliott Ridge before."

"Not even in the Calamity Year?" Carter laughed at her expression. "Dennis told us about it. He says it's happening again. Claims troubled women will be flocking here because I allowed Amanda to stay."

"I hope not. That's just an old story, anyhow."

"I'm sure he's wrong." Carter turned to give himself a once-over in the mirror. He wasn't much of a clothes-horse, but he looked good, he decided.

"Amanda is one lucky lady to get you," his mother said. "Carter, I'm so proud of you. For everything."

"Thanks, Mom."

"Here's your dad. He'll want a word with you. I'm going to find my seat. Love you, Carter."

"Love you, too, Mom."

He watched his parents exchange a few words before his father entered the room and closed the door behind him, leaning heavily on his cane. He looked Carter up and down.

"Well," he began. "Never thought the youngest would marry first."

"Neither did I," Carter admitted warily.

"You found a good woman, seems like. Amanda likes it here. Says she wants to stay."

Carter nodded, not knowing how to answer that. His father's hip replacement was coming up at the end of the month. Carter hoped it went smoothly. He could tell his dad was in pain.

"You do right by her."

"I will."

"Keep your eyes on the goal. Don't make her leave the home she loves—" His voice grew gruff. Carter's throat grew thick as he felt his father's pain. Did his dad think that's what he'd done?

"I'm trying—" he began but his father waved him off.

"Be a man she can be proud of," he finished. "Do your best."

"Always, Dad." Carter wished he could say everything he wanted to say. That Mom didn't regret leaving Elliott Ridge. That all she wanted was for her husband to be healthy and safe. That's what they all wanted.

They'd never been good at putting their feelings into words, though, so he clapped his father on the back. "Means a lot to me that the two of you are here today."

"Wouldn't miss it for the world."

"I'm sorry—that I was part of the reason you had to leave here to begin with."

There. He'd finally got that out. He'd wanted to say it for years.

"Wasn't your fault." His dad shook his head when Carter began to protest. "No sense talking about the past. You're here now. That's what counts. You came back."

Carter knew he'd have to be content with that.

After his father left to take his seat, his brothers filed into the room to round him up, all of them in dark suits, ready to stand with him at the altar.

"Better get going. Don't want to be late to your own wedding," Nate said.

"Why is Warrington here?" Lincoln asked from the window.

"Warrington?" Carter came to see, then hurried downstairs, his brothers following at his heels. Outside, he slowed as the man's flashy truck idled in front of the house.

"Did you invite him?" Hudson asked.

"No." Carter went down the steps to meet the intruder as Warrington parked and got out.

"Came to offer my congratulations." He came around his truck, his hand extended, but he didn't look like he was in a celebratory mood. In fact, Carter thought he might have been drinking.

"Cut the crap," Hudson said, pushing past Carter. "What are you really here for? You tried to kill our subdivision application."

"You got what you wanted, didn't you?"

"Yeah, we did," Gage said quietly, coming up on Carter's other side.

Warrington lowered his hand. "I'm here to tell you that you may have won this time, but I still want this land, and I intend to do whatever it takes to get it. Am I making myself clear? I offered you a very fair price for it. I'm not going to let you carve up the place and make it harder for me to develop. It's time for you to sell. Now. My offer still stands."

"You can take your offer and shove it up your ass," Carter said.

"Is that your position?" Warrington demanded of Gage.

"Damn straight," Gage said. "Rod found out what happens when you cross an Elliott. Be careful, or next time it'll be you."

Warrington spun away. Walked a few paces, then turned back. "You are now my enemies. All of you. I'm going to get this land. When I do, you're going to wish like hell you'd taken the money when you had the chance." He stalked back to his truck, got in, slammed the door, revved the engine and took off with a spray of gravel. A few latecomers had to dodge away from him as he drove around the Circle and down the hill.

"Hell of a way to treat a man on his wedding day," Hudson said.

"Not very neighborly," Carter agreed.

"He can't touch us," Lincoln said.

"He's going to try," Gage said.

"But there's nothing he can do today," Nate pointed out. "And today Carter is getting married, so let's focus on that for now. Tomorrow we'll figure out what to do about Warrington. Deal?"

"Deal," Carter said.

"THANK YOU FOR asking me to be your bridesmaid," Megan said, coming to stand by Amanda to look in the floor-length mirror she'd installed in the master bedroom of number twenty-three. "We haven't known each other that long. I feel honored you'd choose me."

"I hope we'll be good friends," Amanda said. "I don't know a lot of people in Chance Creek yet." And it wasn't like she'd ask her sister to take on that role. She hadn't spoken to Melissa again after their last call. She didn't want people in her life who'd gamble with her safety for their own financial gain. She was going to focus on the people who had her best interests at heart. Her mother was downstairs, and that was good enough. Lately they'd talked almost every day.

"I'm glad you're staying," Megan said. "I'd miss you if you left now."

"I'd miss you, too." They'd gotten together for coffee several times lately and found out that they had lots in common, like their desire to give back to their community, to have work that kept them engaged, their love of the outdoors—and their struggles with crafty things like knitting. They'd gone kayaking once on Elliott Lake together. Had planned a couple of hikes for the future.

Meanwhile, Amanda had stepped into the role of town manager. She had a credit card linked to the Elliotts' joint bank account and was learning to handle affairs that affected the town as a whole, in addition to her other duties. Her days were full and varied. Her nights with Carter wonderful.

"Your house has turned out so well. I love that hutch Nate built for you. Someday I'd like one like that."

"You should talk to him. I bet you could commission one." The lovingly crafted piece of furniture was beautiful, and she was proud to have it in her dining room.

Megan's smile faltered. "I don't think I'll buy any new furniture for my house right now. I need to get my career on better footing first."

Amanda leaned forward. "Are you doing all right?"

"Oh, I'm fine," Megan assured her. "Really. Things will turn around soon, I'm sure. Selling Gage's house helped me buy some time. Hopefully, I'll be able to help you guys sell some houses up here soon."

"You should have taken the commission on Carolyn Snyder's sale."

"I couldn't do that—take a cut when someone was buying a house they lived in before," Megan asked. "Don't worry; I'm not upset about that at all. Let's just hope the rest of the old-timers who used to live here don't all come back to claim their homes, or I'll be in trouble."

"I'm sure you'll get some real sales," Amanda said. "I want you to be as happy as I am."

"I'm not sure that's possible."

The door opened, and Amanda's mother came in. She fluttered around her, straightening her veil. When she was satisfied, she leaned in. "There's a strange man downstairs asking to see you. Lincoln said his name was

Dennis?"

Amanda bit her lip, holding back laughter. She could only imagine what her mother would make of the rough old codger.

"Send him up."

"Are you sure?"

"I'm sure. Dennis helped save my life. He's the one who noticed my dad's campsite on the Ridge and told Carter."

"I thought Gage found the truck you took that day and he was the one who sounded the alert."

"He did, but Dennis was the one who gave Carter his gun. If he hadn't, I could be dead."

"Don't even say that." Her mother took her hands. "I couldn't stand it if that were true. I can't believe your father could do such a thing. And Melissa. I knew she worshipped your dad, but to put you in danger…"

"That's all over now. Go get Dennis and send him up, okay, Mom?"

Her mother nodded and left the room. Amanda knew they'd have long talks in their future as the two of them tried to come to grips with what her father and Melissa had done. Her mother had told her she was back in counseling. Amanda had spoken with a counselor several times, too.

She wasn't sure if she'd need to continue with that. The life she was creating here with Carter had shored her up, and she felt stronger than she ever had before. Melissa and her father were gone, but she had more people around her than she'd had in years. People who cared. In a few weeks, she was going to Houston to help her mom prepare to sell her house. She was grateful her mother was building a community for herself, as well.

"I'm going to go freshen up," Megan said. "Be back in a minute." She disappeared into the hall.

Heavy footsteps sounded outside her room a few moments later. Amanda moved to the door. "Come in," she told Dennis.

The old man did so, fidgeting with his clothes, which were obviously new and uncomfortable.

"You look very handsome," Amanda told him. He was part of her community now. She was grateful to him for helping to save her life. She'd never doubt him again.

"Never you mind about that," Dennis said gruffly. "Came to give you my congratulations."

"Thank you."

"I wasn't very welcoming—at first."

"You were right. I did bring trouble."

"Wasn't your fault."

"Do you still think it's going to be a Calamity Year?" She softened her words with a smile.

He nodded gravely. "Lots of weddings last time, too. Still, I want to wish you good luck on your day. Hope I didn't offend you."

"You were worried for the Elliotts," she said. "I love you for your loyalty to them. Besides, I owe you my life."

"Carter saved your life."

"Because you gave him the information and weapon he needed to do it with." She touched his arm. "I'm glad you came to talk to me, because I have a favor to ask you." The idea had only just popped into her head, but she knew it was the right thing to do.

"What's that?" he asked suspiciously.

"Will you walk me down the aisle? My father isn't going to—obviously. And my mom—well, it hurts her to have to stand in for him all the time."

Dennis looked like a deer caught in the headlights. "Don't want to mess it up."

"You won't mess it up. You'll take my arm and walk beside me. At the end of the aisle, you'll give my hand to Carter and then you'll go take your seat. You can do that, right?"

"Suppose so." His gaze was darting around the room, as if he was searching for a way out of a trap.

"You'll do great," she assured him. "I'm relying on you."

Her mother came back into the room, followed by Megan. "It's time," her mother told them and took a deep breath. "Amanda, would you like me to walk you down the aisle since your father is… not here?"

"Dennis is going to do the honors if you don't mind," Amanda said.

Her mother looked relieved, then perplexed. "You sure?" she asked.

"I'm sure."

"Okay, then. Let's get going, ladies—and gentleman." She nodded to Dennis. "Time to get to the altar."

"IS SHE COMING?" Carter asked Nate, who stood beside him on the beach where the wedding planner, Mia

Matheson, had constructed a flower-bedecked archway. In front of him, rows of guests sat on folding chairs. Behind him lay the lake itself. Reverend Halpern, from the Chance Creek Reformed Church, was presiding. They had considered holding the ceremony in the chapel, but neither he nor Amanda could resist celebrating their wedding outdoors. They'd been rewarded with a beautiful day.

"I don't see her yet. Wait—there." Nate jutted his chin in the direction of their parents' house. Megan Lawrence, in a peach-colored bridesmaid gown, had rounded the side of the house and was walking down the steps toward them.

"Megan's looking mighty pretty today, right, Gage?" Hudson asked.

"Stow it," Gage said.

"There's Amanda," Lincoln said.

Carter didn't hear anything after that. He was too busy looking at the woman he was about to marry. Dennis was walking her toward them. Carter wondered how that had come about, but he was happy she had someone to support her on this journey, especially since she was working hard to keep the voluminous skirts of her gown out of the sand.

They reached the top of the aisle between the rows of chairs, where Mia had laid a runner across the beach. Amanda let her gown fall straight, squared her shoulders, took a breath and nodded.

The music changed as their procession down the aisle began. Carter couldn't keep his gaze off the woman he'd grown to love so dearly. He'd almost lost her, something he was aware of every day. He woke in the mornings and reached beside him to make sure she was still there—still safe and alive. Every time she reached back for him, his heart filled to the brim until he wondered how there could be so much happiness in the world.

They had a lot of work to do, but Amanda seemed as excited to get to it as he was. It was nearly the summer solstice, and while the long, light-filled days would soon begin to wane again, his love for her—and for the Ridge—increased every day.

When Amanda lifted her eyes to him, he saw so much love shining in them, he knew he'd done the right thing in asking her to marry him, even if they'd known each other such a short time. Number twenty-three was almost finished. So far they'd managed to meet their deadlines for the lumber contract, and he'd drummed up several more so they could increase their earnings. Soon they could place ads for permanent workers to replace the temporary ones.

Even Gage seemed happier these days, especially since their folks had been in town. He'd taken it upon himself to stick close to their father, helping him to negotiate the stairs to the house and keeping him from climbing a ladder to check out the roof. Lincoln had finally purchased two horses, and Nate had bought one, as well. Carter, Hudson and Gage were looking for mounts of their own.

More importantly, their internet provider had finally

set a date for running fiber optic cable to the Ridge—
although that wouldn't happen until mid-July. Many of
the subdivision houses had been gutted, cleaned and
given a fresh coat of primer on the interior walls. It was
time to sell them. As soon as the wedding was over,
he'd get it done, he promised himself.

He didn't have to worry about it today, though.

Megan made it down the aisle and took her place to
the side. Now Carter could see Amanda clearly. She was
a sight to behold in her beautiful gown, a fancy affair
that hugged her curves in all the right places, but then
he thought she was beautiful in his bed with nothing on.

By the time Dennis put Amanda's hand in his,
Carter's heart was beating hard.

"Thank you," he said to Dennis, hoping the man
knew how much he meant it.

Dennis nodded and slipped away, skirting the rows
of chairs to take a position standing in back.

Carter squeezed Amanda's fingers. Did she know
how happy he was?

She tilted her head to look up at him.

He blew her a kiss and she smiled.

"DEARLY BELOVED," THE minister began. Amanda's
heart was beating so rapidly she could barely make out
his words. She was getting everything she ever dreamed
of. A man she loved. The possibility of a family. A
growing community. Work that was varied—and fun.

As the minister spoke, she couldn't help looking up
at Carter. His firm grip on her hand gave her strength.

His shoulder so close beside hers made her think of comfort and security—things she'd always craved but never thought she deserved.

Over the past weeks, Carter had taught her she was worth paying attention to. Worth being protected. Worthy of true love that had no ulterior motives. Carter was part of the foundation on which she could build the rest of her life. No matter what happened with Elliott Ridge, he'd be there for her.

She meant to be there for him, too. And to give everything she could to this tiny town she'd grown to love so much. She was taking her position of librarian seriously and was learning everything she could about town governance. She knew she wouldn't be head cook forever, so she'd decided to enjoy it while she could, taking pride in feeding her big, new extended family. The possibilities for the future were endless here at Elliott Ridge.

"You may now kiss the bride."

No sooner had the minister said the words than Carter turned to her, gathered her close and kissed her so thoroughly, Amanda felt they'd never come up for air. When they finally did, it was to find their guests standing and cheering. Amanda was sure she was blushing, but she was also so happy she thought her heart might burst.

"I love you," she told Carter.

"I love you, too," he said. "Ready to start the rest of our lives?"

"So ready."

Read on for an excerpt of
House for Sale Soldier Included.

"**W**HEN ARE YOU going to find a wife?"

Lincoln Elliott lifted the last of his parents' luggage into the bed of his truck, which sat parked in front of the large, white house he'd grown up in on Elliott Ridge. It was June and the sun beat down from a clear blue Montana sky, sparkling on the wind-ruffled water of Elliott Lake. He'd known the question was coming. His parents had returned to the Ridge last week for his brother's wedding. His mother, a self-designated romantic at heart, would have had to acquire a whole new level of self-restraint to leave town without asking.

The question had been on his mind, too. After all, he was fresh home from a twelve-year stint in the Army. He was working with his four brothers to make their lumber mill profitable again and resurrect the small town his family had owned for generations. Under any other circumstances, it would make sense for him to look for a partner.

Unfortunately, he had a debt to pay before he could do so.

A big one.

He came around to shut the door as his mom settled in the passenger seat. She held out a hand to stop him. "Well?"

"I have no idea, Mom." He pushed gently on the door again and this time she allowed it to close. As he made his way to the driver's seat, he counseled himself to have patience. She wasn't judging him for being single. She was simply in a celebratory mood now that she'd seen Carter, her youngest son, wed.

"You didn't bring a plus one to the wedding," his father pointed out from the back seat as Lincoln got in behind the wheel. Sitting beside him, grinning, was Carter's new bride, Amanda. Lincoln knew she found his whole family mighty entertaining. He supposed it was a good think she didn't think they were annoying. All the Elliotts were strong-willed.

Stubborn, even.

"You're right. I didn't." He hoped his tone made it clear he didn't want to discuss the matter anymore. The truth was, he'd be happy to find a woman like Amanda to spend his life with. These days Carter strode around the place brimming with energy and enthusiasm for the future. It had been a long time since Lincoln had felt like that—and it was his own damn fault.

He fired up the engine, backed out of the driveway and drove around the Circle, which encompassed a grassy area at the centre of the community.

When he and his brothers arrived back at the Ridge in April, they'd returned to their childhood bedrooms in number one Elliott Way as if nothing had changed. A month later, Carter moved out again. He'd claimed one of the town's empty houses for himself and had been partway through renovating it when Amanda arrived. Desperate to keep her here, he'd offered to sell it to her for a dollar. His ruse had worked. Amanda had moved in and the two of them had swiftly fallen in love.

"What happened to Katie?" his mother persisted.

"Who's Katie?" Amanda piped up from the back seat.

Lincoln sighed. "She didn't last through my last deployment." He wasn't broken up about it, either, which showed she wasn't the one, as far as he was concerned.

"What about the women around here?" his father grumbled. "None of them good enough for you?"

Lincoln glanced at him in the rearview mirror as he made the turn onto the county highway that led to Chance Creek. He and his dad hadn't spoken very much during his parents' time here, which was probably because Lincoln had been avoiding him. Throughout his visit, Carter had tried to get their father excited about all they'd done so far, but while he seemed happy to see Carter married, he hadn't found much else to praise about their efforts.

"Not yet. Only been here a couple of months, Dad."

The day Carter had brought their father to inspect their progress at the mill, he'd gone over the contracts they'd managed to secure so far and had introduced their father to some of the temporary workers they'd hired back in April.

354

"Pretty soon we'll be hiring permanent workers," Carter had told him. "I'm working on getting us a contract that will keep us busy for the rest of the year. We can raise the wages we're paying and attract some real talent."

Their father grunted. "I remember when this mill ran with full shifts around the clock."

Lincoln had caught Carter's eye behind their father's back and shook his head. There was no appeasing their dad where the mill was concerned. Not until they'd paid back the equipment loans that had gotten their family into this mess to begin with.

Their father was right; they were operating at a fraction of their historical capacity, but if Lincoln had his way, that wouldn't be the case for long. He was in charge of running the mill now. It was his responsibility to get their capacity up again.

His responsibility to pay those loans.

"I saw Hudson flirting with some pretty young thing at the wedding," his dad said, breaking into his thoughts.

"Hudson's always flirting with someone," Lincoln said. "It doesn't mean anything." He was pretty sure he'd seen his brother putting the moves on at least three different women that night. His brother was like that. Charming. Boisterous. Fun. Identical twins ought to have the same luck with women, but while women flocked to Hudson, Lincoln wasn't made that way.

"Stop comparing yourself to him," his mother said as if she'd read his mind. "You're not interested in flirting with a dozen women. You want one special one who's going to be just yours."

What the hell did you say to a pronouncement like that? "Sure thing, Mom."

His mother waved a hand at him. "Scoff all you want. It's true. Remember, Elliott men know when they meet *the one*. Right?" She turned in her seat to face her husband.

"That's right. Moment I saw you, I knew how it would all turn out," his father said complacently.

Lincoln thought about that as drove the rest of the way to the airport, his parents pointing out all that had changed and all that had stayed the same in Chance Creek County since they'd last lived here. He didn't buy the family legend about Elliott men and love at first sight. Any pretty woman could get a reaction out of him. That didn't mean anything in the long term.

And he wanted something long term. He wanted what his parents had—a partnership that lasted through thick and thin. They'd had to admit defeat and leave their home twelve years ago, and then create a whole new life in a brand-new state. His father had health issues, was taking medicine for his heart and was recovering from a hip replacement. Still, his parents treated each other with respect and care. Were genuinely happy to spend time together. Seeing them dance at Carter's wedding had eased his fears that a decade in North Carolina might have left them bitter and unhappy.

Still, they missed the Ridge. He'd heard his mother

heave a sigh or two when she first entered her old home—especially when she took in the view of Elliott Lake from her old back deck. Once, he thought he'd seen his father close to tears. They'd been down at the beach by the old barbecue pits where his dad used to hold court at family gatherings and community picnics. His dad had always loved to see all his people around him, knowing he provided jobs and homes for everyone who lived on the Ridge.

"A year ago, you could have knocked me over with a feather if you'd told me you boys would all live here and Carter would marry," Lincoln's mother said. "I'm so glad he did, though," she added, looking over her shoulder at Amanda.

"I'm glad he did, too," Amanda said.

Lincoln hid a wry smile. A year ago, his parents had received an offer for the town from Blake Warrington, who was developing the back side of the Ridge into a golf resort. They would have had to take it if Lincoln and his brothers hadn't come home and gotten the mill up and running again. Unfortunately, they still had ongoing expenses, loan payments and a large balloon payment coming due next year for the mill equipment they'd bought just before the crash. The clock was ticking. It was late June now. Eleven months and change to go before they either succeeded or had to leave a second time.

Lincoln turned on the road that led to the Chance Creek Regional Airport and found a parking spot near the small terminal. He helped his parents get their luggage out of the truck and wheeled his mom's suitcase up to the entrance. Inside, the whole party stopped near the departures ticket desk.

"I hope your trip home goes smoothly," Lincoln told them.

"I'm sure it'll be fine," his mother said. "You take care of yourself. Take care of your brothers, too—and Amanda. Don't let Hudson get into trouble."

"I won't." It was a familiar admonition, as if he was his brother's keeper. Since when had he been able to stop Hudson from doing anything? While Lincoln had joined the Army and served with the special forces, Hudson had chosen the Air Force and flying fighter jets. Hudson was addicted to adrenaline. Lincoln was steadier. He liked having his feet on the ground.

"You kids are getting old. I didn't see Hudson up a tree once this whole week," his father said. "No logging going on, either. Guess he thinks he's got all the time in the world."

"Hudson has been helping with the mill. We needed to get that up and running first."

"Wait until you run out of logs. You'll wish you'd done things differently, then."

"Oh hush," his mother said to his father. "They're doing what they can."

"Plenty of timber left in the High Ridge parcel," his father said. "Someone should get busy harvesting it."

"I'll bring that up with Hudson when I get home," Lincoln told him. Leave it to his dad to get talkative at the last minute.

"Should have seen me back in the day. I could climb a tree faster than Hudson ever did."

"No, you couldn't," Lincoln's mother said. "No one is faster than Hudson."

"I could, too."

They were still arguing about it when they said their goodbyes. His father shook Lincoln's hand before they parted. His mother gave him a bear hug. They both embraced Amanda.

"Come for another visit soon," Lincoln told them.

"Got my surgery coming up. Won't be going anywhere for a while," his father said.

"Hope that goes smoothly, too."

"It'll be fine." His father turned away, but his mother hung back and gave Amanda another hug.

"I'm so glad you're part of our family now."

"Me, too," Amanda said.

Lincoln's mother turned to him. "Find a wife," she said again, hugging him, too. "Bring us back for another wedding."

"I'll see what I can do," he promised her and watched them go, cataloging the changes in them since they'd all left the Ridge the first time. He'd been nineteen then. Now he was thirty-one. His parents were in their early sixties. There were more lines on their faces. His father wasn't as certain in his gait anymore. Lincoln had a feeling the heart surgery he'd had years ago had undermined his confidence, although he'd never admit that. Once as muscular as any of his sons, his arms were thinner now, his face more angular. His hip replacement operation was scheduled to take place in four days. His dad had been nonchalant about it through his whole visit, but Lincoln was sure he was nervous about it.

"Ready to go?" Amanda asked softly when his folks were out of sight.

He nodded but it was hard to turn towards the door out to the parking lot. It killed him to know it was his fault Elliott Ridge had emptied out twelve years ago. Those dark times were nearly over, though.

He was already supervising twenty mill workers along with his brothers. Soon Hudson, and maybe Gage, would peel off to start up the logging operation, but for now all of them helped out in the mill. He was older now. Wiser. He had a lot more experience with the world under his belt.

He wouldn't screw up this time.

Lincoln scanned his surroundings automatically as he and Amanda walked outside, a habit he'd picked up in the military. A couple to his left were in a heated discussion, showing each other the screens of their cellphones while their little girl bent over a rigid plastic pet carrier, murmuring to the animal inside. Just past them stood a knot of men in business suits, something you didn't see that often at the Chance Creek airport. To his right, a pretty brunette in periwinkle-blue scrubs rummaged through her purse.

Lincoln focused on her. He hadn't seen her in Chance Creek before. He definitely would have remembered if he had. Her dark hair was pulled into a ponytail, as if she'd just come from work, but if she was some kind of a doctor or nurse here in town, she must have moved here while he was away. She hadn't gone to Chance Creek High, like he and every other kid in Chance Creek County had. He'd have to ask around about her.

Find out where he could see her again.

"Thanks for bringing me into town," Amanda said. "I just need a couple of things at the store before we head back."

"No problem," Lincoln said distractedly.

"Mr. Fluffy!"

The childish shriek made Lincoln stop short. An animal streaked past him, heading for the parking lot. The brunette looked up and their gazes met—just for an instant. Her eyes were wide. Her lips parted in surprise.

Something pure and hot shot through Lincoln like a bullet from a gun.

She was the one. She was the woman he was going to marry.

He couldn't say why or how or—

"Stop! Mr. Fluffy!" A small girl raced past.

Lincoln's attention snapped to her, and he launched into a run. Girl and cat were heading straight toward oncoming traffic.

Could he reach them in time?

He scooped up the girl in two strides, but the animal was faster. Lincoln kept going—

Hoping against hope he wasn't too late.

"GOTCHA!"

Charlotte Holmes closed her eyes and breathed a thank-you that the handsome, dark-haired man had snatched up the calico cat right before it ran into traffic. She'd watched in horror as first the animal and then its owner—a little girl no more than four or five years old—had raced toward the busy road that led out of the airport parking lot. Shock had frozen her in place. Thank goodness the man now carrying the girl and her cat had reacted so swiftly.

"Audrey, how many times did I tell you not to let the cat out?" the little girl's father cried. Both parents rushed to retrieve her.

"She's okay," the handsome stranger assured them. "So is Mr. Fluffy."

"No, he isn't! Mr. Fluffy's hurt! I let him out because he's bleeding!" Audrey cried, tears streaking her round cheeks. She struggled in the man's arms and he handed her over to her mother.

"Bleeding?" Audrey's father took the cat, who writhed and hissed. Sure enough, its paw was streaked with red.

"He is hurt." Another woman joined the group, a cheerful blonde who put a hand on the handsome man's arm. Her wedding ring glinted in the sun and a tiny twist of disappointment filled Charlotte. "I'm Amanda Elliott by the way. This is Lincoln."

"We're the Davies—Cliff and Enid," Audrey's father said.

Charlotte shook her head at her wayward thoughts. So Lincoln Elliott was married. So what? It wasn't like she was looking for any entanglements.

Not when she was on the run from a killer.

Charlotte glanced around, scanning the people streaming past out of the airport. Just the thought of Ivan Gasperyn's eagle-sharp eyes catching sight of her made her shiver. He was cruel and ruthless, and she had no doubt he was hunting her down.

She pushed her dark thoughts aside determinedly and stepped forward to join the group surrounding Audrey and Mr. Fluffy.

"Can I help? I'm a veterinarian."

At least, she had been until Ivan Gasperyn killed his brother, Lewis, putting an end to her career. The brothers had been raised with unbelievable wealth and privilege, and Lewis had used his inheritance to become a giant in the horse-racing world. Working with him had been a dream come true until Ivan moved back from Europe with a head full of schemes about how to use Lewis' success for his own purposes.

Now Lewis was dead.

Three days ago, she'd left her home, her job, her possessions and her friends behind and she had no idea when she'd be able to return to claim any of them. Ivan Gasperyn was capable of anything.

She had proof of that.

"If you hold him steady, I'll just take a look at that paw," she said to Cliff.

"Thank you." The man held Mr. Fluffy steady, while Audrey whimpered in her mother's arms.

As she bent to take a look at the animal's paw, Charlotte wondered if she had left a trail Ivan could follow. She wasn't a criminal mastermind. She didn't even watch detective shows on television. She preferred reality television, although she'd never admit that to anyone other than her closest friends. The people who starred on them got to do all the things she never did. Her job required her to be professional, to keep her emotions in check and to keep her opinions to herself. The people on TV did whatever they wanted and to heck with the consequences.

Charlotte had been on the move since Monday. It was Sunday now. She was so far past exhausted she could barely feel fear anymore. She'd hopscotched the country on seven different flights, paying cash for the last three of them. She hoped that would make her impossible to track, but who knew what Ivan could do?

He had many friends in high places, after all.

"Mr. Fluffy will be just fine," Charlotte assured Audrey, trying to forget about Ivan for the moment. "Looks like he gave himself a scratch during the flight. When you get home, clean the area and put a little peroxide on it. Mr. Fluffy won't even notice he was hurt."

She stepped back as the family thanked her. Cliff put the cat carefully back in its carrier.

"Let's get Mr. Fluffy home," he said to his daughter. "He'll be happier there and we can get him all fixed up. Okay?"

Audrey nodded.

"Thank you. Both of you," Enid said to Charlotte

and Lincoln. "I don't know what I'd have done if Audrey had been hurt."

"No problem at all," Lincoln said. "Bye, Audrey."

The little girl buried her face in her mother's neck.

"That was quick thinking," Charlotte said when the family was gone. "By the time I pulled myself together, you'd already saved the day."

"I know what you mean," Amanda said. "I didn't realize what was happening until it was all over!"

"Just glad I got there in time. Do you have a practice around here? I've only been back in Chance Creek for a couple of months and I haven't had a reason to call a veterinarian yet." Lincoln studied her, his dark gaze taking her all in. Charlotte wondered how she looked to him. She was dressed in the scrubs she'd been wearing when she made a run for it. She'd managed to buy a change of clothing along the way and now she washed an outfit every night in the sink of whatever local motel she found to sleep in and alternated what she wore. She pulled her hair into a ponytail each morning and didn't bother with makeup, not wanting to call any attention to herself. Soon she needed to find a place to live, replenish her wardrobe and get a job. Otherwise, she'd blow through her savings in no time.

"Just got here myself."

"No bags? Or did you forget to pick them up?"

Charlotte looked down, embarrassed. "This is all I've got with me." She lifted her large shoulder bag. "Traveling light, I guess you could say."

"Are you staying at the Evergreen Motel?" Amanda

asked. "It's the only one in town," she explained when Charlotte turned to her.

Charlotte hesitated, buying time. Could these people help her? "I was hoping to find a vacation rental. Or even a regular rental. Somewhere less expensive where I can stay long term."

Lincoln looked her over again and Charlotte had the feeling he was taking in the wrinkles in her clothing and the smudges under her eyes.

"What kind of a place do you want?" Amanda asked. "Something in town? Something in the country?"

"In the country," Charlotte said firmly. "Something quiet. Where I'll be left alone."

"Are you on vacation?"

"Not exactly. I... just a need to get away for awhile. To re-evaluate my life choices. Do you know a place where I could do that?"

We do." Amanda smiled at her husband and bumped his shoulder with her own. "It's remote, though. Forty-five minutes from town."

"Sounds perfect," Charlotte said. "What kind of accommodation?"

"A house," Amanda said. "In a ghost town," she added dramatically.

Charlotte cocked her head. "A ghost town?"

"Elliott Ridge emptied out a little over a decade ago. It's a company town. My family owns it," Lincoln explained. "My brothers and I are trying to resurrect the place."

"There are 29 houses for sale and a bunch more for

rent," Amanda put in. "They're all really cute. There's a swimming lake and a big town hall. We even have a library. I'm in charge of that."

Her smile was contagious and for the first time in a week, Charlotte relaxed. "Sounds pretty wonderful. I love to swim."

"There's a lot that needs to be done to get the place up and running again," Amanda said. "We're looking for people who don't mind pitching in now and then. Folks who want to build real community."

"I'd be happy to help out where I could," Charlotte assured her. "As for community, that depends on who's part of it."

"Of course. We're good people." Amanda bumped her husband's shoulder again. "Tell her, Lincoln."

"We do our best." Lincoln was still sizing her up and Charlotte wondered if he had reservations about inviting a stranger to their community. There was a military air about him she recognized. Something in his posture. The way his gaze flicked up to scan their surroundings now and then. She supposed he'd be protective of his wife.

Disappointment tugged within her again. She'd have liked for him to be protective of *her*.

He's taken, she told herself sternly.

"We Elliotts pride ourselves on our high standards," Lincoln went on. "I have four brothers. All of us served in the military for twelve years. We came home a couple of months ago to resurrect our family's town. We've got a lumber mill and a logging operation that we're bringing back to life. Elliott Ridge was a thriving concern for over a hundred years and we've committed ourselves to making it that way again. We'd love to welcome a veterinarian to town."

"What kind of vet are you?" Amanda asked.

"I specialize in horses."

"Lincoln has horses. Two of them."

"I'm sure there will be plenty more on the Ridge soon. We've got stables and paddocks," Lincoln said. "Chance Creek is teeming with horses, too. There's always need for a veterinarian in a cattle town."

"I don't know how long I'll stay."

His gaze sharpened. "Do you have somewhere else to be?"

"No. It's just… I don't know anyone here."

His slow smile did something to her insides and Charlotte tried in vain to steel herself against it. "You do now."

Amanda leaned closer to him. "Lincoln. Is the newcomer deal still on?"

"Newcomer deal?" Charlotte repeated. "What's that?"

"Something I hope will make you want to stay."

End of Excerpt

The Elliotts of Chance Creek Series:

House for Sale Navy SEAL Included
House for Sale Soldier Included
House for Sale Airman Included
House for Sale Marine Included
House for Sale Ranger Included

The Cowboys of Chance Creek Series:

The Cowboy Inherits a Bride (Volume 0)
The Cowboy's E-Mail Order Bride (Volume 1)
The Cowboy Wins a Bride (Volume 2)
The Cowboy Imports a Bride (Volume 3)
The Cowgirl Ropes a Billionaire (Volume 4)
The Sheriff Catches a Bride (Volume 5)
The Cowboy Lassos a Bride (Volume 6)
The Cowboy Rescues a Bride (Volume 7)
The Cowboy Earns a Bride (Volume 8)
The Cowboy's Christmas Bride (Volume 9)

The Heroes of Chance Creek Series:

The Navy SEAL's E-Mail Order Bride (Volume 1)
The Soldier's E-Mail Order Bride (Volume 2)
The Marine's E-Mail Order Bride (Volume 3)
The Navy SEAL's Christmas Bride (Volume 4)
The Airman's E-Mail Order Bride (Volume 5)
The Navy SEAL's Second Chance Bride
(Volume 6)

The SEALs of Chance Creek Series:

A SEAL's Oath

A SEAL's Vow
A SEAL's Pledge
A SEAL's Consent
A SEAL's Purpose
A SEAL's Resolve
A SEAL's Devotion
A SEAL's Desire
A SEAL's Struggle
A SEAL's Triumph

The Brides of Chance Creek Series:

Issued to the Bride One Navy SEAL
Issued to the Bride One Airman
Issued to the Bride One Sniper
Issued to the Bride One Marine
Issued to the Bride One Soldier
Issued to the Bride One Sergeant for Christmas

The Turners v. Coopers Series:

The Cowboy's Secret Bride (Volume 1)
The Cowboy's Outlaw Bride (Volume 2)
The Cowboy's Hidden Bride (Volume 3)
The Cowboy's Stolen Bride (Volume 4)
The Cowboy's Forbidden Bride (Volume 5)

About the Author

With over one-and-a-half million books sold, NYT and USA Today bestselling author Cora Seton has created a world readers love in Chance Creek, Montana. She has thirty-five novels and novellas currently set in her fictional town, with many more in the works. Like her characters, Cora loves cowboys, military heroes, country life, gardening, jogging, binge-watching Jane Austen movies, keeping up with the latest technology and indulging in old-fashioned pursuits. She lives on beautiful Vancouver Island with her husband, children and two cats. Visit **www.coraseton.com** to read about new releases, contests and other cool events!

Blog:

www.coraseton.com

Facebook:

facebook.com/coraseton

Twitter:

twitter.com/coraseton

Newsletter:

www.coraseton.com/sign-up-for-my-newsletter